VENETIAN STORIES

VENETIAN STORIES

JANE TURNER RYLANDS

PANTHEON BOOKS, NEW YORK

Copyright © 2003 by Jane Turner Rylands

All rights reserved under International and Pan-American Copyright
Conventions. Published in the United States by Pantheon Books, a
division of Random House, Inc., New York, and simultaneously in
Canada by Random House of Canada Limited, Toronto.

Pantheon Books and colophon are registered trademarks
of Random House, Inc.

Grateful acknowledgment is made to Harcourt, Inc. and Faber and
Faber Ltd for permission to reprint an excerpt from the poem
"Hollow Man" from *Collected Poems 1909–1962* by T.S. Eliot.
Copyright © 1936 by Harcourt, Inc. Copyright © 1963, 1964
by T.S. Eliot. Reprinted by permission of Harcourt, Inc.
and Faber and Faber Ltd.

Library of Congress Cataloging-in-Publication Data

Rylands, Jane Turner, 1939–
Venetian stories / Jane Turner Rylands.

p.   cm.

ISBN 0-375-42232-3
1. Venice (Italy)—Fiction. I. Title.
PS3618.Y38 V4 2003
813'.6—dc21   2002035674

www.pantheonbooks.com
Book design by Virginia Tan
Printed in the United States of America
First Edition

2   4   6   8   9   7   5   3

for Philip and Augustus

CONTENTS

VENETIAN STORIES

POSTMAN

When the last quarter of the twentieth century opened throttle for the millennium and the Venice of today, the neighborhood of Salizada San Samuele was still a backwater that figured on no tourist route. Local shops and local people carried on a symbiosis hardly altered since the dawn of commerce, making forays into the wider world of Venice more a matter of style than necessity. The Salizada itself had not yet filled up with shops and drew its homely character from its service as the crossroads of its small community. Like all such neighborhoods that once flourished among the teeming footways of Venice, it was exclusive and had its own dramatis personae. Every weekday morning there were the housewives, today with their shoulders hunched and collars raised against the cold, hurrying through its broad expanse to the shops around the corner past the two sentries in the dry cleaner's, Marta and Bella, where they stood ironing in duet and caroling through the glass to this one and that one to come collect her waiting goods, *per favore.*

Around half past ten entered Mario the trash collector pushing his cart, followed by Zic the handyman. Together, in front of the dry cleaner's, they reviewed the day's take, smoking and making a show of anything *divertente*—an old hookah, a portrait of a long-forgotten granny brooding behind a dirty glass, a length of carved stone from a cornice that could have fallen on someone's head, a pair of faded curtains as long as the street was wide—before adjourning to Bar Bacareto, the broad-fronted *osteria* that presided over the top end of the street like a rosy monument over its avenue.

In those days, before the workers moved virtually en masse to the mainland and the *borghese* gave up on pets in favor of accessory dogs, the *calli* and *campi* were atrot with Identikit mongrels, each one recalling several different breeds but looking like none of them. In the neighborhood there were always some of these in the role of "good boys" on leads, looking for pats, and some "bad boys" on the loose, looking for trouble—but never with the cats who snoozed on sunny doorsteps impervious to their erstwhile predators, just as the pigeons waddled safe in the *campi* of the Serenissima. Coming in from the street of shops, deliverymen pushing *carrelli* cried out for room to pass—"*Attenzione alle gambe!*" Look out for your legs!—then dropped their carts and wandered off to join the trash collector, the handyman, and all the other regulars for the morning's *ombra* at the Bacareto. While over all, the maids, appearing here and there at balconies and windows, broadcast their industry in dust clouds from the heights.

But no one paid the slightest attention when Luigi Esposito approached the Salizada, as a beetle might venture from under a baseboard, pausing to see if the coast was clear, then scuttling along the nearest edge. Had anyone bothered to notice, his inelegant livery might have suggested something in common with the trash collector, but in fact no nexus joined them. For this stranger was not a *spazzino,* nor any other kind of steward of the Most Serene Republic. He was a *postino,* a minion of the State of Italy—and San Samuele was not even his appointed round. Luigi Esposito did not belong to this neighborhood. Furthermore, at eleven o'clock on a working day he belonged on his postal route several neighborhoods away. Luigi was only too aware of the anomaly, in all its applications, and halfway down the Salizada surrendered to its spur, breaking into a clumsy, skipping run to deliver himself into the sanctuary of Calle dell'Anzolo.

Safely out of sight, cosseted in dimness, Luigi Esposito braked his run to the lumbering gait that suited his stocky build, a stature that conspired with his dark eyes, his black curls, and his outfit of government issue, to present to the Venetian eye the perfect image of a Southerner, a *meridionale.* That was one of his problems. Another was that even though he was only thirty-three years old, he was clearly a character settled in his ways. As he walked along the *calle* he slouched forward to ease his progress. He let his hands ride idle in his pockets and let his elbows bounce at his sides so that his shoulders gave a little shrug at every step.

Ahead of him, toward the end of the *calle,* the palaces leaned closer and closer together until the confusion of eaves and chimney shafts let pass hardly enough daylight to mottle the pavement even at midday. The effect was suggestive, and many an intrepid stranger to Venice, venturing off the beaten path, had peered with misgiving into the depths of Calle dell'Anzolo and turned away convinced that he had come upon one of those fabled "assassin's alleys" where brooding ghosts lingered for revenge. Even Luigi Esposito, who had lived in Venice for nearly a dozen years, had approached this place one foggy morning not long before and shuddered to make out in the floating gloom a figure in a fluttering cape bearing down upon him. He had been about to fall to his knees and cry out, when he recognized the broad hat of the English *Reverendo* whom he'd seen coming and going from the great black door that loomed in the darkest part of that sunless reach, but who always said *buongiorno,* and let him pass unharmed.

Yet only a step or two beyond this darkness a small bend in the *calle* brought into view not merely the reassuring light of day but the spectacular flashing expanse of the Grand Canal. This was a bright winter's day, and it was toward this shimmering vista that Luigi Esposito was plying his footsteps through the deepening shadows.

From his shoulder swung the black leather bag which declared him unequivocally a deliverer of the post. He had, only minutes before, been going his rounds pressing doorbells, crying *"Posta! Posta!"* into a crackling intercom, or upward toward a querulous face peering down from a window ledge. In and out, heaving waterlogged doors over the undulations of ruined floors, feeding envelopes and magazines into mean, defiant slits, or tapping his feet in the cold while an old woman lowered a basket so she wouldn't have to come downstairs, he had resisted until he arrived at Campo Sant' Angelo. And then, even though he hadn't finished, and it wasn't time for lunch, he had given up and headed for San Samuele.

Emerging from the shade, he stood now at the water's edge, blinking in the brightness of the reflected sunlight. Almost opposite he could see the midmorning crowd milling on the *pontile* at San Toma, waiting for the vaporetto. Here and there at the edges of the Canal, islands of debris bobbed on the shoulders of the dancing waves. Near the steps where he stood, in a wreath of straw and flowers and grapefruit peels, floated a drowned cat so swollen it looked like a man's head. Beside it a writhing newspaper drifted slowly to the bottom. Farther out, where the current was stronger, a glinting motor oil can caught his eye and made him smile.

His son, Paolo, had found just such a can a few days before with some oil left in it. So he'd brought it home.

After Luigi had poured the oil into a jar, Paolo had chucked the can out the window into the canal. But someone in the neighborhood, probably right there in his own building, had called the police trying to make trouble. When the police knocked on the door and called out "*Vigili!*," Paolo had been frightened, but Luigi rose to the occasion. At first he pretended not to know what the police were talking about. Then, he stepped out into the corridor and complained in a loud voice that he, who had no boat, no motor, and no cause to have motor oil, let alone an empty motor oil can, had to submit to such questionings when there were others, taxi drivers and deliverymen with boats, who lived in the same building—he would be glad to show the good *vigili* where to find them. The silence that gripped the house in the wake of these declarations attested to the respect the hidden auditors felt for the *vigili,* and went a long way toward restoring the good humor these agents of the peace had lost in climbing the six flights of stairs to Luigi's door. Luigi was proud of himself.

But afterward, when the police had gone away, his wife had told him in front of the boy that it was wrong to lie. And later, when they were alone, she had scolded him again for setting a bad example. Sabrina was getting religious again: these days she ran to the priest about everything. His mother was religious too, but her case was different. What with chasing Babbo out to work at the brickyards every morning, and fetching him home from Bar Sport every night for thirty years, she had a right to some consolation. In actual fact, when Luigi was about ten, the job of fetching Babbo home for dinner fell to him, which meant tearing himself away from his comic book, from the hypnotic spell of *Paperino,* of Donald Duck. He would run as fast as he could and hope that Nando, the *barrista,* would be looking out the door and see him coming, because if he was, Nando would give him the thumbs-up sign and go straight over to the card tables and send his father home, so Luigi didn't have to come all the way. Nando was a pillar of the community as important as the priest, Don Gennaro, who happened to be his best pal. Nando harbored the menfolk after work and always attended to the wives and children. Sometimes he would call out, "Tell Mamma Rosa she can throw in the pasta," and Luigi would tear back home to snatch a few more minutes with *Paperino* until Babbo arrived. Sometimes if Mamma was ready to serve up the plates and she heard Babbo on the stairs, pulling himself up by the banister singing "*Valderi! Valdera!,*" she would shout to Luigi to go help his father. Going to the door which his mother had left open on purpose, he would find Babbo in the passage, rebounding from one wall to the other, trying to pot himself into the doorway. Then it would be dinner in the kitchen, then arguments, which sometimes included him, and which, after he learned the technique, he enjoyed, and then bed, and the world of *Paperino* until he fell asleep.

No wonder his mother used to love mending socks and

baking cakes for Don Gennaro who patted her hand and said how lucky her husband was. The priest regretted, however, that she had only the one child. Then one day soon after Luigi had gone looking for a good job up north, Babbo got himself crushed under a load of bricks falling from a crane. When his companions dug him out and saw how done in he was, they were loyal enough to make sure he was dead before the ambulance got there, so he never had to live with it. Then they saw to it that his mother got the workman's insurance and the pension. The owner of the brickyard was touched by the eleven strong men who came on Rosa's behalf to appeal to his better nature.

Anyhow, little Paolo had been thrilled at the way his father had won out over the police. Luigi smiled with pleasure then frowned at the thought that his wife's friends would say she was right. He would tell Paolo that he had seen his oil can making its getaway to the Lido. That would make him laugh.

He watched three women in fur coats being borne across the Canal on the *traghetto.* He scowled at their swaying backs as the labors of the rowers propelled them away.

He became aware of footsteps behind him. They stopped. A door opened and slammed. There was no further sound. He turned and walked back up the *calle,* scanning the upper stories as he approached a low doorway. As he unlocked the door and pressed his weight against it, he looked about once more.

In an instant he was inside leaning against the closed door and bolting it before feeling for the light switch. When the bare bulb flared over the cellarlike room, a sharp hiss made him start. In the far corner a gray tiger cat arched its back and swayed. Luigi realized with annoyance that it must have crept in when his mother came to leave more boxes. It hissed again, showing needlelike teeth. Its upper lip was quivering and its pupils were dilating and contracting as though trying to measure him. He picked up a pebble and threw it. The cat leaped forward, snatched a dead rat in its teeth, and dragged it under the trestle which held stacks of boxes and crates above flood level. Without taking its eyes off Luigi, the cat began clawing and biting at the rat's flesh. Luigi placed a chair in front of the iron stove and sat down with his back to the cat. Animals, when they showed their lack of feeling, revolted him.

He was sitting, safe at last, in the *magazzino* which he rented from his wife's uncle Gino, who had tried for years to get a high rent for it as a "workshop in the best neighborhood." Only one innocent had ever risen to the bait: a young carpenter who had quarreled with his *padrone* and was desperate to set up on his own. But it was too small even for a novice, so he had given it up at a loss and Luigi had been allowed to have it for the boxes and trunks he had no place to keep in the one-bedroom apartment where he lived with his wife and seven-year-old son, and now his poor widowed mother, dragged up from Naples to sleep on a sofa in a city where she would never feel at home. But she'd helped to make space for herself in the apartment by moving boxes of things to the *magazzino* with her shopping cart. In fact, it had become almost a mania with her, and no one knew exactly what she was packing and taking away. Sabrina said she hoped his mother might be planning to go live in the *magazzino*.

To make matters worse, there was probably another baby on the way. His mother had heard Sabrina being sick in the bathroom several months ago. But Sabrina still hadn't mentioned it. He lit a cigarette and blew out a cloud of smoke. He wondered why Sabrina couldn't manage better. The priest would gloat as if he'd made it happen himself. In a sense he had. Priests were always after more babies. The thought made Luigi reach for the wine bottle. He unscrewed the cap, took a deep swig, and gazed into space, waiting for comfort. The truth was that the *magazzino* was useful for more than storage. The real reason he had wanted it was because it was near his postal route and gave him a place to stop for a little rest, *un rifugio,* on a bad day.

Bending forward, he opened the door of the stove. He grabbed some wood shavings from the floor, held them to his cigarette lighter, and threw them inside. A small flame shot up and he reached into his bag for something to keep it going. He found a postcard. With his lighter he lit around the edges and added it to the fire. He watched it burn and curl, as though shrinking with pain. Someone he met once had worked in a crematorium in England and told him that corpses would sit up in the fire and scream. He stared at the words sinking into blackness, and only just in time remembered to scoop up some more sawdust and shavings to keep the fire burning.

Luigi lifted the bottle from the crate and took another gulp. As he did so, he noticed a loose strip of wood on the crate's side, which he grabbed with his free hand. He gave a sharp yank and pulled it off. Through the gap it opened, a child's wooden block rolled onto the floor. He snapped the strip over his knee and put the pieces on the fire. He picked up the block, which had a letter on each face; he turned it around and around, looking for his initials, then threw it too into the flames.

The stove began to give off some heat. Luigi pulled his bag onto his lap and fumbled among the bills in the bottom for the remaining letters. Letting the bag drop to the floor, he arranged the letters on his knees with their addresses downward. Facts spoiled the ritual. On top there was an air letter from Australia. He dug in his pocket for his pen-knife. With the sharp blade he cut a splinter from the crate beside him, but it was too thick and blunt, so he threw it into the fire. He cut another, thinner one. He put his knife back in his pocket and with the splinter ripped open the sides of the air letter. He unfolded the flimsy blue paper and scanned it hastily lest the fire should go out.

Someone was starting a farm . . . needed rain . . . last letter took over a month . . . had met a lot of Italians . . . helped with everything . . . missing Italy . . . all well . . . hoped to have money to visit next year . . . hearts . . . children's scribbles. Nothing important. He was glad it was good news, and he added it to the fire with a benevolent smile that showed no teeth, like the one the Pope was wearing blessing the little children in the picture that Sabrina had taped up in the bedroom the other day.

He stuck his finger under the lid of a coarse envelope and brought out a letter scrawled in such clumsy writing that he could hardly make it out. As he unfolded the paper, a soft ten-thousand-lire note floated into his lap. "Our dearest ones," the letter began. Luigi stared at the scrawled words for a while and then looked up in disgust. It was written in some dialect.

He could imagine what it said. It would be two old farm people who lived in a shanty, who grew everything they ate and never had any money unless they sold a rabbit, or some eggs. They had a daughter who was too beautiful for her own good. She had run away from home and they hadn't seen her for years. One day she came back. She had with her two little children, but no husband. He was dead, she told them. She stayed with the old folks for a few weeks, but then she couldn't stand it away from the city any longer. So she took the two children and left. She wrote to the old folks now and then telling them her latest address. They wrote to her saying how much they loved her and sent her money so she could come and bring the children to see them again. But she never came. His throat ached with feeling as he told himself the story.

He looked at the banknote and wished it had not been his fate to open that letter. And yet, being touched by such good and simple people was a blessing in itself. He laid the letter in the flames and, placing the money in the envelope, laid that too in the fire as an offering, near the edge. He watched as the envelope turned brown and then caught fire. Quick as a flash he plucked it from the fire, dropped it, and stamped out the flames. Ruefully, he removed the ten-thousand-lire note and pushed it into his pocket. Without looking up he tossed the envelope back into the stove. He would, he resolved, as he noticed the cracks in his shoes, put five thousand into the poor box at church to show his gratitude to God that there were still such good people on earth. He felt a grace descend over him. Perhaps, he pondered, it would be wrong to give any of it away. He could use it, God knew. And who but God had put it in his way?

Luigi's finger hurt where he'd burned it on the envelope. He looked at his hands and saw the dirt under the nails. The hands of a workingman, he thought with a sigh, and poured some wine over his finger before sticking it in his mouth to soothe it.

The cat had finished with the rat, and stalked to the door not to be locked in a second time. It sat licking its paws and waiting.

The cat was right. It was time to go. He arranged the remaining letters like a hand of playing cards and chose one, which he put on the crate beside him. The rest he opened and spread on the fire without bothering to read them. He uncapped the wine and took two more gulps.

He ripped the end from the last envelope and brought out a sheet of paper covered with flowing lines of elegant script. It was in French. Carefully he studied the sentences for words of love. Once when he was working in a hotel he had fallen in love with a French girl. All one afternoon he had memorized words from a dictionary, and that evening, after a *passeggiata* in the Piazza to the music of Florian's and Quadri's, he had drawn her into a doorway and whispered in her ear, "*Baisez moi,*" whereupon she had slapped his cheek as hard as she could.

He pulled a face at the memory and, finding no mention of *amour,* decided the letter had to do with thanks for a favor. "*Merci, merci beaucoup,*" they were saying at the end. Someone on his postal route had gone to some trouble for someone in France and they were deeply grateful. He understood the situation perfectly. His countrymen were always performing acts of kindness toward strangers who didn't know what to make of their openhearted and friendly ways. They were sympathetic and understanding in their very natures. We are, he murmured to himself, probably the kindest people on God's earth. He put the letter into the stove, but the thought stayed with him.

In a reverie he watched the last letter disappear into the merest crumpled ash. And at this evidence of human vanity his heart welled with sentiment that flooded his whole being. Hot tears sprang to his eyes. Unashamed, he turned and let the staring cat see them roll down his cheeks.

ARCHITECT

B efore Vittorio Falon was even sixteen, he had been in the best houses of Venice. The experience opened his eyes and worked to his advantage. Even in the short term it gave him a certain confidence that riding down the Grand Canal with his schoolmates he could look up from the vaporetto and know who lived in this palace, or that one, and envisage the rooms that looking up from the Canal one can barely see. But Vittorio was discreet beyond his years and never let on to his peers. Now, nearly twenty years later, he found himself welcomed once again into these great houses, but the people who invited him seemed not to recall his former visits. So he never reminded them.

His reticence had partly to do with the fact that he knew himself to be one of a dying breed: a Venetian with a future in Venice. But there was more to it than that. For as long as he could remember, he had been teased by the notion that the stream of fate which had conveyed his father, at the early age of twenty-one, to the surprise inheritance of a draper's shop in the Merceria, was transporting him too toward some unforeseen destiny. His only fear was that when his moment came, he might not be as apt as his father, or worse, that when it came he might not even recognize it.

When Secondo Falon inherited Morello & Figli, from a great-uncle without *figli,* the beauty of the business was that it was stable, so that being continued on established lines, it would continue to yield a comfortable living to a hardworking proprietor. The awkwardness was that Secondo's good fortune revealed to him that he had no heart for drudgery. What he saw sparkling in his overflowing cup was not so much the money as an unexpected sense of romance. And that was the sense in which he welcomed his new destiny: the mantle of Venetian merchant had fallen to him; he would embrace the legacy to the full. So with the ardor of youth he jettisoned his uncle's stock that had served the prosaic needs of so many for so long, and spangled his shelves instead with the princely sheens and midnight rainbow hues of the handsomest furnishing fabrics money could buy. The radiance set off against the antique shelves and paneling was overpowering. Under Secondo's rule, Morello & Figli was less a shop than a conjuror's den crepitating with notions of potentates and power. His advisers reproved him with the proverb of sinking one's fortune in a single ship, but Secondo had his own maxim: the love of luxurious goods was as ingrained in his fellow Venetians as in himself, and they would suffer to go without dish towels and aprons if their sumptuous furnishings hung in the balance. It became the stuff of legend. Morello & Figli flourished as never before.

But while the tide of prosperity was at the flood for Morello & Figli, in the highest quarters of Venice the tide was low, and getting lower, as reservoirs of ancient wealth ebbed slowly away. In due course, when the old families could no longer afford to run their *palazzi* and were constrained, one after the other, to divide them into apartments, Secondo's business multiplied like images in a shattered mirror, for he was called upon to furnish each fragment with the richness implied by the whole.

In any case, his business had never been solely with the great, for all who aspired to share in the gorgeous atmosphere of Venice bought from him: the rich bought fabrics by the bolt, but the less rich bought many bolts of fabric by the meter. And he had the good sense to accord these customers their full weight as the anchor of his business whose steady custom kept him stable. He favored them also because it made him feel munificent, as though he conferred a blessing by helping them to their rightful share in the splendor which their city flaunted all around them. He would spend hours with them advising on the best fabric to cover a single side chair, or even a footstool.

Secondo's wife, Donata Manina, took a different attitude, and was a perfect complement to him. She enjoyed above all the custom of the noble families and the rich foreigners who came to live in Venice. She loved to serve their every whim as they gilded and regilded their grand *palazzi,* or even their rented *piani nobili.* Indeed, after the birth of her only child, Vittorio, the moment when she might have been expected to retire, she redoubled her interest in this part of the business. Eventually all the great commissions came directly to her. And she personally attended to each one. She herself went with an assistant to show books of swatches to her customers, to take measurements, to consult and give advice, to avoid the simultaneous appearance of similar fabrics in the houses of neighbors, or even worse, of friends. She became The Indispensable Guide.

When Vittorio was fourteen, she taught him how to take measurements with an efficiency and a dignity which inspired confidence and respect. He was a quiet, serious boy and, as an only child often does, he kept mainly the company of his parents. After school, and in the summer vacations, he was his mother's assistant. Sometimes she would coach him to make suggestions that she knew would be received with enthusiasm. The two of them were a great success together, and Vittorio gained such pleasure and poise from the consideration accorded him, in spite of his youth, that he was eager to begin taking over from his father as soon as he could put his schooling behind him.

But his mother had other plans. She wanted him to become an architect. She inured in him the benefits of that training, coupled with his present knowledge. He knew he would be wise to continue to follow her advice. He set out to specialize in interior design, but while he was still a student in Rome, his father died. Vittorio was ready to come back and take his father's place, but his mother would not hear of his abandoning his studies. Instead, she brought a manager from Milan to run the business. She chose well: Dott. Verdi was not merely capable of the day-to-day operation of the shop, he proved to have an excellent touch for the grand business as well. At this, the mother retired, ceded to Dott. Verdi the apartment over the shop, and found an apartment for herself and her son on the Grand Canal. The location was something she had insisted upon, but she had been obliged to compromise on certain amenities in order to afford it.

Nowadays when visiting in his mother's house it infuriated Vittorio that he was every night, and several times a night, startled awake by thuds and squeaks followed by prolonged shudders, capped by the arrogant *clang!* of the vaporetto's gate being shot violently into place. Footsteps and voices echoed around his bedroom. *Why*, he could not understand, she persisted in the martyrdom of living in this apartment. Everything was wrong with it. The layout was impossible: an entrance into a long, dark corridor onto which opened first two bathrooms side by side, followed by a kitchen with a dining room opposite, then two bedrooms to which the faraway bathrooms theoretically related, and then at the end, the *salone,* or drawing room, with two windows—this was the *pièce de resistance*—overlooking the Grand Canal.

A view of the Grand Canal, yes, but at what price! Immediately below these windows was a vaporetto stop: all day there was a murmur of activity there, which peaked every ten minutes as the boats arrived. Very late at night the boats became less frequent. So their arrival came as a sudden shock. He had begged her to move to a different location, but she was stubborn on the issue. When he came home to stay with her, especially on weekends, she would often sleep until ten o'clock, and then excuse her tardiness by saying that she had been kept awake by the noise. But she would always add that she didn't usually notice it, that maybe she noticed it more when he was there because she knew it bothered him.

Tonight it particularly irritated him. He was beginning to feel superior and protective toward his poor old mother. She didn't seem to have any interest in her life apart from him. He listened for sounds from her bedroom, but there were none and he concluded that she had probably been lying awake for hours anticipating this racket. He wondered how often she was kept awake like that. She had been living here for nearly fifteen years, since when he was at university. She used to say she'd got used to it, but would move someday. Now he perceived it was beginning to wear her down. Soon, he surmised, her health could begin to fail.

He was glad that he had started to pay more attention to her again.

When he had first set up his practice as an architect, he had been eager to establish himself outside her influence. Also, somehow, he did not quite like the idea of reasserting in the public mind the direct association with Morello & Figli; at least not at first, even though his Roman girlfriend, Flavia, was impressed by it and thought it extravagant to leave it for others to manage. But he categorically refused to turn his attention in that direction until he had made his own name. Flavia's ambition to manage Morello & Figli did not convince him, and it was his opposition to it which prompted him to avoid introducing her to his mother for fear they might hit it off. Little by little Flavia lost interest in coming to Venice and eventually she gave up on him. So for a while he had no women in his life at all.

But somehow, as he began to acquire bigger projects and important clients, he felt himself drawn into his mother's company again. He marveled at how much she still knew about life in Venice and especially how much she was able to tell him about the patrician families who used to be her customers. When he told her about the commission he was about to receive to create a mezzanine apartment for the Decardi son, who was getting married and coming back to Venice to live, she had advised him not to turn away other work on the expectation of being occupied with that project as there was trouble about the marriage and the wedding had been postponed; it might even be called off. They would probably do the apartment anyway, she maintained, but they would not be in a hurry. She ventured that it might be tactful for him to suggest that they take some time to think over the plans. He did that, and the Decardis were so delighted with him for being so easy to deal with they invited him to a cocktail party that same evening. He met there the Patristis, and out of that meeting he had acquired a large, prestigious project in their enormous *palazzo.*

His mother had somehow divined the right course so many times recently that their old harmony returned. He began to confide in her and seek her opinions. But he would not come to live with her. Nor, to be fair, did she want him to. She wanted him to get married. But she begged him not to marry just any ordinary girl; she wanted him to have someone elegant and bright who would be a help to him. That was her sole reservation. When he told her that Flavia had drifted out of the picture, she actually clapped her hands with spontaneous delight.

His mother's cleverness as a manager of situations he had always accepted as one of his natural advantages, but coming back to it after a time, he was more impressed by it than ever and wondered how his mother, retired these many years, managed to be so well informed about the private lives of the *alta società.* He knew that she had no companions and rarely visited other people's houses. But when he asked her how she kept abreast of a world she didn't even inhabit, she reminded him with an injured air that she had known these people, many of them, since before he was born. And although they weren't really social friends, she saw them out for coffee and about the town; they trusted her not to be too interested in their private lives and so were less guarded with her than they would be with most of their friends.

As Vittorio lay in bed now, awake and thoughtful, he felt a wave of childlike admiration for her, which was followed by a wave of affectionate concern. He wondered if she wanted someone to talk to, lying awake in her room. Almost an hour had passed since they said good night. He could hear people walking down the *calle* to the vaporetto. The opera must be over, he thought. And though they were laughing and talking in an undertone befitting the time of night, they might as well have been walking through his bedroom, so clearly could he hear their echoing voices. It was, he knew, an effect of being near the water that amplified every *ciao-ciao,* clip-clop, cough, slam, or mutter, and he wondered if Venetian politicians in the cloak-and-dagger days had been wise to the perils of giving utterance near a waterway, or was that the unknown factor by which so many of them came to grief. It was precisely because one heard so much from the *calle* that he always took this room when he was home, although he knew that when he was away his mother often slept here herself. This practice he regarded as evidence of her loneliness for him.

He arose quietly and tiptoed to the hall to look into his mother's room. But a rustle made him look into the drawing room. The light from the vaporetto stop glowed through the window that gave directly onto it; his mother never closed the shutters there because, she claimed, she had paid so dearly for the Grand Canal view. In the lower half of the window where she had trailed ivy over the iron grillework, the light flickered through the leaves. Suddenly he made out her form silhouetted against it. She was sitting by the window with her back to him. She seemed to be doing something with her hands. He heard another rustle and saw that she was writing with the quick, short jottings he knew from the days when she used to have detail consultations with clients. But what was she writing? He heard some voices from outside the window. Two women were below talking in an undertone. He guessed that they had decided to hang back from the *pontile* until the boat arrived so they could talk privately. He concentrated on the voices; they became more distinct.

"But are you sure?"

"Oh I *know.* Listen to this: Matteo was coming back from staying with a friend in Bergamo. As Edmondo was in the country, I thought it would be a good idea, since Matteo's only twelve, if he met his train in Verona and came back with him. But by a twist of fate Matteo's friends put him on an earlier train, so he had to get off at Verona and wait. He was wandering about the station when he happened to look in the window of the bar and see Edmondo kissing a woman. And guess who it was: his ex-secretary; the one who left Venice last year and then came back, Marda Segusio. Somehow Matteo managed to keep his wits about him and succeeded in boarding the train he was supposed to be on without their seeing him. Then he watched them get on separately. Five minutes later they pretended in front of Matteo to be amazed to meet. So now Matteo has seen for himself what a *buffone* his father can be."

"How awful for him."

"He can hardly stand to be in the same room with him, he's so embarrassed for him. Just like I felt the first time I caught him."

"But the poor boy. Twelve is the worst age for that sort of thing. What about little Esmeralda?"

"She's only four so she doesn't know anything about it. For her it will all come later. But I've promised Matteo that this time I will get a divorce."

"Couldn't you wait? Maybe it's just a passing fancy."

"Oh you know as well as I do that this thing's been going on for years. And before this one there was Moceniga Carrara. I almost divorced him then, but it's better this time. He couldn't *possibly* bring himself to marry his secretary; he's such a snob. But she's *very* ambitious, and *very* determined. It will be fun watching him squirm. I'll bet you *any-*

thing he comes right out with it and asks me to stay married to him until he can get rid of her. He's so *spoiled.* Anyhow, keep it quiet for now. I don't want my mother to find out or she'll start an *intervento* to save her daughter's famous marriage. Since she made it, she thinks she has artistic rights over it. *Eccolo,* there's our boat. We'd better join the others. Won't they be thrilled when they find out? Something to talk about."

"You can trust me. It's too sad to talk about."

He heard them walking down the ramp and could just see their heads as they walked across the *pontile.* The one was Baronessa Bonome, the other was Sofi Patristi. Vittorio was dumbfounded. He had been invited to drinks by Edmondo Patristi at Palazzo Patristi only two days ago to start work on the restoration. She had been with them. People said it was her money that paid the bills.

The vaporetto thundered up to the *pontile* and Vittorio took the opportunity to creep back to bed. He had lost the desire to interrupt his mother's sleeplessness. He felt changed, as though invested with a forbidden power. All at once he was gripped by the desire to laugh. Of course—his mother's information: *that* was how she got it. People came to the vaporetto stop from the Teatro La Fenice, from the Gritti Palace, from the Monaco. And late at night, when there were few people, they talked. And the meetings for coffee? She had said she *saw* them at coffee, not that she had coffee with them, and they trusted her—yes, he could see it all now—they trusted her, an old woman sitting quietly at the next table occupied with her newspaper—or more likely her notebook—they trusted her by not even noticing her. After all, she was nothing more than a familiar face, like the hundreds of familiar faces in Venice that one nods to in the narrow *calli* day in and day out all through the seasons, year in, year out, without quite being able to place them. And so she knew all, carefully overheard conversations at Café Florian, Paolin, the Gritti Terrace, the bar at the Monaco. And then the nightly vigils. He smiled in the dark. He wondered whether he would tease her about it in the morning or whether he would let her keep her secret. He decided to hold his peace. But he would bring her breakfast in bed at ten o'clock. *Mamma mia!* No wonder she gets so tired.

He must have dozed off, for he was startled by the sound of footsteps, slow, heavy, weary footsteps coming along the *calle*. Automatically he slipped out of bed and crept soundlessly toward the hall. It amused him that he had caught the habit after a single exposure. Like mother like son, he concluded as he reached the door of the drawing room; but he was surprised, in spite of himself, to find her still watching. So she hadn't even taken a nap. He admired her stamina, her determination, but he wondered if it could possibly be worth it at this hour. He checked himself: for he could see on the *pontile* the head of Edmondo Patristi. She is following a pattern she knows, he realized. He watched Edmondo move as though to straighten his tie and stretch his back. The man was tired, it was obvious from the way his shoulders sagged. He saw him put a handkerchief to his lips and wipe them and then look at the handkerchief. He made a quick gesture. He must have thrown it away, Vittorio decided. The distant hum of the vaporetto increased to a roar as it approached. Vittorio shrugged his shoulders at the noise and under its cover returned once again to bed. Shortly afterward he heard his mother's bed squeak and he fell into a sound sleep.

When he awoke he was troubled. Something had happened to him since last night, something important. He got up slowly and opened the shutters. He looked up the *calle* and then toward the vaporetto stop. He remembered those strange, incredible things that had happened in the night. This morning he was the same man, Vittorio Falon, architect and interior designer, and yet he had acquired a new dimension; he had glimpsed the world from Olympus. What fools these mortals be, he grinned to himself, and then remembered his mother. He would go and make breakfast to pass the time until she woke up. He longed to see her and speak to her, despite his resolve to say nothing of last night's adventures.

He dressed but decided not to shave right away. She wouldn't scold him if she didn't have to sit opposite him.

He would shave while she was having her breakfast in bed. But he took his shaving bag with him to the kitchen anyhow, since it was halfway to the bathroom. He was pondering for the thousandth time the conundrum of how one might rationalize this badly designed apartment when he turned in to the kitchen and found his mother already there.

"Good morning," she smiled at him. "Did you get enough sleep?"

Vittorio wondered for an instant whether she knew that he had been with her last night.

"I couldn't sleep very well because of the horrible racket," he ventured. "I don't know why you ever sleep in that room. One hears everything."

"Yes, I think you're right. Last night I slept like an angel. Perhaps I should always sleep in the other room."

Vittorio dismissed his suspicions. The brioches were already on the table, so he sat down. She brought the coffee and sat down opposite him.

"Sorry I haven't shaved. I was going to bring you breakfast in bed," he said.

"Dear boy!" she exclaimed. "I am so glad to be up early. I don't like to make you late. I know you like to catch up on your work on Sundays. Tell me all about what you're doing. What are your new jobs?"

"Well," he began cautiously, "I told you about the two public jobs, and I told you about the Palazzo Patristi. There's nothing more, really."

"Ah," she replied. "Palazzo Patristi. Isn't that a big job?"

"Yes. Yes it is. A big job. It's complicated. They haven't done any work for years and it needs a general structural repair and a lot of remodeling and restoration."

"That sounds expensive," she observed, taking a hungry bite out of a brioche and gazing thoughtfully at the jam oozing from the stump. "Where does the money come from? Do you believe the rumors that the money is hers?"

"Oh, I don't know. But when I spoke to them she took an interest in the money side, I can say that much."

"I see. So you know them both—Barone Edmondo *and* Baronessa Sofi."

"Yes . . ."

"She is lovely, don't you agree? Beautiful, charming, and, it appears, very rich. I think she's an excellent young woman. It's a pity her husband doesn't think so."

"*Mamma!* How can you say such a thing!"

"*Vittorio!* How can you talk to me like that? I know a great deal about your clients Patristi, and I speak only to you. If you'll listen to your mother like a good boy, I'll tell you a thing or two. Then *you'll* have to be discreet."

"Of course, Mamma." He dreaded hearing her retail the conversations he had heard for himself.

"Haven't I helped you before?"

"Indeed."

"Well then. You should pay attention to me; I'm only trying to help you. Now listen: Barone Edmondo is in love with another woman. The Baronessa has discovered this and she intends to send him away. Very soon." She stopped, surprised by her own strident tones, to compose herself.

After a pause, she added quietly, "I hope that when you are there working with Baronessa Patristi, you will include young Matteo in your discussions. He will be interested in your designs, and you will want his approval."

As the words settled over him, Vittorio blinked like a man emerging from a bank of clouds, thunderstruck at where he found himself. He recognized his future beckoning to him over a ground plan—and though it was only roughly sketched at the moment, he saw perfectly how it could be developed, and realized.

His mother dusted the crumbs from her fingertips and pushed her chair away from the table. "I had a good night last night, Vittorio," she yawned, "but I think that once you're married, I'll give up the view and move to a quieter place."

COLLECTOR

As Ermintrude Gotham looked back over her many years in Venice, among the most vivid extrusions she saw marking the landscape were antagonisms, some of which persisted for many years and changed, for an interval at least, the social orientation of her life. Sometimes they entangled others, sometimes even—such was the nature of Venetian life—they had little to do with her personally but entangled her anyhow. Some divided the whole of Venetian society and determined the shape of great social events, of charity balls, and royal visits. Turning the pages of her photograph album was illuminating; one could note the missing and then flick ahead to see some of them come back again, older, and perhaps wiser. There were those that one never would have expected to see again, and others that one never would have expected to disappear, even for an interval. Of the two, the former cases were by far the more interesting ones. There was, of course, a third case, of those who disappeared never to return, which was least interesting of all. Baronessa Notabene's *uscita di scena* was one of these.

Ermintrude Gotham, better known as Trudi Gotham, came to Venice by an unusual route. She was the daughter of the great New York book collector German Gotham, whose vast collection had been generously apportioned to five universities after his death. To his daughter he left his important name, a sizable fortune, and a winning character. She started collecting autobiographical materials, more specifically diaries, virtually by accident.

When she finished her university degree at Grenoble, she went to Praglia, near Venice, to learn from the *Frate* about book restoration, then accepted an offer in London to join the staff of the famous antiquarian bookseller Bertrand Quatriem, where she encountered the great amateur bibliophile and serial marrier, Viscount Cato. After a brief friendship bred among the incunabula, he acquired her. As Lady Cato of Lievedon Hall, she became a famous hostess, and she might have continued as such had it not transpired that one of their more illustrious guests left his diary behind and unwittingly won her away to a new career.

The maids, thinking the handsome book to be one of the many thousands belonging to the Hall, put it in the library to be shelved by either Lord Cato's secretary or Lady Cato, who shared this work between them. The diary proved a problem for the secretary, who left it for Lady Cato with a note asking her to give it her attention. It turned out to be an enchanted portal through which Trudi Cato eventually found her way to Venice.

As it happened the maids couldn't remember in which bedroom they'd found the anonymous volume, but Lady Cato was sure she recognized its author by both his tone and his handwriting. Nevertheless it was an awkward situation, as the entries describing the author's stay at Lievedon were largely devoted to musing about the mismatched marriage of Lord Cato to the forthright, but curiously shy, young American. In that character, Lady Cato wrote to the author asking whether he had left a very handsome book at Lievedon and avoided calling it a diary, specifying instead *8. vo, full calf, gilt borders with tooled gilt eglantine motif on spine, 200 pp, watermarked paper, ca. 100 ms, F.* He, being none other than her former employer Bertrand Quatriem, wasn't fooled. His reply took the form of a bread-and-butter note praising his hostess and saying that he had not left the book. Having said that, he went on to observe that the folly of keeping a diary was its pernicious tendency to encourage idle speculation. She took the point. And they remained friends.

But his folly was the world's fortune. When he denied ownership of the book he removed any scruple Lady Cato might have felt about reading it, thus opening the way for her interest in the way people live their lives. Like Lady Cato herself, the interest was principled and serious, with no quarter for wickedness. When in due course she divorced Lord

Cato, she set off straightaway in her father's footsteps to become in record time a noted collector. Her fame came partly from the fact that her collection was unusual. No collector before her had focused so closely on diaries and letters, particularly on modern and contemporary ones. She was convinced that hers was an era in which life stories were of special interest, a conviction she based on the observation that the world was changing so fast that a personal account offered the opportunity to ponder change and diminish the sense of loss. Her fame came also from the fact that she encouraged the writing of journals and diaries by awarding financial grants to promising young writers, artists, actors, scientists, in fact to anyone of sufficient interest who came to her attention, to keep a diary for one year, which would at the end of the year become a part of her collection, and, if it had exceptional merit, would make possible the extension of the grant for a further period. Many young geniuses wrote diaries for Trudi Gotham for five or ten years to finance their early careers. Some, who later became famous, felt that their diaries were worth more than they had been paid for them, and begrudged Trudi her share in their success. They realized that in a sense, they were still working for her. Their ingratitude deterred Trudi no more than the condescending speculations in the diary which brought her collection into being. But there was a more interesting phenomenon at work. The effect of frequent success among her diarists mimicked Calvin's doctrine of predestination, becoming almost a doctrine itself: a person with a Gotham grant was among the elect and therefore would succeed.

She had lived for a time in London but, finding herself too much in the shadow of her former marriage, moved to Rome, where she was known as Trudi Cato. While in Rome she commissioned some diaries on her usual basis, but had problems with people who had taken the money and written the diaries, then decided that they would rather keep them or publish them for more money. As she already had considerable experience in the matter and took great care over her contracts, she always won the day. It became a joke in Rome, an exclamation by someone who felt he'd been seduced with money to make a deal he later didn't want to keep: *Sono stato trudicato!*

In truth, there was one instance of a contract which she didn't enforce with such ease and which festered in the legal system for a number of years. She discovered in Rome an interesting but strangely rootless young man who seemed to know everyone and be invited everywhere. He was called Manfredo Nofretti and she ran into him frequently. He seemed to know several of the clever young people who had grants from her. So when he asked her, point-blank, if he could have a grant and write a diary, she was cornered. She wasn't accustomed to being accosted by social acquaintances asking for grants, and while she had no doubt that Mani was intelligent, he didn't seem to do anything except appear at cocktail parties and receptions, and the last thing she wanted to sponsor was a volume of idle gossip. Finally, she explained her terms and her position on social chatter, and drew up with him her usual contract. Within a month she had evidence that she had done the right thing; two people, both of them grantees, rang her to say that they had seen Mani's first chapter and it looked promising. Later she began to hear at regular intervals from different people that they had read extracts from his forthcoming journal, which were simply brilliant. Trudi was delighted; for one thing, she was eager to increase the Italian section of her library; for another, this diary promised to be a new departure, which always pleased her. But when the diary fell due, he refused to hand it over. He said it wasn't quite ready. When she offered to extend his grant on the basis of her evaluation of what he had so far written, he hinted that he thought he could earn more by taking it to a publisher. At that point, she turned it over to her faithful lawyer, Davide Bari, who never failed her. Nevertheless, Manfredo Nofretti proved a difficult nut to crack, and he was still holding out against Bari's unflagging efforts and diverse tactics long after Trudi moved to Venice.

Her discontent with the metropolitan sprawl of Rome asserted itself within months of her arrival, inviting fond thoughts of Venice, with its human dimensions, where she had spent her summers before her marriage and which she knew well. After a few years in Rome, she heard through friends of a vacant palace on the Grand Canal not far from

San Vidal. It had belonged to Glorio Colana, a much-loved playboy in pre-war Venice, who had died in the war. His wife had gone back to her family in France "for the duration" and never reappeared. After long litigation, Palazzo Colana had finally come up for sale. Trudi Cato bought it and brought her library to Venice. She took back her maiden name and went on commissioning diaries.

Palazzo Colana was perfect for her purposes: the ground floor had space for a porter's apartment and various offices, the first *piano nobile* had the traditional huge *salone* running from front to back, ideal for a reading room, with rooms on both sides for stacks and other deposits as well as offices and workrooms, while the upper *piano nobile* was equally grand but somewhat cozier, and on the top there was a guest apartment with beautiful views. There was only one problem. Although her architect had succeeded in acquiring the building permit to make the physical adjustments required for her library, her Venetian lawyer could not seem to get the permit for her to run the library as an institution and open it to the public.

When she moved to Venice, she had followed the established practice of taking recommendations from local friends before commissioning an architect and choosing a lawyer to steer her various applications for permits through the authorities. In both cases, she had chosen the professional recognized by the upper crust as having the best rapport with the requisite authorities. The young architect, Vittorio

Falon, had lived up to his name and without a false step had galloped over and around the difficulties like a *palio* winner at Siena, whereas the lawyer, Corrado La Strada, of a much nobler pedigree and the universal pick for winner, was instead getting mired down at every turn. His excuses were becoming so complicated and long-winded that Trudi stopped listening to them, even at cocktail parties; she could imagine the hours he was charging to her account on the basis of these elaborations. When at last the works were finished and the house was ready for occupation, both as residence and library, Trudi had a tense conversation with Avvocato La Strada. The next day he came up with a temporary solution which, though bad, was better than nothing. He recommended a temporary oral agreement which amounted in fact to a postponement for perhaps a year of an enforcement of the ban on running such institutions without a permit. There were two drawbacks he felt obliged to point out: the deal would be expensive to arrange, and could, conceivably, militate against her being granted the permanent status she was seeking. However, if she wanted to avoid further delay, there was no other option. Trudi entertained a stream of unholy thoughts concerning Byzantium and accepted the terms.

Trudi Gotham had met Patrick Mayer in London after her divorce. He had come out to visit her several times in Rome, where he had once lived and knew even more people than she did. When he visited her for the first time in

Palazzo Colana, she was on the verge of acquiring her temporary permit, or rather stay of prosecution, for opening the Gotham Library of Autobiographical Materials to the public. From the first he had been interested in her collection, and even recommended candidates for grants. During his visit, they passed the time shelving books, installing the card catalog, and working through correspondence from people who wanted to consult materials in the library. There was a backlog of work, much of it too esoteric for her new secretary, evaluating proposed research projects and assessing fees, which Patrick was able to expedite as well as Trudi could herself. He knew many of the writers who applied to consult the library, and many of the people whose materials were being consulted, so he was an invaluable aide. But perhaps most important of all, he was amusing to be with and amused to be there. She hired him as chief librarian and gave him a suite of rooms on the top floor with a view over the rooftops toward San Marco and the Campanile. She paid him generously, but obliged him to join her famous dinner parties on a regular basis. He was the one detailed to answer questions about the GLAM and after dinner, over the coffee cups and brandy snifters, to let escape an indiscretion or two about the authors or the collection, so that guests were dispatched home with stomachs and ears full of delectable morsels. It worked a treat: esteem for the collection soared, Pat Mayer became nearly as famous as Trudi Gotham herself, and hardly anyone noticed that it wasn't spontaneous, that behind it all was the deft instinct of wily old German Gotham's heiress.

Hardly anyone except for a few aged society dames, that is, who saw only too well that it was not merely calculated, this persistent accretion of fame and worth, but that it was undeserved. They would have loved to be essential to the phenomenon, but they had made a mistake, which they always referred to among themselves as *Her First Big Mistake.* When Miss Gotham came to live in Venice, as she met new people, she routinely invited them to her parties, and she made no exception *vis-à-vis* the elder ladies of the nobility. Although Ermintrude Gotham was grand in her own way, she was unpretentious, and forthright to a fault. For her, an acquaintance was an acquaintance and an invitation was an invitation. And likewise, a "no" was a "no." Among themselves the ladies agreed to apply the standard strategy of not being in a hurry to accept her, certain that she would come to appreciate them better as a result. In fact, they had nothing against her except that she was coming on a bit too fast. Through a rite not entirely different from the courtship routine of pigeons—in which the suitor struts and preens while the lady feigns aloofness over repeated supplications until the suitor's ardor wanes, then at last the lady all at once relents and they come together to perpetuate the society of pigeon life—the ladies initiated the ritual by turning down Miss Gotham's first invitations with hauteur. But Trudi Gotham, having been brought up where a spade is a spade, took their behavior at face value and let them go. Although she didn't register the fact at the time, it was nevertheless true: her star was rising, theirs was sinking. She hardly missed them, but these few never forgave her for being so unsophisticated as to fly away at the first rejection. Their leader loomed one more time on Ermintrude Gotham's horizon.

Baronessa Notabene was the Anointed Queen of Venetian Society. Everyone knew how she stood in her own regard. Even workmen dusted their shoes on the mat with ridiculous care and smoothed their shapeless clothes with absurd self-consciousness before presenting themselves in her courtyard. Her sway among the grand elders, among her own generation, knew no bounds: her wishes were commands. She had several daughters, but there was no dauphiness among them. She had ascertained this when they were still in their teens. She looked no further afield. She committed her court to a course of *après moi le déluge* and reigned as if she were immortal.

The Gotham Library of Autobiographical Materials had opened under its temporary arrangement and after only a few months seemed well on its way to becoming an established institution, a circumstance that pleased Trudi and reassured her that she would get the necessary permit in due course. Less reassuring was the reaction of Avvocato La Strada, who seemed concerned rather than pleased. One morning he telephoned to say that his close friend Baronessa

Notabene wished to pay a private visit to the library before opening hours. Could Miss Gotham receive her the following morning at nine o'clock? Trudi was mystified but agreeable. She was left wondering: What on earth could be of interest to Baronessa Notabene in the Gotham Library of Autobiographical Materials?

The following morning Trudi Gotham presented herself in the Library to meet the Baronessa. Her lawyer brought her guest slowly up the stairs; she was holding his arm and carrying a silver-headed walking stick. The Baronessa was dressed in black, with a black hat and a short veil pulled down over her eyes. At the door, she avoided looking at Trudi and acknowledged her greeting by nodding to the Avvocato. She looked around the room.

"The Baronessa would like to look at the books," said the Avvocato. "I'll show her around." Trudi followed as he guided her first to the French section. She scanned the shelves for some minutes, then raised her stick and indicated certain of the racier volumes. They moved on to the Italian section where she performed the same review. Trudi continued to follow silently behind. In the English section, the Baronessa was more cursory, but as they came to the modern section she grew more intent. She seemed to be looking for something in particular and Trudi was about to ask if she could help when the Baronessa stepped back again and indicated with her stick several volumes, among them *A House is not A Home*.

"Oh!" exclaimed Trudi, "I'm surprised you know that book."

The look on the Baronessa's face dropped the temperature ten degrees. The Avvocato stepped quickly away, taken by the need to cough. The Baronessa followed him and said something *sotto voce*.

Recovering himself, the Avvocato turned to Trudi: "Where do you keep the contemporary materials, the ones you commission? The Baronessa would like to see that part of the collection as well."

"Those are not so beautifully bound," said Trudi. "We keep them in the closed stacks. Come with me." She led the way into the side rooms flanking the reading room. "At the moment," she continued, "these are being filed like the Cotton Library in order of acquisition, beginning with the earliest at that end," she indicated to her right, "and continuing toward the most recent . . ." She started to indicate in the other direction, but the lawyer and the Baronessa had moved on while she was still talking. She rejoined them as they were scrutinizing the acquisitions of the last year.

That operation completed, the lawyer turned to Trudi.

"The Baronessa used to come here when it belonged to Prince Colana. She would like to see upstairs."

"With pleasure," said Trudi, leading the way to the stairs. "I hope the maid isn't doing anything too drastic today," she added as she opened the door and held it for her guests.

The Baronessa looked up and down the handsome *salone*.

The lawyer guided her through the dining room and study, leaving Trudi to follow. In the drawing room, the Baronessa cast her gaze around like a detective after stolen goods, then returned to the *salone*. She looked at the Avvocato and nodded, pointing with her stick toward the bedrooms.

"My dear friend would like to see the other rooms as well," said the Avvocato.

"My pleasure," said Trudi, but she had to hurry to get through her bedroom door before they did. The Baronessa looked around for several minutes, then turned and hurried into the adjacent bedroom without waiting for Trudi, and then into the next. She even looked into the bathrooms.

"Would she like to see the kitchen and the pantry?" asked Trudi, addressing the Avvocato, who consulted his companion in an undertone.

"No, she wouldn't. My friend says she once met Patrick Mayer in Rome. Where does he live?"

"Oh no!" Trudi laughed out loud. "His apartment is upstairs. He comes and goes through a completely separate entrance. If I'd known you wanted to see him, I could have phoned him and asked him to come."

The next day Patrick Mayer announced that he had been invited to dinner by Baronessa Notabene. He pretended to be annoyed that he had to wear black tie, but secretly he was delighted to be invited with the old guard. At first, Trudi was a little hurt, but then she decided that she had nothing in common with those people, so *tant pis*.

That same afternoon Trudi's Roman lawyer, Avvocato Bari, telephoned to say he was coming to Venice and needed to talk to her about the Nofretti case. There had been an unexpected development. Could he come see her?

The butler put the coffee tray on the table between Trudi and Avvocato Bari.

"Thank you," said Trudi. "Just leave it there. I'll pour it."

"Look," said Avvocato Bari, pulling a thick sheaf of papers from his briefcase. "This is the story so far. Normally, we would have had a judgment by now, but this Nofretti is slippery. For some reason he thinks he's invulnerable, so I've been trying to find out what his story is. When I tell you what I've discovered, you'll understand why I had to talk to you in person."

Trudy leaned forward in her chair.

"I have a cousin—I won't tell you her name, because you've met, but she's very grand and moves in the best circles in Rome. I told her about your problem with Nofretti and about my problem trying to solve the case. I have to swear you to secrecy, but here's the story. This man lives on an allowance from his putative godmother, who kept him in Swiss boarding schools and summer camps from the time he was small. He has made his own way in society by using this connection, but he did it without her blessing. In fact, it seems to be her nervousness about him that makes him feel impregnable. The received opinion is that he's figured out the godmother is in reality his grandmother and that she will do anything to keep his true identity secret. And this is where my problem starts. She is none other than Baronessa Notabene, who has enough judges and lawyers and politicians in thrall to block virtually anything she wants to keep from happening."

"Oh my prophetic soul!" said Trudi, putting down her coffee cup. "She's just been here with Corrado La Strada, her friend but *my* lawyer. Afterward I felt sure she was looking for ways of discrediting me and shutting down the Library. She's also started cultivating Pat."

"It's a good thing I came to see you. Describe this visit."

"The Avvocato won't keep you waiting more than a minute," said the secretary. "But please sit down."

Trudi gathered from the secretary's manner that her standing with La Strada had altered since Davide Bari had come to see him.

"Ah, Trudi, there you are. Come upstairs." It was La Strada himself come down to fetch her.

He pulled a chair toward his desk for her and went around to the other side. "Now then, I have here the permit for the Gotham Library of Autobiographical Materials, signed and sealed, about to be delivered. All we need is your signature on this waiver saying that you relinquish all claims to the diary commissioned from Manfredo Nofretti and that you undertake to keep the entire matter confidential." He showed her the pages, then opened the door beside his desk and asked his Notary please to join them. The *Notaio* picked up each page as she signed, then retreated with the pages through the door into the adjacent office.

"Very good. And now here is the document you've been waiting for, backdated to the actual day you opened. Good work?"

"Wonderful. But now that I've signed the release and promised not to say anything, couldn't I just take a look at the diary for my own satisfaction, since I went out on a limb to commission it? I might learn something from it."

"I think you've already learned all you can from this experience. Anyhow I can't show it to you."

"Oh, come on."

"I didn't say I won't. I said I can't. I don't have it. He says he didn't write anything. He swears it doesn't exist."

"But what about all those people who said they'd read wonderful extracts from it?"

"They could have been lying. I hope they were. He has that capacity to coerce people into doing what he wants them to do—a trait not unknown in the family."

That was the first indiscretion Trudi had ever heard pass Corrado La Strada's lips since he'd been working for her.

Contrary to her principles, she began to think more highly of him because of it. "Well, what a bore," said Trudi, getting up to go.

"Worse for me," he said, standing up. "Baronessa Notabene is waiting for me to bring her the surrendered diary this afternoon. I think she was looking forward to owning it herself, having deprived you of it."

CONTESSA

"Maria?"

The Contessa looked down from the landing and called into the darkness:

"Maria?"

She was perplexed that the *piano nobile* was still shuttered for the night when it should have been shining with daylight.

"Maria?"

The French clock sent up a sigh from the shadows and pinged a grudging five . . . six . . . seven times. The Contessa listened as she descended the stairs, then switched on the chandelier and checked her watch. Of course: it was nine. The clock needed winding. So where was Maria? The house should have been opened over an hour ago.

The Contessa crossed the *salone* into the *sala rosa* and picked her way through the dim shapes. Bright slivers glared through the shutters, bleaching the darkness around the windows and casting a de Chirico strangeness over the room.

She dispelled it in a flash, throwing open one set of shutters after the other, down the side and across the front, until the four great windows, affording a sweep of bright sky over gardens and the Grand Canal, seemed to set the house free. She glanced over her shoulder to see how the airy lightness celebrated the room's august style that she loved. It was strange that the children cared nothing for the classic dignity of the *sala rosa;* they cared only for the view—and Bobo was the same.

Then it dawned on her why the maid wasn't there. Ever since last month when the Contessa had stopped taking breakfast to lose a pound or two, Maria had taken to coming upstairs late whenever the Conte was away. It was a concession the maid had usurped and it was bothersome— not least because it cried out for confrontation, something the Contessa sought always to avoid.

She leaned over the sill to enjoy for a minute the buoyant life down on the Canal. A terrier frantic to chase seagulls pranced on the prow of a barge, while the boatman, impudent as a genie with his arms crossed and back swayed, straddled the tiller and steered with his knees; a siren cut the air as a police boat shot past in a stylish curve, leaving a gondola bucking on its wake and the gondolier bawling after it; farther on, a vaporetto heading for San Marco performed a stately *chasse-croisé* with a landing stage on tow toward the Rialto; and over on the *fondamenta* the usual fisherman was laying out his tackle with the seriousness of a new altar boy. The Contessa was so absorbed in the vignette that she didn't hear Signorina Biso come in with the coffee tray and set out their notebooks.

When she turned, she felt a twinge of dismay at being caught daydreaming by her secretary. The day was not getting off to a good start. The Contessa gestured for Signorina Biso to sit down and took her place opposite. The vague sadness that had come over her when she first opened her eyes was still there shadowing her thoughts. She was relieved that they had no correspondence nor accounts to deal with today so they could work up here over the coffee table and not have to go down to those dreary offices on the mezzanine.

Seated on matching *settecento* settees, each with notebook and pen, each in a smart *tailleur,* each with blonde streaks in her shoulder-length hair (the secretary modeled herself on the Contessa), they fell in with the symmetry of the room like two weights in a balance. Yet any Venetian could tell between the secretary and the *Nobil Donna* which one counted for more in the world, if only from the different ways they wore their clothes: the one with hauteur and the other with nonchalance.

"*Cara,*" said Contessa Panfili, sliding the coffee tray toward her secretary, "we have to work on this dinner for the Minister on Thursday. I was looking at the list and it's all the same old people. We have to jazz it up. If you ask me, it needs foreigners. Ring Lady Boodle's secretary in London and ask her if Venice Rescue has anyone exciting coming out this week. And do the same with the U.S. for the Venice office here. If we don't get any ideas from those two, try our contacts in the embassies in Rome. This has to be a modern Italian dinner, cosmopolitan and"—she snapped her fingers—"with it. We could go up to sixteen or eighteen if we find that many good people. Only don't end up with fourteen. I must have told you about my mother's inviting fourteen and my uncle's being so late that they had to go to table or spoil the risotto? No? Well, no one would go in with thirteen, so my father took down the portrait of my great-uncle and put it in Uncle Giò's place. But when Uncle Giò showed up and the butler started to take away the portrait, there was a thundering crash in the *salone.* A whole window, frame and all, had fallen into the room. Of course everyone knew why it had happened and it was cited for years as the absolute proof of why you should never take a chance on fourteen for dinner.

"But three weeks from Saturday," her voice trailed off as she turned the pages of her diary, "we'll have a different kind of party. Old-fashioned . . . Venetian . . ." She put on her reading glasses and looked toward the windows for several seconds before returning to the business at hand: "It's Conte Bonlin's sixtieth birthday. Find the invitation list for the party we gave Barone Brando last year, and we'll work from that. We'll get his favorite *prosecco* from Contessa Brenta—and that reminds me, make a note for tomorrow to tell the Hotel Monaco to send over their zabaglione dessert with amaretti for sixteen or eighteen—however many it turns out we're going to be on Thursday—for the Minister. It's his favorite. And let's have them make an enormous *meringata* for Alvise, for Conte Bonlin. But let's wait on that. If I'm going to invite everyone in Venice, plus the Veneto, we're talking about forty or fifty people. We'd have to use the Tiepolo Room. We'll talk about this when you've got the list from Barone Brando's party, and I've had a chance to think."

Signorina Biso put a stack of cards on the coffee table: "These are the place cards for tonight. Do you have time to arrange them now?"

"I'd better do it later. I have to go to the hairdresser, then straight from there to lunch at Malcontenta with the Italian Heritage Board. *Caspita!* I don't have time to go all the way out there! But since I persuaded them to use the place to help Bitsi's business, I have to show up. Tell Maria that I'll be back around four, and to bring me tea in my room at five, just tea, no biscuits. Look at me: I could hardly button this skirt this morning. Tell her to have ready both my blue Valentino, that old one with the big sleeves, and my new Armani dress, the gray one: I haven't decided which one to wear tonight. It depends on how fat I feel. Have Maria bring up the place cards at five on the tea tray. It's getting late; I have to get moving. Can you come tomorrow?"

Signorina Biso scribbled and smiled and nodded as the Contessa talked, making a droll face when the Contessa mentioned being fat to show that, with all respect, she didn't agree—for the Contessa had an almost perfect figure and the face of a forty-year-old, despite her fifty-five years with three children raised and out in the world—Marco and Bobino both in Rome, and Carolina in Milan. As the Contessa rose to leave, Signorina Biso stood up, still scribbling.

Crossing the courtyard, Giulia Panfili felt the sun on her face and saw what a beautiful day it was. She looked up at the bright blue sky and thought, What a perfect *Venetian* day. As she closed the great door of the palace behind her, she had a thought that made her turn and ring the bell.

"Maria?" she said into the intercom. "Good morning. It's me. Go down to the kitchen, please, and tell Mina to go to the Rialto this morning for the fruit and vegetables. It's a lovely day, and the food will be much better than the rubbish Vianello sent us last time."

Her route to the hairdresser took her past the errant greengrocer. His teeming spread of fruits and vegetables was so exceptionally appealing that she couldn't help smiling that she'd chosen this day of all days to punish him for taking advantage. You could never outmaneuver Venetian merchants. Some fiendish god protected them, now as ever. She hesitated for a minute looking at a crate of smooth brown champignons, ranged in files like a toy infantry. Signor Vianello stepped forward.

"*Cara* Contessa, what can we offer you today. Look at those beautiful mushrooms. They were the best in the Rialto at six o'clock this morning. I bought all they had. That's the second box; we just put them out."

"*Sì!*" she replied with an involuntary laugh, disarmed by his lie. Everyone knew that his produce was delivered by a contractor with a barrow that blocked the *calle* every morning at eight o'clock. "Give me two or three hundred grams," she surrendered, "they do look good."

She watched him fussing to pick out the best ones and she felt a slight remorse about her decision to send Mina to the Rialto. When he had weighed them, she told him to send them around to the house, as she was on her way to the country.

"At once," he smiled, bowing. He watched her disappear around the bend in the *calle,* then dumped the mushrooms back onto the display and refilled the bag from a crate under the counter. He motioned to his son.

"Take this over to Palazzo Panfili. Tell the maid the Contessa selected these especially and asked us to send them straight over."

At Campo San Stefano, Contessa Panfili looked up at the clock on the corner of the church. She had time to go in. The *Parroco* had telephoned again yesterday asking for help to get the high altar restored. It might give her something to talk about at the Italian Heritage meeting. She waited while a band of tourists in thrall to a furled umbrella trailed past. They were mostly women, but not a skirt among them: American, she concluded. Possibly German. Picking her way through the stragglers, she crossed over to the church.

Coming into the rosy light of San Stefano on a weekday morning always gave her a feeling of stifled joy. It was her parish church, and to her the most beautiful church in Venice; one day Carolina would be married here. With its soaring roof and side aisles lined with stately porticoed altars, it seemed an avenue of heaven. The crowning glory was the high altar faced with a tapestry of colored marbles, porphyry, lapis lazuli, malachite, and mother-of-pearl, all trimmed into figures of fat birds and handsome chalices with bright flowers and trailing leaves.

But it was ruined: a century and more of slow degradation followed by the poverty of the war years had ruined almost everything in Venice. Daily the priest and the sacristan gathered up the fallen pieces. They had a shoe box full of them. After a spate of urgent appeals, a government functionary had made an inspection and offered to have the altar wrapped in plastic. It was the best they could do under the current restraints. A typical story: Giulia Panfili knew from experience. She would hear the same story again and again at the meeting today.

The sacristan approached her with a timid smile.

She greeted the old man with affection. "I should like to see the *Parroco,* if I may. It's about the high altar."

The sacristan bowed without speaking and shuffled away toward the sacristy.

He was the same sacristan with the stutter who had been here all those years ago when she used to come in with little Marco of a morning, before Bobino and Carolina were born, to light a candle for a happy life. On the front of a side altar were two marble babies standing at the same height that Marco then was. While she was saying her prayer, he used to fondle them like dolls; she would hear him prattling to them in the most ingenuous way. Sometimes the sacristan would stand nearby saying, "*B-b-bambino f-f-f-freddo,*" and Marco would turn and look at him, his little face shining with pleasure. So sweet it was to remember.

In those days when the children were small, she had loved everyone. A stranger to malice. But now—now it was hard to think of someone she really liked: a few old friends, some timeworn relationships, comfortable loyalties; the family, of course. But not even Bobo could ease the pain of losing Marco to that terrible *romana.* The memory lay jagged in her subconscious like a mantrap in a leafy path. She had stepped into the drawing room looking for Maria, and found them necking. She'd tried to step back, but the girl, staring over Marco's shoulder, had fixed her with such an evil look that she'd hesitated and seen the girl slowly stick her tongue into

Marco's mouth, then close her eyes in a swoon of wicked satisfaction. It made her sick to think of it; like a horror film where aliens change people with spells. How could he have got mixed up with such a person? Where did he find a runner-up Miss Italia? Miss Swimsuit. That was her title.

The Contessa gazed at the cold babies behind the candle rack; still waiting under the altar, still the same. Had she changed, or had Venice changed around her? She went over to the rack before the statue of the ascending Virgin and lit a candle. She worked a folded banknote into the slit in the tin box, thinking how she used to save small coins for Marco to pay with, to make the clinking game last longer. And then one day he'd asked for more coins so he too could light a candle. That was the first time he'd ever prayed in church. He prayed for the cold babies to be warmed. She crossed herself and whispered: "Mother of God, give me a happy life again."

She looked up and saw the priest watching her from the steps of the sacristy. She hurried to him.

"Father, I've been thinking about the altar. There's a board meeting of Italian Heritage today and I thought I might be able to arouse some interest."

"Oh, if only you could," he inclined his head in an attitude of appeal. "I've spoken to so many people in the last few days. Here, I've printed a pamphlet. Tell me what you think of it." He watched her closely as she leafed through the pages describing the altar, its history, its condition, the work necessary to save it, and the cost. She nodded: it had everything she needed.

"Believe me, Father," she said, pressing the report to her heart, "I love this church, and if Italian Heritage can't help, I will keep trying until I find a way."

She rushed from the church, through Campo San Stefano, toward the hairdresser. She hadn't left herself quite enough time, but her sense of mission put wings on her feet. She glimpsed her speeding reflection in the window of Lord Nolesworthy's new antique shop; dark, open by appointment only. She wondered whether she should, after all, invite Blair and Luisa Nolesworthy for the Minister's dinner. They would give the party what it lacked. But the consequences for her would be devastating. Her heart sank to think of it. The Minister would forthwith turn his attentions on Luisa, with all her international connections, and start ringing her, instead, to say when he was coming to Venice. Giulia Panfili would be forgotten, thrown back into the tableau vivant of Venetian life. It was more than disloyal; it was unfair. How could Venetians figure in the modern world if all anyone ever wanted of them was to wallow in their heritage, then prance away like a scented poodle.

It made her temper rage. Venice had fallen to the *canaglia,* people who could *never* be a part of one's true life. In the old days a man of Bobo's class would have been more than a minister. With his sense of humor and patience, Bobo would have been a distinguished senator. He might have been Doge. Then she would have been the shadowy figure in the background, *La Dogaressa.* She could have been so happy then. And the children wouldn't be in Rome and Milan, but here in Venice, sharing a life with their family, the boys following in their father's footsteps, and Carolina marrying young into a family of friends.

But Marco and Bobino had no desire to be like their father. It was something they wanted to avoid: an emarginated life with imaginary occupations. Every morning Bobo read the financial newspaper *Il Sole 24 Ore,* but he had no way of using what he gleaned from it. He went to look at the farm and visit the vineyards from time to time, but Gino was the manager. In the country he had his horses and his shooting; in Venice he disciplined himself not to play bridge too often at the Circolo. Everywhere he was known for his old-world courtesy, and his good nature.

For a time she had chased after the great captains of Italian industry and invited them to her parties, but gradually she had realized that none of them was going to invite Bobo to join their ranks. After dinner they would bask like puppies in the comfort of his charm, but before long, grown restless, they would tumble into lively exchanges among themselves, leaving the aristocrats like gentle borzois to sigh before the fire about their farms and their palaces and old times, the happy days when they were waiting to inherit their places in the world. That their way of life had been one of the secret casualties of the two great wars, they had learned too late. It had been kept from them by their parents and grandparents, who facing their disintegrating world with disbelief had turned away to build of common memories a phantom world. Later, as one by one the older generations faded from the scene, little by little the bright cloud vanished.

One morning at breakfast, a few years after Mammina died, Bobo laid his *Il Sole 24 Ore* on the table with a strange little cough. He leaned back in his chair and looked out the window over the neighboring gardens:

"*Cara* Giulia," he murmured, "what should I do?"

The despair in his voice had touched her to the quick. She had tried to be lighthearted.

"*Carissimo,* we're dinosaurs. We missed the ark. We'll just go along as we are. At least the children will be okay; that's the important thing."

It had been much harder for Bobo than for her.

She arrived at Armando's with a minute to spare. From the far corner Armando tossed his black ringlets and waved a hairbrush in salutation. He dispatched a young man to escort her to the basin and wash her hair. As she was sinking into the chair, the phone rang and she heard a girl's voice cry out:

"Armando. It's Laidi NAWlaisvarti; she wants to know if she can have a quick comb-out before her guests arrive for lunch."

At the sound of Lady Nolesworthy's name, Armando lifted the hairbrush he had been drawing through a sea of wine-dark waves, flung it onto the cart beside him, and capered like a faun between the chairs and carts to the telephone.

"*Sì, sì, sì. Cara* Laidi NAWlaisvarti. *Sì, sì! A presto!* See you soon."

He hurried back to his purple masterpiece, flushed with importance.

Giulia Panfili got up from the basin holding a towel on her head and walked over to Armando:

"Armando, I have to go to the country today for lunch and need to do a few things on the way. Do you think you could do me next?"

She wanted to be out the door and far away before Luisa came breezing in, perfectly aware that she had alerted everyone in the place to her lunch party. Armando's salon was famous as a gossip center; they called him *Radio Armando*. She went back and sat down in front of the mirrors.

Armando appeared behind her chair, beaming at his reflection.

"You ladies are always so busy," he cooed. "You work as hard as I do." As he spoke his famous black eyebrows jumped up and down.

"Yes," she smiled, trying to match his tone, "Venice is back in fashion. Did you see in *La Nuova Venezia* yesterday that Ministro Tasca is coming?"

"Oh yes," he said, falling on the scent. "I saw it in *Il Gazzettino*. And will he be coming to you?"

"Yes," she answered in the careful inflections she used for dictating to Signorina Biso. "I will give him a cocktail party on Thursday evening."

She didn't mention the dinner; she knew that Luisa and Blair would never come to drinks if they knew that they would be among a small group obliged to leave while others stayed on. She would ring Signorina Biso from Piazzale Roma and tell her of the new drinks party before the dinner, and that she should get busy at once telephoning Lady Nolesworthy and a few others, perhaps the British and American consuls. She would have to say that Contessa Panfili is out of town today, and be sure to specify that the party is from six to eight, which everyone would understand to mean that the Minister had another appointment. She would herself check to see if the President of Italian Heritage would be around on Thursday.

"*Cara* Contessa," he enthused as he combed her hair. "We will soon have to give these streaks some attention. I see so much gray. We will have to find a day when we have more time. That was Lady Nolesworthy on the phone. She begged me to fix her up a bit before lunch. She is having twenty people today."

The Contessa watched him in the mirror as he warmed to his discourse.

"She is a very good customer; I couldn't say no. But last

week she told me she was going to let her highlights grow out for a while. Her hair is in very good condition and she has always kept her highlights to perfection; so I asked her why. She wouldn't give a reason. It's very strange. You know what?" he whispered to her in the mirror, "I think she may be pregnant." He pulled the face of a little boy who has seen something naughty, then went on, "It's the only thing I can think of, why she would change like that. And she had that sort of contented look, you know? Well, we'll see. It's a secret that will come out. Soon we shall all know. Perhaps you and I are the first to guess it." Armando smirked at his generosity in allowing her to share credit for his discovery.

Contessa Panfili felt her spirits dive like a skier out of control. It was probably true. She could feel it. It would be Luisa's luck to get a boy; she was one of those people who got what she wanted. How uncanny: just the other day, Sofi had speculated about Luisa's having a baby. She'd pointed out that even if she had a son, it would never have a title, because Blair's peerage was only for his lifetime. They agreed it made you feel a bit sorry for Blair and Luisa. Nobody has everything. It's important to remember that.

It was always a tonic to talk to Sofi. She was sensible. Even the way she was managing her separation from Edmondo: not a cross word between them so far. Edmondo had even accepted her new architect friend, Vittorio Falon, and they were all collaborating on the restoration of Palazzo Patristi. Sofi had surprised everyone. But she was probably right to look for a man with a career, even if she had to go downward a little.

You can't live in the past; the children had figured that out. Still, for Alvise's party the situation was awkward. They had to have Edmondo; he was one of them. And Sofi the same. It would be okay in such a big party. But Edmondo's mistress, never. Sofi's architect was different; everyone had taken to him. After all, Venice was a republic before it was Italian; Venetians used to make their own rules. She could have the Decardis invite him to come with them. They had known him first. Vittorio would understand that we can't insult Edmondo, even though he's behaved like a donkey. What a pity that nice, sensible Sofi is ten years too old for Marco. One would never have had to worry about him again.

She walked back through Campo San Stefano and down to the *traghetto* to cross the Grand Canal to San Tomà. The gondolier helped her in with that roguish gallantry that always sparked her affection for those vagabonds from the past. The thought that these ferries had been functioning for a thousand years made her sigh. The last remnant of old Venetian life that still survived, they harked back to the age when time was money and dithering tourism didn't exist.

Before you knew it, you were being bundled up the other side and sent about your business.

When she got to Piazzale Roma she stopped to ring Signorina Biso, then crawled into a taxi and told the driver to take her to Villa Malcontenta.

Settled into the backseat, the Contessa unfolded *La Nuova Venezia* to the Venice page and read, under the headline "Venice Prepares for the New Preservation Act," "Ministro Tasca has moved forward his visit to Venice and arrives today at 12.00 for a series of engagements before the deliberations." It struck her like a blow: twenty for lunch. That explained everything. After months of trying to avoid it, the impact came almost as a relief. She had known from the beginning that it would be hopeless to compete with Luisa for someone like Dion Tasca. She wondered who had brought them together. In any case, her fate was sealed. The Nolesworthy billions, the Nolesworthy contacts, they would run her down like a speeding juggernaut. She steered her floundering thoughts forcibly toward how she would galvanize Italian Heritage to restore the altar of San Stefano.

Usually it accosted her how the modern ugliness of the road to Malcontenta confirmed the aptness of the antique villa's name, but today Contessa Panfili's thoughts were so far away that she didn't even see the smoking industrial landscape that framed the great house like the wrong backdrop in a play. She was brooding about the life of a Venetian in the modern world. She told the driver to be sure to pick her up at 3:45, and walked around to the portico. She could hear the babble through the open door and decided to greet everyone, then find a quiet place where she could read through the priest's report.

The luncheon bore the pallid stamp of the standard Venetian caterer: the mélange of sea minutiae followed by the risotto followed by the sea bass in the company of Russian salad, green beans, and green salad, followed by the fruit tart, followed by coffee. She ate so little she thought she might fit the Armani after all. On her right and left were two businessmen, champions of industry, who had taken up Italian Heritage as they might choose a tie. It was the ideal cause: patriotic, suggestive of good breeding and cultivated taste, while at the same time an emblem of high station in keeping with a large, expensive house, a family smartly dressed, and knowing the Gritti concierge by name. They were, like most of the people she saw ranged along the head table, as good as traitors to the Venetian cause. She wished she could expose them.

The waiters had cleared the plates and swept away the crumbs. The President stood up and opened the meeting with some tangled observations about the central place Italian Heritage held in his busy life and how many projects had been brought to glorious fruition during his happy term of office. There were certain indications that he had neither prepared his speech nor bothered to go easy on the wine. Her mind turned to Luisa's lunch party. She could picture the Minister now tossing back his wine and strewing the air with colorful indiscretions like confetti at carnival, while the other guests sat pinching themselves with disbelief, imagining that they were privileged, witnessing something historic, and torn between the fascination of what he had to say and the impatience to rush out and report what they had heard. This was his way with an audience. He never let down his host. Suddenly she heard her name. She looked up and realized that the President was calling upon her to say a few words of welcome. He was passing her the hot potato! What a cad! As she stood up, the priest's report slipped from her lap, but she didn't even grab for it. One of the businessmen picked it up and placed it facedown on the table before her.

"As a Venetian, I would like to welcome you," she plunged in without quite knowing where she was going, "to our hinterland. It was decided that the Venice meeting should *not* be in Venice itself, for the convenience of those coming from elsewhere. This villa is the closest of the Venetian country villas to the city proper—*as you can see by its proximity to the Marghera industrial zone.*"

The bitterness of her irony surprised even herself, and brought forth from the audience an uncertain titter.

"I wasn't aware that I was going to be invited to speak today, but I'm glad to have the chance," she waded on, "because, as it happens, there are some things that I have wanted to say for a long time." In a daze she surrendered to the tide of the morning's emotions.

"As I go about my daily life in Venice, I see everywhere the evidence that our city is treated with less consideration for its welfare than any other important city, not just in Italy, but in the world. I see you relax at the reference to the world, thinking that I'm going to talk some kind of philosophical rubbish about the plight of ancient civilizations. But I'm not. It is Italy, our own Italy, that is responsible for the slow destruction of Venice, and that includes us Venetians."

She saw the audience exchanging polite glances, and thought how pleased with themselves, how narcissistic, they all were.

"Under the guise of love—and with a constant pious reference to love for the place—our masters have stripped Venice of every form of life-giving enterprise and left it to die, deprived of everything a city needs.

"Let me show you the effect of ignorance on this city— and stupidity. Venice is a natural center for such 'clean' industries as government—" an automatic burst of laughter, triggered by a reference to clean government, erupted from the crowd and rattled the Contessa. "I mean clean in the sense of not causing acid rain and the like, not *morally* clean, of course. Anything but that." She paused to let the laughter subside. "Industries such as banking, the stock market, research, and administration. But instead, everything is leaving Venice: even the banks have moved their seats to the mainland. And why, in this electronic age? Because, as our own government representatives tell us, it is too inconvenient. Not being able to move about by car puts Venice out of reach."

Here and there friends nodded ruefully. She wondered what they were agreeing with. She paused and leaned toward her audience. "But wait a minute. What is ruining *your* cities—Milan, Rome, Florence? What makes transportation such a problem in every major city of the world? Oh yes, the car.

"Yes, they tell you, but Venice doesn't even want motor-boats; they undermine the foundations. Okay, that's true. But the absence of cars and motorboats doesn't make Venice inaccessible. Let me tell you something: the most efficient means of transport in Venice is the means that was designed for the job a thousand years ago. A gondola can slip from the railway station to the Piazza in less time than it takes to struggle by taxi from Milan Central Station to the Borsa. Ah, I hear you say. But we businessmen can't lie in a gondola enjoying ourselves on company time. Oh, please. Do businessmen choose the least comfortable way to travel? And are we a Protestant country, that we have to deduct the pleasure and the beauty of a thing from its usefulness?"

Their laughter washed over her like something foul. She couldn't go on much longer.

"In spite of all the horrible things that have been done to Venice for the sake of the car—the bridge, the Tronchetto parking island, Piazzale Roma, the petroleum industry here at Marghera, the petroleum tankers coming through the lagoon—it's still a city of waterways and walkways. If we only did such a simple and obvious thing as make the gondola the official form of transport, and ran the service like a business, *many* of our problems would disappear."

Several women gave her looks that seemed to say, "What a sweet idea!" They were completely at sea, lost in a vinous haze. It was madness to try to have a meeting after lunch.

"The problem is that the gondola exists only as a frivolity. Apart from the *traghetto* ferries, it exists for tourists, weddings, and the Regata Storica. No wonder the gondoliers have become lazy and dishonest. They're demoralized. But worse, what is true of the gondola is true of the whole city. Venice has been declared a playground. Anything serious must be taken away to clear the space for tourist shops, restaurants, hotels, that sort of thing. The Venetians who have to deal every day with this situation have gone the same way as the gondoliers.

"Let's not be a party to this. Let's open our eyes. There's hardly a building in Venice that can't be reached easily and quickly by foot or by gondola, or adapted to commercial use without losing its character. This is the ready-made commercial capital of the future—which even most of us Venetians, merchants that we are by heritage, are too blind to recognize. As for the national government, it's never sorted out a Venetian problem in all the years since unification, so let's stop looking there.

"You businessmen on the board of Italian Heritage—" She glanced down at the men on either side of her; they looked up, puzzled. "When are you going to wake up?" The two men blinked. "You should be racing to be the first to put your headquarters in Venice." They nodded vigorously. "Others would follow you." The homage to their leadership brought forth smiles, which waned as they sank back into their reveries.

"One day some intelligent people are going to see Venice for what it is. And when they do . . ." She looked around the room and saw the glassy eyes of vacancy. "And when they do," she was struggling, "Venice will be saved. And then," she finished with a shrug of resignation, "our sons and daughters could come back to live and work where they belong."

She was exhausted when she sat down. She could hear applause and even a few sympathetic bravas, but she couldn't look up. She hadn't meant to talk like that, and she knew that she hadn't achieved anything. Worse, she'd spent her credit and lost the chance to bring up the San Stefano altar. And she had given her word. Now she would have to find some other way to save it. She felt discouraged.

. . .

As the taxi pulled into Piazzale Roma, a sudden stop flung her against the seat in front.

"Goddamned Romans! Can't you read the signs?" The taxi driver was leaning out the window, shouting. Gathering her handbag and papers from the floor, she glanced through the front window and saw that a car ahead with a Roman license plate had stopped to let out some passengers. Two young men got out. The taxi driver was still yelling but had lapsed into broad Venetian. The young men turned around, laughing at his language. Giulia Panfili jerked her head behind the headrest and peeked through. It was *Marco* and *Bobino;* they were waiting for someone else to get out. A girl. It was Natasha Fierazzo, an old school friend of Bobino's, Sofi's little sister. She was at university in Rome. They must have all found a ride back for Cesco Carrara's going-away party; he was leaving for America tomorrow for a year.

The driver turned to her and shrugged his shoulders. "I can't get you any closer. These foreigners aren't going to move. You might as well get out here."

She was still hiding behind the headrest; she didn't want to intercept them like that.

"Could I have a receipt, please?" She watched them walking toward the vaporetto, and smiled at the fatigue of youth; they never walked anywhere if they could ride. While the driver scrawled the receipt, she pleasured her heart watching her beloved sons going about their Venetian lives. Bobino was chattering and waving his arms, making Marco and Natasha laugh. Then she noticed that it was Marco who was carrying Natasha's bag, and as if by magic, at that moment, he put out his arm and drew the girl toward him in a gesture so unmistakable, so exactly the way Bobo used to tuck her against his side as they strolled along, that a wave of giddy happiness lifted her spirits like a bobbing cup, so that she couldn't wait to be on her way.

As she opened the door, the driver held out the receipt. She laughed in amazement. What did she want with that? She gave the driver a banknote and said, "Oh forget the receipt and keep the change."

Along the *fondamenta* by the Rio Nuovo, her feet sailed over the stones, through Campo Santa Margherita, over the bridge beside the fruit-and-vegetable barge. It was a gaudy, beautiful sight, spinach and tomatoes. There were some more of Vianello's exclusive champignons. She laughed out loud. She walked on and on without thinking where she was headed. On Fondamenta della Toletta she realized that she was taking the long way; it would have been quicker to cross over in the vaporetto. But she had not the fatigue of youth. As she crossed the Accademia Bridge she looked up at the bright blue sky and thought how fortunate she was to be who she was, and where she was. She let her feet take her where they would. The church was open. Stepping once more into the rosy atmosphere, she could hear the old women saying their Ave Marias in the sacristy. She went straight to the statue of the hovering Virgin and knelt down before it.

"Maria," she heard her own soft voice in the empty sanctuary. "Mother of God, thank you for being with me. Stay with me. Now and always."

She crossed herself and started to rise, half turning to go, but sank down again on one knee, pushed back by the swelling tide of her old happiness, so long dormant. Inclining again to the Blessed Virgin, she added, her face shining with joy, a simple benediction. "And bless any new baby boys who might be on their way to Venice—even an English one."

SOCIALITE

Beauregard—a rare moniker, in a precious setting: van Dongen Bourbon Benson—was a typical New York socialite. Nobody in his family had ever lived in New York before he set up there, and nobody there knew his story. On the other hand, everybody who was anybody knew the name. From that intelligence grew the perception that someone, probably his mother, must be from the South. So it wasn't too difficult for the more learned of the gadabout crowd to arrive at the consensus that his mother was of French nobility by way of Louisiana. His detractors countered that he must surely hail from Alabama—Mobile, to be precise. But for most Venetians, the heritage of being a New York socialite with visible wealth was more than sufficient recommendation to accept his invitations and let him prove himself. They called him Beau—or Bò, depending on the context—and asked if they could bring their friends.

· · ·

That Beauregard van Dongen Bourbon Benson was born in the South was a verifiable fact. And although the Bourbon in his name was a tribute to the inspiration for his conception rather than to his lineage, it was no less Southern for that. The source of his family's wealth was too prosaic to let drop among the demitasse—though in a sense that was the perfect place. His father had started out buying, piecemeal, the failing sugarcane factory where he was employed. He succeeded in turning it around and refocusing his supply source from Cuba to South America. He also took an occasion to buy a sugar beet factory. He later diversified into importing and canning South American fruit. Beauregard would have preferred a seasoned wealth from ancient cotton plantations or tobacco, or even from horse breeding, or banking, but in fact for him it made little difference as he had nothing to do with the actual business of earning the money he spent with such elegance. His sister and her husband looked after the business and did everything in their power to make it easy for him to stay up north or in Europe.

Difficult though he was in character, no one, not even his sister, could deny that Beauregard was a handsome cuss to look at. By the time he arrived in Venice, he was no longer young, but he might well have been in his prime. His steel-gray hair brushed back in waves over his ears, falling almost to his collar, and his trim Van Dyck beard were eye-catching, and as perfect a match to each other as a bespoke handbag and shoes. His Southern antecedents were not evident in his manner: he had neither a warm look nor a warm presence. In fact his grayness of eye, hair, skin made him seem more limed oak than flesh. Even his voice was reedy and his conversation of such studied formality that it seemed nearly petrified. But in Beauregard's walk there was an unmistakable grace, and even a hint of the dancer's splayfoot mince that betrayed his interest in theater and dance.

His university, Tulane, was hardly the academic byway it might seem; nevertheless it dispatched him, a new Bachelor of Arts, without a clear avenue to travel. He had been editor of the school newspaper, so he prevailed on his professors to get him a job on the local paper covering cultural events. He took up the work with so much enthusiasm that the professors in spite of themselves began to envisage for the University a beautiful new Benson Auditorium, funded in gratitude. But it was not to be. The first feature that Beauregard wrote, about a visiting ballet company, he fortified with all the wit, style, and analysis at his command. When his masterpiece came back from the editor completely revised, he was dumbfounded, hurt, and furious. His beloved ideas were like puppies flattened by a steamroller: the outlines were still discernible, but they'd lost their appeal. Beauregard Benson didn't have to put up with this. Journalism lost its appeal. Instead, he went to New York where he could learn more about theater and ballet than anyone in Louisiana could ever hope to know. He became a patron of the arts, and artists. So successful was he that two decades later New York seemed to him as provincial as Louisiana. He sponsored a *Festa della Danza* and took up Italy, and eventually, Venice.

As his first Venetian residence, Beauregard Benson rented a floor of Palazzo Benzon, a large, gaunt palace on the Grand Canal not far from Sant'Angelo. He was too savvy to pretend for even a minute that he was a Venetian Benzon, but he enjoyed the coincidence and in a subtle way it enhanced his aura nonetheless. Old-fashioned folk discomfited by the box-office trend in society took a subliminal comfort from going to dine with a Benson in Palazzo Benzon. As for the others, they surrendered to the rich man's advantage that what people want to believe, they usually can.

Straining to charm his Venetian guests, with their camaraderie and easy frivolity, Beauregard crackled with vexation and faced their compact world with fear, but he soldiered on anyhow, engagement, after engagement, after engagement, winning his way in a short time to a frenetic social life. He got himself onto committees, attended important gatherings, and entertained with a gritty resolve to win renown as the host with the most, even though it meant suffering the friction of social contact that often raised painful sparks both for him and for his guests. Sociable Venetians bent on diversion recognized that they could no more avoid it than hurdle the nylon carpet down at the watergate, which happened to be endowed with much the same character. They took the course of least resistance: they balanced his eccentricities against his hospitality, and kept an eye on the scale.

The fact was, and the Venetians had recognized his problem the first time they met him, Beauregard Benson was wanting only one thing to set him straight, and that was a wife. He himself was not aware of his need, but all Venice was, and that in itself was sufficient to guarantee that he would get one. They had already started working on it: an informal committee of formidable noblewomen, led by the most formidable of all: Baronessa Notabene. Under their tutelage Beauregard's social life literally went to pieces, from a flood to small pools. From moving freely through large gatherings he now found himself, night after night, at the center of small intense candlelit dinners seated opposite a would-be wife, with both of them flanked by whichever elders of society were betting on that particular match. It was a stressful time for the high-strung stallion, for the rejected mares, and especially for the ad hoc trainers and promoters who took exception to being flummoxed by some inscrutable caprice. Beauregard was not making friends and he knew it. Each morning he opened his eyes jittering with dread. When he closed his eyes at night, his nerves hummed "The Typewriter" song.

This phase in Beauregard's social career was brought to a sudden close when for the first and possibly only time in his life he was called back to Louisiana on business. Beauregard had finally recognized that his sister's managerial character might be called in his defense. By the time he got back to Louisiana, he was a wreck, fit for nothing. At the same time, his sister perceived, he was ripe for anything. She couldn't help admiring how the Venetians had spurred him into the home stretch.

Yet no one was more surprised than they when Beauregard next showed up in Venice, on his honeymoon. His choice of bride was another surprise. Mrs. Beauregard Benson, the former Carmenina Bolivar, was only twenty-eight. She was South American from Colombia, a sugarcane heiress, and judging from her name she appeared to be of excellent stock. She was little more than five feet tall, with a robust build that made her look in the bloom of health, if somewhat "hammered down." In Broadway lingo she would have been a "wide doll," and some of Beauregard's cronies in New York actually nicknamed her among themselves Lola Sapola. But the allusion was neither kind nor entirely apt. Wide she was. That much was obvious. But she was a gentle girl, as square in comportment as in shape, and she hadn't the faintest notion how to "step in with the punch." Though as time wore on, she too learned ways of defending her sweet husband from wickedness.

From the beginning she defended him from women who liked to squeeze and kiss their host and hostess. She did the smooching for both of them with an enthusiasm that made everyone happy, none more than Beauregard. Standing at the door greeting and saying good night to their guests, they were in perfect contrast. She was short, plump, with dark hair, olive skin, rosy cheeks, and an affectionate, fun-loving demeanor. He was tall, slender, pallid, and reserved. She thought he was elegant and wonderful, like a god. He was content to let her flesh out the bare bones of his charm, and he did his best to fall in with other aspects of her Latin nature on an ends/means basis.

The following year they returned from their travels with a king-size perambulator, a South American/Italian nanny, and a bouncing baby boy: Bingham de Bienville Bourbon Benson Bolivar—known as Bingo. The pram sported a large monogram, and was so recognizable that in no time everyone had flagged down the nanny and peered inside to confirm that the little passenger was a real Benson—as indeed he was: a bona fide (dozen double Bourbons) Benson. The ménage spent the next few years on intimate terms with a number of nanny search agencies while zigzagging among New York, Venice, Louisiana, and Bogotá—Beauregard and Carmenina and nanny with little Bingo, first as a bundle, then as a toddler, and before they knew it as one almighty handful.

When Bingo turned four, Beauregard and Carmenina settled in Venice. They had perceived how Venetians coddle the little ones, and they recognized the perfect ambiance for their *bambino adorato*. They moved from Palazzo Benzon to a *piano nobile* in San Samuele because it was convenient to Campo San Stefano—the importance of that proximity being its distinction as the best playground in the *sestiere* of San Marco.

Campo San Stefano is a great prairie of a *campo* that spreads toward the Grand Canal, extending first into Campiello Pisani and then to Campo San Vidal. In those years it was blessed with a restaurant, two bars, and the famous ice cream parlor, Paolin's, each with an apron of tables in the *campo,* and had virtually no shops. Through its center passed the main route from the Accademia Bridge to both Piazza San Marco and the Rialto, making it a meeting place for adults as well as children. In the afternoon, when the sun shone on Paolin's, the *campo* swarmed with children who had spent the morning confined either in nursery schools or on compulsory shopping expeditions with mothers or nannies. Many mothers, and the richer nannies, passed the time sitting at Paolin's eating ice creams and drinking cappuccinos, along with the local community and passersby. For Bingo, visiting this oasis was the high point of an afternoon's play. He would wander among the tables pretending to look for Nanny or for Gianni to give him a glass of water, but hoping to find something better, like friends of his parents who rarely thought a mere glass of water sufficient for a growing boy.

The *campo* was also furnished with two wellheads, one at each end, ideal for mothers and nannies to lean on while they chatted, with curbs around the bottom, perfect for children to sit on; and the great white monument of Nicolò

Tommaseo standing in pensive pose, almost always with a pigeon on his head. For Venetian children, this too was playground furniture, with its base of four short flights of steps divided at the corners by flat planes worn slick by generations of sliding *popò*, but perhaps most of all because of a whimsical detail in the statue's execution: Tommaseo balancing on his high pedestal was braced by a stack of books rising behind his legs, with a final book, spine upward and partly collapsed on its pages, making the supportive connection under the coat to the sculptural mass, but creating, from a child's-eye view, the impression that the books were cascading from within the coat as—*Cacca Libri,* the monument's playground epithet.

Bingo rolled up on his tricycle to address the little girl called Lala who was sitting on the curb of the well, cradling her doll.

"Here," said Bingo, "you can play with my tricycle." He left it next to her and headed for Paolin's. He was pretty sure he was going to get an ice cream cone. Baronessa Notabene and Contessa Dicadoro had been watching him playing in the *campo* and were motioning him to come to their table. His nanny was sitting at Paolin's too, but over on the edge with a table of her friends, so there was nothing to stop him.

Bingo's dark curls were long and brushed back like his father's. He had big brown eyes with tones of gray in them, pale olive skin, and he was slender in the body like his father, but square in the shoulders like a Bolivar. He had acquired a name for being too beautifully dressed, but he was not to blame. He pulled out his shirt, let his trousers slip down to show his belly and baby builder's bum, and took every chance to sit on the pavement, slide down the monument, climb on the wellhead, or do anything possible to foil the excess of doting parents. Even as he approached Paolin's, he was intent on having ice cream down his shirt, and was ready to work to make it happen. He negotiated his way through the forest of chairs and tables, piled with jackets and parcels, his curly head disappearing and reappearing ever nearer, while the Contessa and the Baronessa monitored his progress, strangely elated at the prospect of his company. Bingo was an entertaining child, who from the time he learned to talk started laying claim to the role in Venetian society that he occupies to this day.

Arrived, he gave them his best smile and even offered to kiss their hands, which sent them into ecstasies. From the first, Bingo had this way with dowagers.

"*Ciao Bellissimo,*" the two ladies cooed over him. "How are you? Climb up here."

Contessa Dicadoro pulled out the chair nearest to him. He climbed in headfirst, one knee up and then the other, getting a sustaining pat on the bottom as he ascended. He turned around with a satisfied smile, a little prince enthroned. He surveyed his hostesses.

"Would you like a cup of coffee?" It was their favorite joke. He put his hands over his mouth in horror. It was the response they were looking for. Things were looking good. "Would you like a glass of water?"

He shook his head. "No, thank you."

"You wouldn't like some ice cream, would you?"

He nodded. "Yes, please." The effect was immediate. "*Cameriere!*" Contessa Dicadoro waved her hand.

"*Senta!*" commanded Baronessa Notabene, fixing the waiter in her sights. She drew him to the table. "Gianni: this young gentleman needs an ice cream cone. Chocolate?" She looked at Bingo for confirmation. Gianni looked at Bingo and nodded. He knew him well; at almost four years old, he was already an important customer. Bingo nodded happily. Life was perfect.

"Bring him some water as well," said the Contessa.

"With bubbles?" nodded Gianni, looking at Bingo.

"No," said the Baronessa, "flat. Children shouldn't have bubbles; it's bad for their digestion."

"Where is Mamma?" asked Contessa Dicadoro.

"She went away," said Bingo, who enjoyed these catechisms.

"You mean she went home."

"No. Away to lunch."

"You mean she went to the country?" asked the Baronessa.

"In a car."

"Who's giving a lunch today?" mused the Contessa to the Baronessa. "Could it be Loredana? No, hers is tomorrow."

"Where is Papà?"

"Gone in train. Make a festival."

Ever since Beauregard's social life had become so much easier, he had returned to his vocation of sponsoring theater and dance. He had even gone so far as to establish an organization to bring American companies to festivals in Europe, which made it necessary for him to travel often.

"Is your grandmother, your *nonna,* still here from South America?" inquired the Baronessa with a kindly interest.

"Gone away now." As he talked, Bingo never took his eyes from Gianni, who still hadn't brought his ice cream cone.

"Did she stay with you at home?"

"No."

"Why not? I thought you had spare bedrooms."

"She can't. She gives Papà heebie-jeebies," he giggled. "Last year he got itchie scratchies."

The Baronessa couldn't believe her ears. "You mean he caught them from her? Isn't she very . . . clean?" She looked at the Contessa with amused alarm.

"No, no," Contessa Dicadoro nipped the nascent libel. "I'll explain later. It's just an American expression."

Bingo sailed calmly on, "Noooo," shaking his head but still watching Gianni. "Not clean. She put cacca with her shoe. Made a stink. They took the carpet. She said a dirty word. Not clean." He shook his head the way Nanny did when something was naughty. Gianni came out the door with an ice cream cone, headfirst in a bowl, and a small bottle of water. He held the tray up high as he approached to show Bingo that it was for him.

"I'm sorry, young man, there was a long queue at the ice cream counter and they forgot our order. But now it's here. *Buon appetito.*" Gianni poured the water and picked up the cone and handed it to him upright, then spread a napkin in his lap. "He's a real little gentleman," he said to the ladies as he tucked the bill under the dish.

"Where does she stay," asked the Contessa, "at the Cipriani?"

"Swimming pool," said Bingo through the ice cream.

"Do you go there to see her?"

"In a boat. Last night Papà hid behind the little houses and scared Mamma."

He laughed and thrust both hands up over his head, sending the ice cream cone into an alarming tilt. "Mamma screamed and made the *vigili* come."

The two ladies were rapt but puzzled, and as hard as they tried they couldn't quite figure out the story from Bingo's recital of events; but they thought they'd got the gist. Nevertheless, for retailing the story they were seriously hampered. Bingo was still very young and the story was complicated. Even among the participants no one was sure who understood what—nor much wanted to find out.

95

. . .

Carmenina and Bingo had said goodbye to her mother, Bingo's *nonna,* who was leaving early in the morning. As they sat in the hotel motorboat approaching San Marco, Bingo cuddled up against his mother and closed his eyes. Carmenina instantly regretted not waiting to call a taxi.

"Darling don't, don't, don't go to sleep. We have to walk all the way back home and you're too big to carry. Come on. We have to get out now. Let's go." She pulled him by the hand from the cabin and up the steps. The boatman helped them onto the pier.

"I'm tired," whined Bingo, putting up his arms. "Carry me."

"I can't. You're too big. And too full of ice cream. Here, give me your hand. We can hurry because there are no crowds. Look. All the little souvenir shops are locked up." They hurried down the empty Molo in front of the souvenir huts lining the wall along the Royal Gardens. She didn't like keeping Bingo out late in the Latin tradition, and above all she didn't like being out alone at night even in Venice. In fact, she thought she heard something behind the huts. She slowed down. There was something moving. She stopped. Her heart was pounding. A man stepped out from between the huts. Carmenina's eyes opened wide and her jaw dropped. A little South American scream—Casey Jones on the brakes *fortissimo*—cleft the night and froze him to the spot. From all directions *vigili* came pouring in pairs. Bingo, who had been stumbling along with his eyes closed, woke up, saw the joke, and started to laugh. He slapped his knees and clapped his hands. The six *vigili* were less quick to understand, and stood panting from their run, looking from the man to the woman and back again.

"It was a rrat," said Carmenina, relapsing instinctively into her native accents. "I only saw a rrrat. He went back therrre." She pointed behind the huts where her husband had been. "Therrrre," she pointed again, insisting.

The *vigili* looked squeamish and continued to glance from Carmenina to Beauregard in uncertainty. They did not want to go behind the huts. At this point four of them took the opportunity to say that they were on duty elsewhere, and said good night.

By this time Bingo was in his father's arms, with an arm around his neck, smiling happily at the *vigili*. Beau looked as miserable as a man can look with an adoring son in his arms. He walked over to Carmenina.

"Could you just hold him for one minute, darling?" He turned to the two *vigili* who remained. "I'll go with you."

The three of them walked behind the hut, Beauregard trying to look relaxed with a hand in his pocket. In less than a minute the three of them came out from behind the huts, the two *vigili* trying to look relaxed, each with a hand in his pocket.

"Signora, the rat is nowhere in sight," said one of the *vigili*. "But this is part of our beat, so we will keep checking and keep the area free of infestation." They bowed and headed back toward the Piazza.

"I'm sorry," said Beau to Carmenina as they walked along the Molo. "The meeting broke up and I was in a hurry to leave. I should have gone in the restaurant."

Carmenina sighed. "Anyway, now you can carry him. I was having trouble getting him home. I didn't bother to call a taxi because I wanted to leave and he was so full of energy until we got in the boat."

Beauregard was sitting at Paolin's with Carmenina trying to feel like a family man watching Bingo ride his new bicycle with the training wheels up and down the *campo*. It was Nanny's day off and he was on his best behavior keeping Carmenina company because he was leaving again in the morning for Rome and making a dallying return by way of Positano.

"He's like a machine: back and forth, back and forth," said Beauregard putting down his *Messaggero*. "Seems a shame we can't harness him to make something, like a rug, with all that energy; or maybe electricity." He could never think of anything to say to his wife.

Carmenina looked at him with the eyes of one awakened from sleep. Her mother had sent from Colombia her favorite photo romance magazine. She was lost in one of the stories.

"Is he all right?" she asked seriously, leaning forward to look down the *campo*. Just as she located Bingo down near the monument, she saw three *vigili* approach him. She stood up to see better.

"What's wrong?" said Beauregard, leaning forward himself to have a look.

"What are those *vigili* up to? Why are they talking to him?" Carmenina was on Red Alert.

So much was the sprawling *campo* known for its unsanctioned public function as a playground that the *vigili,* when feeling out of sorts or bored, were known for their perverse habit of heading for San Stefano to impose the Letter of the Law, forbidding balls, bicycles, and sometimes even games like hopscotch which deface the paving stones with chalk. For the *vigili,* the incentive for these occasional forays into law enforcement could hardly have been the castigation of the children, so it must have been the fun of engaging the mothers and nannies, when they descended from their mustering point at the northerly wellhead.

These pitched battles between Common Sense on the one hand and the Rule of Law on the other achieved incandescence in seconds, with the two Forces of Right gaining and losing dominance as passersby joined their ranks and then drifted away. Sooner or later someone would mention the Mayor.

"I went to school with Mayor Bullo's daughter and I know that he would be appalled at this gratuitous assault on the children of Venice."

"Good heavens yes. Dino Marchiori is on the Council and lives right in the next *campo.*"

Finally, someone would negotiate a retreat for the *vigili* saying that the good men and women were only doing their jobs. And the *vigili* would make a break for it, granting an amnesty until the morning, when they swore to return and distribute fines to all offenders. As the *vigili* retreated toward the Rialto, laughing and gesticulating among themselves, the children went back to their bicycles and toys, dizzy with pride for the performances of their mothers and nannies.

As Carmenina stood watching, one of the *vigili* took hold of the new bicycle and gestured for Bingo to get off.

Carmenina was already on her way, a one-woman flying wedge in a pincer movement with the detail arriving from the wellhead.

Beauregard wondered whether he should go with her, but as he watched he recognized the very *vigili* of their earlier encounter. He thought better of it. Anyhow, it was a woman's battle. There were about six of them haranguing the *vigili;* if he went down there he might find himself on their side and then he would be in trouble with Carmenina. Also, he was pretty sure that Carmenina wouldn't recognize them and that they wouldn't recognize her. But they would probably recognize him. In fact they were already coming this way. He opened his newspaper. When they had passed he looked around for Carmenina and Bingo. They were over at the wellhead with the army talking excitedly about the battle. Bingo and three other children were acting out the battle, first as a boxing match and then as a Wild West shootout. The women were at one moment infuriated and at another amused. Eventually Carmenina came back.

"That didn't take you very long," said Beauregard admiringly.

"*Uffa,*" said Carmenina. "What a nuisance. They say they'll come back tomorrow and give everyone fines. So Bingo will have to play with something else for a few days, until they forget."

"They forget everything," suggested Beauregard pretending to be half interested in his newspaper.

"No they don't," said Carmenina. "That's how I got rid of them so fast. I told them that instead of picking on children, they should have the courage to chase away people who really do harm, like molesters."

"You really said that?" asked Beauregard, amazed at her militancy, and at a number of other qualities slowly coming to light, like her competence, her reticence, her providence. And her prescience? *Let not thy divining heart,* he thought, and changed discourse.

"Would you like something to drink?" He turned to Carmenina, but she was lost in her magazine. He looked at Bingo, who had resumed breaking the law, riding up and down, up and down on his bicycle. He reached down and felt his ankle to see if it was still sore from not landing straight when he was trying to learn from Dieter in Berlin how to do a capriole.

MASON

He jerked back his hand and looked. It was empty. Something behind the paneling had reached out and pulled the thing away; something invisible—that could only be a ghost. He felt the hair on the back of his neck start to rise and fear taking him with such force that when he turned and saw the hunched figure beckoning to him, black against the light, he couldn't stop himself from charging headlong past it, mindful of nothing but the open door and daylight.

Rocco Zennaro sank down on the church step and put his hand on the door to steady himself. He could feel the bolts sliding shut and hear locks clicking inside. He felt sick in his heart. Why had this happened to him, a man who never looked for trouble? What had he done to get drawn into this? He felt as if he'd been dragged through time immemorial, yet he remembered, like it was yesterday, the casual act that caught him. In fact it *was* yesterday, at quitting time, not even twenty-four hours before.

"*Ohe!* Where's my towel? I've got soap in my eyes. Come on!" Shouts of horseplay echoed through the ruined house. The men were in the old laundry room washing up and changing to go home. As he moved from room to room attending to his chores, Rocco could feel their banter holding back the gloom that settles on an idle building site. Because he was the foreman and had to check over the workplace before closing down, Rocco always waited to wash-up last. He filled the time with tidying and planning the next day's work. This evening, resting on his broom, he noticed that he felt tired. The idea that he might be coming down with something was just forming when he glimpsed a coil of twine peeping out over a wooden lintel in the broken wall. He jerked it free and stuck it in his pocket without even looking at it: salvage was a reflex. What interested him was the door frame itself.

Bricked up in the last century, it was a piece of Venetian craftsmanship from five or six hundred years ago. He looked at how carefully joined it was, and strong, but low and narrow. Rocco had uncovered it that morning when he was stripping down the plaster. Finding forgotten doors and windows intrigued him. He liked seeing how things used to be, once-upon-a-time. When he was demolishing a wall, he could understand by the way the bricks were laid, by their shape and color, when the wall had been built, where the bricks had come from, and the quality of the craftsmen who had done the work. He examined recycled sills and, if there was a sack-wall, he turned over the rubble that filled the cavity between the walls of brick or stone to see what part these pieces might have played before sinking through time to such a humble role. For Rocco, the story of Venice was in its walls. Right from the beginning, tearing down and rebuilding had been as constant and as natural as the seasons, a process carried out by people like himself. He felt a bond with those fellow journeymen, brothers who had performed his same job, in the same place, partitioned only by time. He admired their ancient and accepted practice of reusing old elements in new buildings, of making sure that nothing ever went to waste.

Nowadays Rocco would go around picking up quantities of brand-new nails and screws that the young carpenters swept into heaps to throw away. For him, those boys were from a world more removed from his own than that of the man who built the door all those centuries ago. The young ones liked to tease him. The other day when he was gathering up some nails, one said, "Don't bother with those, Rocco; they're no good: they've got the heads at the wrong end." And then another one said, "No, no. Rocco's right: we can use them when we get around to the other side." But underneath the jokes, they admired him for being a true artisan, and they listened to his lore. Looking at old beams, he could tell by the splits in the grain whether the trees had been cut down at the waxing or the waning of the moon. When he helped to replace a beam ravaged by such splits, he rued the perfidy of the woodman, however many centuries before, who had traded integrity for expedience.

Rocco had started in the building trade when he was only thirteen. He had begun as a general laborer, but soon got himself apprenticed to a mason and proved himself to be obedient, silent, and quick to learn everything he was taught. For the rest, for picking up the special knack that made a true artisan, gleaning those tricks of the trade that no one would give away, Rocco kept his eyes open and watched how the old ones worked. Day by day he picked up the secret skills that made all the difference, and by the time he was eighteen, he was qualified to a high standard as a bricklayer and stonemason.

The fact that it was a manly trade, heavy work carried out among men, suited him down to the ground. He couldn't have tolerated working in a supermarket like his brother on the mainland, with all those women chattering and giving advice. Men don't talk as much as women. And when they're working hard in the dust, they often don't talk at all, which is even better. He got all the chatting he wanted at home, from Marina, who saved it for him especially to go with dinner. For her it was a wifely duty to keep him up to date and to compensate for the boredom of a job that never gave him anything to talk about.

The door was a curiosity. The beams had peculiar marks

lined up like words; not part of the grain, but cut into it. The timber he thought might have come from a ship and been treated in some way: he had never known mortar to stick so fast. By the time he finished hacking it off, he was sweating and so dizzy he had to rest against the wall. He thought he might faint and when he closed his eyes, a stream of green images flashed by like a dream, of islands in a sea, of palaces in gardens, fields with orchards, with a warmth of people, rich and poor, which faded back into the room only after his eyes had been open long enough to blink, and blink again. It gave him a turn.

He was not a man given to fantasy and where this flight had come from he couldn't imagine. Of course he had in his head, from school, the story of Venice, how it grew: the islands linked by wooden bridges, then by stone bridges, and finally, after buildings filled the islands, how they were linked now, as Marina always said, by people at windows looking across the canals straight into one another's houses, so that today Venice is just like anywhere else and a Venetian thinks about being a Venetian as much as a dog thinks about being a dog. She was probably right.

Rocco ran his hand over the powdery surface: it was perfectly flush. He kicked the base. Solid. But the question was what was behind it. He and the architect had worked out that there was a thin slice of the room he was standing in hidden behind the wall. As a situation it wasn't remarkable. Venetian houses abound in spaces appropriated, somehow, from a neighboring apartment. But normal or not, it posed a technical problem that had to be resolved.

Architect Falon had stopped by just before lunch. He was in his usual rush, but he was always considerate with Rocco; he never forgot that it was Rocco's steadiness that made it possible for him to run his own fleet of workers and avoid calling in a big company every time he did a job.

"Just look at this," he called as he ran up the stairs, holding up an envelope charred on one end. "It's a draft notice for the Decardis' younger son. As I'm coming in the door, this *postino* stops me and hands it to me, saying he doesn't want to put it in the letterbox without explaining how he'd saved it from being thrown into the incinerator with some rubbish. He didn't want to get anyone into trouble, as it was just an accident, but he thought the Decardis should know why it was burned and he wanted to be sure it arrived safely, and on and on. What he really wanted was a tip, so I had to fork out a fifty. It was the smallest note I had. What misery! He probably put a match to it himself. He looked like a Southerner. Would you give it to the Decardis' maid tomorrow, Rocco? I'll ring the Decardis and tell them about it. Thanks. And now for this unwelcome wall. I looked at the neighbor's plans. The space isn't shown. Even if they've got some opening into it, they can't claim it. So that's it: we open it up."

The area had been included in the measurements on the original plan, but unfortunately the architect's staff had corrected the measurements because the wall didn't appear on the plan and they couldn't see that there was anything behind it. That was the problem. Falon said that if the authorities came to look at it, as it was so old, applying for a variation in the plans and getting permission to take it out could hold up the works for months. The Decardis had left their apartment upstairs and gone to the country to get away from the noise and the dust, but they wanted to come home. Furthermore, they weren't just clients; they were his friends.

"Tomorrow, Rocco," he said, "make it disappear. I can put the measurements back the way they were by registering a correction; we'll just say we measured it wrong. I'll bring you extra help first thing in the morning." Rocco sighed as he leaned the broom in the corner; for some reason, he didn't look forward to tearing out that door and pulling down the wall.

He walked back through the empty rooms one more time to check that the windows and shutters were closed and the work sites ready for the morning. On this job there were usually four or five men assigned to him. Tomorrow there would be seven or eight. As he opened the door to the laundry room, all the others came filing out, clean and ready to go, the young helpers first, with their faces shining and their wet hair combed back. They laughed and said "hello" and then "goodbye." It was the moment when their spirits soared, setting out for their trains and buses to the mainland.

Rocco took off his dusty clothes and started to wash his face and arms. Of the whole crew, he alone still lived in Venice. He had only to cross over to the Giudecca and he was home, while all the rest of them would still be sitting in the train or bus, the young ones telling jokes and the older ones catching forty winks.

When he was dressed, he transferred his money and his handkerchief from his work clothes, tacked the scorched draft notice on the wall where he wouldn't forget it, turned off the electricity at the mains, double-locked the front door, picked up some splinters on the steps and put them on the heap in the courtyard, pulled the outer door firmly to, shook it to make sure it was locked, put the keys in the pocket of his jacket, and then, with a mind as quiet as a field, he homed for the Zattere and the Giudecca ferry.

When the sailor opened the gates, Rocco let the crowd push past him into the cabin and took one of the single chairs in the prow, as he always did, summer and winter. After a day cooped up in the dust, he liked the open air. As they pulled away from the landing stage, a November mist was settling over the water. He felt the air growing dense and a tingling sensation coming over him like the beginning of a sneeze. He pulled his handkerchief from his pocket, pulling with it the twisted string. As the vaporetto droned toward the middle of the canal, its points of departure and destination faded simultaneously from view. But Rocco didn't notice the strange effect. He was untangling the string to roll it into a ball. He had unwound only a single coil when he thought he decried, through the vapor, something queer about it. He took a better look. What he saw made his heart thump. The bundle of string was not what he had taken it for. There was no mistaking: someone had worked it into the shape of a man, and he knew, from the chill that was slipping from his shoulders down his arms and legs to his feet, that it embodied a spell. The spell was telling him so; he could feel it, but what he couldn't feel was whether it was a good spell or whether it was working for something evil. He couldn't fathom its nature. He coiled the string around the body the way it was before, wrapped it in his handkerchief, and put it back in his pocket, right down to the bottom.

He walked home with his hand on his pocket. All through dinner the string tugged at his consciousness and caused him to put his hand on it from time to time to be sure it was safe. It had some kind of power. That much he could tell. But what its nature was he didn't know and it troubled him.

Marina was furious with old Signora Bordon and served up the *pasticcio* like it was their neighbor she'd cooked for dinner. It had been a day peppered with offenses, but the worst centered on Marina's flower boxes.

"When I came through with the ironing," she jerked her head in the direction of the sitting room, "there was that black cat sitting in the window box watching me—who knows for how long he'd been gawping. So I got the broom and went in and opened the bedroom window so I could knock him off as he ran back home. But just as I leaned forward to see where he was, he ran up and hissed like a snake. Then he jumped right over my head onto the roof next door." She drew an arc with her fork over her head. "That cat has the devil in it; I can feel it. I'm going to write to Giada and ask her to read some cards and tell me about that cat."

Giada was the fortune-teller on television. He wondered whether she would be able to tell whether the string man had the devil in it, but he didn't raise the issue. He wouldn't have known how to begin.

"You won't believe who's got a job at the supermarket over by the Redentore." Marina took his dirty plate and put down a plate of *spezzatino*. "The Conton boy. So he'll have plenty of money now to buy more music. I saw him putting out the milk." She pretended to be lifting a milk carton from a case on the floor and slowly placing it on the table, while patting a yawn with the other hand. "He won't last. He looked like he wanted to speak to me, but I pretended I didn't see him. He has to learn he can't be rude to us and then just go on like nothing happened."

Marina was a good wife. He was relieved that she hadn't noticed how distracted he was tonight.

"And you'll never guess who else I saw today, down by the vaporetto. Old Pisa. Remember him? How he didn't give the priest the money his mother had left for prayers after she died and he got so he couldn't straighten up and they always called him Pisa. Then one day he was cured and stood straight up again, and everyone said it meant his mother had got out of Purgatory, so she'd forgiven him. Well, he's all bent over again. So what do you think that means?"

She didn't expect an answer. She didn't even expect him to think about it. But tonight, while he watched her spooning out the *tiramisu,* he wondered whether such causes and effects were possible between this world and the other side.

"And speaking of Purgatory," she continued in a way that made him wonder what could be coming next, "when you see the architect tomorrow, tell him that I went to see his mother today. She wants me to come Mondays, Wednesdays, and Fridays from ten-thirty to twelve-thirty. She doesn't get up early. She's quite a lady. She says she goes out a lot, for lunches and coffees, so she won't be underfoot when I'm cleaning. Anyhow, it doesn't look like a bad job; it's only her and she's tidy. The house is *bellissima:* Grand Canal, expensive curtains and carpets. It's not what *we* like, but it's rich-looking. That was her job, wasn't it? Furnishing houses? You can see that she was a businesswoman. She writes everything down in a notebook: my name, your name, our telephone number, when I'm supposed to work, the kind of floor polish I think is best; she took it all down. I thought it was a good idea: so as not to forget. I might get a notebook. I keep forgetting to write to Giada."

Marina turned on the television while she washed the dishes. She liked to listen to the horoscopes and watch Giada with the tarot cards. Tonight Rocco didn't feel like watching television. He went in the sitting room and sat near the window. He lit a cigarette and looked out at the mist drifting like spirits around the streetlamps. A faint church bell tolling in the distance reached him over the water. But no; it wouldn't be a church bell, not at this hour. It had to be something for the fog. Strange, he'd never heard it before.

In the night he started awake. He thought he must have been snoring and Marina must have poked him. He looked at her: sound asleep and far away. Perhaps a sound had alarmed him. His heart felt as cold and heavy as a stone. He stopped breathing to listen. Then the dread that had been stalking him since yesterday slowly took hold of him. It was the string man. He knew. It was urging him. He had to do something about it.

But what? But what? Was it good or was it evil? Had it been hidden in the wall as a curse or as a blessing? Without knowing the words whispered by the man who put it there, how could he know what it meant? And how could he know the words whispered by a man dead for hundreds of years?

Lying awake he was visited by thoughts he had never before entertained. He remembered that when each of his two sons was born, Marina had sent him to the shop in Calle della Mandola to buy a tiny pair of scissors in a leather case. She hid them under the drawers in the wardrobe where no one could ever touch them or open them. That was to protect the babies. He hadn't paid much attention to it then. It was a kind of game, a thing people used to do. He supposed it was meant to cast a magic spell over them. As a matter of fact, both his sons had been spared and had children of their own. He wondered.

There had been some narrow escapes, the worst one when Rico, coming home from catechism in a rainstorm one night, had been blown off the high *fondamenta* into the deep Giudecca canal. Despite the darkness, a passing taxi driver not only saw him fall, but managed to find him and pull him from the water. When he brought him to the door, Rico was streaming wet and shaking like a jackhammer, but he didn't even catch a cold. Could it have been the scissors that made the taxi driver look toward the *fondamenta* just at the instant the umbrella and boy flashed through the lamplight and disappeared over the edge? He'd never thought of it before.

A few days after it happened, a gypsy had walked up

to Marina and the boys on the Accademia Bridge. She'd grabbed Rico's hand and looked at his palm, then dropped it. "You're lucky to have him," she said to Marina. "You nearly lost him." That encounter upset Marina more than the accident; she couldn't sleep for thinking about it.

The scissors must still be there in the wardrobe. He wondered if the spell carried on from one generation to the next. He was sure that his boys hadn't done anything like it for their children. They were married to modern women. But it might not matter; the spell might pass on forever, from one generation to the next, as long as the scissors were safe. He thought about finding a safer place; under the floorboards might be better. Then he thought of the ancient door, which before the day was out would be in a boat full of rubble on its way to a landfill. No place in the world was completely safe.

Except a church: the thought came to him like a shout in his head. Yes! He caught himself as he was about to cry it out. If it was a good charm, it would be at home in a church; if it was an evil charm, the power of the church could neutralize it so it couldn't get revenge. A cross can stop a vampire!

Rocco got up and dressed in the bathroom. He scribbled a note for Marina about having to go to the supply yard and slipped out the door. It was not yet daylight. He had plenty of time before he needed to be at work. As he waited for the vaporetto, he looked at the place where Rico had sunk into the dark water. If he hadn't been saved, would they ever have known what had happened to him? Or would they have been tormented all their lives, like Franco Cardin's grandparents, whose son fell off the *fondamenta* while he was playing but his playmates never let on for fear of being blamed. So the parents never knew. Eventually they surmised that he had been stolen by gypsies; there were always gypsies about, and in those days there were no investigations. It was two generations later, after the parents were long dead, when one of the boys, an old man, told the story of how their friend slipped off the edge and how the three of them clung together, watching, for such a long time, waiting for him to pop up. But he never did. Afterward they thought that one of them should have run for help, so they swore never to tell what happened. One of the boys turned bad and went to jail. One became a priest. They all kept the secret until no one cared anymore. But Rico had been saved.

He went to the church he passed every morning in Campo San Stefano on the way to the Decardi house. He was lucky it was open early, but he was unlucky too. A coffin was being delivered for a funeral. He stood in the street. Rocco was not a religious man, but he had done his catechism and knew what was right. Seeing a coffin without crossing himself made him nervous. Even when he had to step aside to make way for the coffins being rolled down Calle della Testa from the hospital, as he often did going to the supply yard, he would scratch his nose and fiddle with his buttons, then check his breast pockets for cigarettes until he had traced a surreptitious cross. He decided to give the undertakers plenty of time to get out of the way. He went and had a coffee at the corner bar.

When he entered the church, he was surprised. It was much lighter than he expected. There were massive altars along both walls. Up near the high altar, an old sacristan looked at him over the lectern he was dusting.

The coffin was a long way up the center aisle, near where the sacristan was cleaning and some florists were placing flowers. Rocco headed to the left aisle where no one was praying and began to examine the joins in the stonework, first on one altar, then the next. He couldn't find the chink he needed.

He heard slippers shuffling toward him and forced his hands into a less frenzied caper over the joins; he knew he must look like he was doing something wrong; which, for all he knew, might be the case. The shuffling stopped.

"What . . . are . . . you . . . doing?"

Rocco stood up. "I'm a mason." He was happy to be telling the truth. "I'm trying to solve a problem—in a job I'm working on."

The sacristan's face brightened: "This . . . church . . . must . . . be"—he took care to see each word steadied before putting down another, like a palsied man setting up a domino chain—"paradise . . . for . . . a st-stone . . . m-mason. The . . . b-best . . . is there." He pointed and set off across the church.

Rocco began to panic. It was getting late. He had to stow the charm and get away. He had the keys to the house. The men would be waiting outside. The architect was bringing extra help. The bell in the campanile began to ring.

"Come." The sacristan looked back and motioned for Rocco to follow him.

Rocco looked heavenward in desperation, and caught in a single glance a hundred perches among the beams and buttresses where his burden might have rested undisturbed for a millennium. He cursed silently, checked himself, and changed it to a prayer: "Oh God, *please.* Help me!"

A phone rang. The sacristan signaled "wait" and made his way to the high altar. Behind a column he lifted a receiver. Standing near a side altar, Rocco saw a crack where it joined the wall. He pulled out the string bundle and forced it, with all his might, into the crack and out of sight. He left the church in a hurry.

Rocco was standing with his foot on the scaffolding, smoking a cigarette and looking at the door frame lying on the floor at his feet. It didn't look like much now. They had torn it apart getting it out. He turned over the lintel with his foot. There in the top was a small rectangular well. That would be where the string man had been. He ran his fingers around it and felt how carefully it had been finished inside, with a rabbet all around the edge. He looked over the rubble and splinters and saw a thin leaf of wood, which he picked up and fitted over it. He wondered how the lid had happened to shift and the string man be exposed for him to see.

Once the door was out, the dividing wall had almost fallen down by itself, with most of the plaster crumbling into powder at the slightest touch. The narrow room looked to Rocco like it might have been a workshop. There were pictures of tools around, maybe marking where they were kept, like the trowel and the square. In the rubble from the wall, he found on a piece of plaster a beautiful picture of an eye. He put it in his pocket for Marina.

The architect had to take two boys away after lunch to work on another site, so Rocco went to see how they were finishing up in the kitchen. One was shoveling rubble into a barrow, while the other one waited; then the barrow boy wheeled the barrow down the hall to the window, where he emptied it through a conduit into a barge in the canal below. While he did this, the shoveler waited. As it was nearly lunchtime, Rocco sent the shoveler down to the courtyard to fetch another barrow, so they could work faster. He got another shovel and helped him to fill the barrow so the barrow boy wouldn't waste time waiting for the shoveler to fill the next barrow. The boys were working well, keeping pace with Rocco, when he saw something in his shovel that made him stop dead. It was taking shape before his eyes. He put the shovel down, picked it from the rubble, and put it in his pocket. The boys said it was only dirty string and not worth anything, but he just shrugged and went on shoveling. He was thinking.

Today Rocco was the first to wash his face and arms for lunch, and the first to leave. He told his apprentice to be the last to leave and to slam the door tight. Then he ran as he hadn't run in years back to the Church of San Stefano. But just as he achieved the front step, the doors slammed together with a bang. In his speed, he fell against them and felt the bolt sliding on the other side. He looked up at the church clock on the corner and saw that it was still a few minutes before twelve, so he turned and ran back the way he had come, past the house where he could hear his men coming down the stairs, and on into the next *campo*, where he saw with relief the open doors of the Church of San Fantin.

As his eyes adjusted to the dimness, Rocco saw the priest sitting in the front with his back to the altar, hunched over a book. The priest glanced up at him, then went on reading.

Rocco put his hand on the string man in his pocket. He felt that he was in serious trouble and he didn't know what to do. He looked at the racks of candles in front of the various altars. He chose the altar with a male saint holding a child. He felt in his pocket for a coin and slipped it into the collection box. He pulled out a candle. But as he was about to light it, he saw that the wick was burned. He tried another, and another. All the wicks were burned. He understood: the priest was multiplying his profits, blowing out the candles and selling them again and again. Rocco was outraged. The devil was everywhere. He lit a candle and prayed to the saint, whose name he didn't know, to help him to do the right thing. The priest was getting up and was coming toward him. Rocco looked over his shoulder. The priest moved past him toward the door, indicating with his head that it was time to leave. The wall beside the altar was paneled with wood. Rocco ran his hand over the surface and felt a gap in the dark corner. He took the string man from his pocket to try fitting it into the crack. He had barely touched it to the wood when it pulled slowly through his fingers, as though drawn away by an invisible hand.

The light of day made him feel better. He got up from the church step and stood for a minute looking around. A cat that had been sleeping in the flower boxes at the restaurant across the way lifted its head and seemed to smile. He felt like smiling back. Were cats always wicked? He wondered. It watched him walk away.

By the time he got to the *mensa* everyone had eaten and gone back to Campo San Stefano to sit on the monument and smoke. He didn't see anything on the steam table that appealed to him. He took a *panino,* a glass of wine, and an apple. He found a clean table and sat down. He looked at his food. It was the kind of simple meal the carpenter who built the door with the string man might have eaten every day. He was still puzzled: what was the string man meant to do? Why had the carpenter taken so much trouble over it? What gave the string man the power to save himself? He was convinced, now, that the string man belonged to some force and that the force wanted the string man to be safe. It must be that the spell could carry on for as long as the charm was safe. By this time, after all those centuries, it could be casting its spell over all that remained of the old Venetian stock: himself, his wife, their children and grand-children; even Signora Bordon who sent her cat to tear up Marina's window boxes, and Gianni Conton's son who played rock music all weekend and made a face like a Martian when you tried to get his attention through the window to ask him to turn down the volume. It was strange to think of power spreading out over the centuries from one carpenter. He wondered if the man whose magic had fallen into his hands had spoken of it, or whether it was a secret between the two of them, over the great divide. Was it he in the paneling of the church with the reused candles?

Rocco stopped trying to answer the questions. He didn't have to be troubled by these things anymore. The work could go on normally now. He felt sure of it.

He pulled a paper napkin from the dispenser and rubbed the apple until it shone, then cut it into four pieces. He lined them up. Of the four pieces, two had bits of worm. He pondered for a second, but he'd had enough. He left the apple and went back to work.

VISITOR

Charles Smithers, barely launched on his maiden first-class flight, was already disenchanted. His legs ached and he thought he might even cry if the stewardess didn't come soon. He had been trapped for nearly an hour behind his meal tray with *The New York Times* divided into its ten or twenty parts cascading over and around his feet and adding weight to his camera, which was balanced on his ankles where he had caught it when it fell from the seat pocket at the start of this cruelly protracted dinner—or was it lunch?

On these transatlantic flights everything is so up in the air. He would have liked to share a joke with someone to get his mind off his misery, but the woman beside him, he could see at a glance, was not the type to give him an opening—least of all in the jocular vein. He hazarded a furtive Dracula smile. He had been warned by his friends, so many times, that the stream of jokes capering through his brain was Marx Brothers at best, usually worse, and never suitable in high places—which this undeniably was.

It was largely out of respect for this woman's emanating dignity that he refrained from hammering, or even pressing, the button to invoke the stewardess to come save him. Here, he thought it more decorous to take the service for granted, so he had held the camera on his ankles all this time for fear that it would roll under the seats and pick up filth or be claimed by someone. These things might not be a risk here in first class, but what if it should slip through the divide and roll down through business into tourist class? He knew the situation back there. It would be lost. And even if it wasn't, he was not sure that he would want it back afterward. While *The New York Times* rustled about his straining legs, he tried reveling in the extra legroom he commanded as a first-class passenger, but he could not escape the irony that he was worse off at the moment than he had ever been in tourist class. There he played the game of defending his share of the armrests and grabbing whatever was proffered. It was difficult to pass the time like this. While waiting he started idly to polish the ashtray with his linen napkin and to rub a mark from the windowsill, but he came to his senses and took up a pose of bland disregard toward the disordered tray and evidence of halfhearted cleaning, as though he were a total stranger to housewifery.

The woman beside him had hidden her tray with a shining Italian magazine which she read with a vague incurious air that transmitted signals of aristocracy! aristocracy! to his antennae and played on his curiosity. His *Octagon,* his *New Yorker,* his *Wall Street Journal* had all gone down in the general slide. He wondered which he wished most to retrieve. He bet himself that the *Octagon* would attract her attention and arouse a flicker of well-bred interest: Spink's was a smart shop. The Baccarat paperweights might be something they could talk about, or the coins—he didn't suppose an aristocrat would object to talking about money in that sense, as *objets d'art*—no one objects to art. Or he could show her the picture of the stirrup cup he might "acquire on behalf of a client" whose horse farm in Maryland he'd once decorated. The cup was shaped like a hound's head and had engraved around the collar:

> 'tis Darling have at him,
> we're in for a run,
> the hounds fly together
> like shot from a gun.

He loved that verse and had merged it instantly into his Ready Anthology of Memorized Poems. Marty, who knew his brain a little too well, was a computer programmer and code-named Char's poetry facility RAMP, and added ANT for And Naughty Thoughts. RAMP was for climbing in society; ANT was crawling about in the dirt. But Marty was right, as usual, to link the two. They were stored precisely there in the same memory and full of dangerous cross-references. It took vigilance—and a limited intake of alcohol—to keep the two files apart. RAMPANT by name, rampant by nature; that was his brain.

The verse evoked in him the perfect joy which reigned in his imagination at a hunt breakfast with everyone suave and secure in his primacy over those who were not members, happy in their smart red coats, which Charles knew enough to pretend were pink. Not for him the mistake of the bumpkin child who blurted out that what he saw was the Emperor's pink body and nothing else. It was a stunning *gaucherie* which made Charles wince for the poor boy. He turned his sympathy then to the king and wondered if he had blushed. Then he would have been red—but this would be one of those times when it was correct to ignore the truth, to deny the royal humiliation and pretend that red is pink, bringing him neatly back to the hunting coat principle. But not quite: a fugitive thought was still tugging at his imagination: would the king have blushed from head to toe, in every part—even the part he feared *too meager for a monarch,* not worth calling to the attention of the flamboyant armorer, and now glowing, a tiny prick of color? Would the little boy have pointed and laughed, with all the other little urchins gathering around him? Charles covered his face and moaned out loud. He felt the elegant lady turn a vacant stare in his direction. But luck was with him at last. The stewardess appeared with a litany of apologies.

There was a man in business class who had booked first

class with his travel agent but had somehow been mistakenly put in business class. The check-in desk had told him that first class was full, but he should ask to see the first-class stewardess after takeoff in case she could do something for him. But in fact there was nothing she could do and she told him so: the flight was completely full in business *and* first class and he would have to take it up with his travel agent when he got back. Whereupon he started to swear and threw his dinner on the floor. They had threatened to have the captain radio the police in Rome to meet the plane. She explained as she cleared away their trays and tidied up around them. Charles sat up straight, glad to regain his equilibrium.

"Listen," he said in his noblest manner, "if it makes so much difference to him, I can survive in business class."

A commanding hand, jewels glittering, extended to silence him. The elegant woman gave him the first meaningful look he had seen on her face since they left New York.

He understood. His heart leaped. She preferred *him.* She didn't want him to leave her. The stewardess understood as well. With warm thanks, she refused his offer. She stowed his camera overhead and helped him to organize his magazines and newspapers. He began to feel good again. He might as well be at a hunt breakfast. Happy as a clam. Happy as a clam at a hunt breakfast, even. His mind's eye locked on a hand taking up a shell and lifting it toward an open mouth. He grabbed *The New Yorker* and thumbed through it furiously searching for something elevating, a poem, a serious article.

Eventually he found a poem about someone who felt sad in a particular house, which he didn't really like, but at least it raised the tone of his consciousness. On the whole, dirges like "Deep caves and dreary main, / Wail for the world's wrong," or the Tennyson one that Marty was always quoting with a long face, didn't do much for him. Here, he and Marty were complete opposites. In fact Marty had been annoyed by his parody "Let there be no moaning at the bar, / When I cruise in to see." He was like a lot of people who enjoy teasing others but can't take a joke on themselves. When they had first started to live together, Charles worked for days to clean up the apartment, and until they'd got affluent enough to afford a maid, it had been Charles who did all the cleaning and tidying. So Marty called him Char, for charlady, and got everyone to call him Char, even his clients, who thought it was short for Charles. That was Marty's kind of joke.

"Are you stopping in Rome?" A beautiful female voice fell on his ear like chimes. It was she, the aristocrat, opening a conversation with him.

"No," he replied, forcing himself not to pant, and to meet her gaze. He took in her cool, blonde, good looks. She was, he thought, probably about forty-five, and not yet facelifted, though she would be, in another ten years. Her eyes were of the palest blue and gave a disturbing Magritte-like impression of opening into an empty universe, an impression contradicted by her formidable presence.

"I'm going straight to Venice to visit an old friend at the Gotham Library," said Charles.

"Are you staying with Mrs. Gotham?"

"No. I'm staying at the Gritti."

"Have you stayed there before?"

"No, this is my first trip to Venice."

"How long will you stay?"

"I don't know," Charles admitted half apologetically, feeling like he'd missed a point in a quiz show. "I can stay as long as I like, really."

"Well, you'll love it," she said approvingly. "And you'll like the Gritti, too. As hotels go, it's one of the nicest. I always send people to the Gritti or the Monaco as the next best thing to having your own apartment. I live in Rome. We'd better reset our watches. Let's see: it's nearly four o'clock in the morning in Italy. We should try to sleep."

She drew a sleep mask from her handbag. "See you at breakfast." She smiled and turned away, pulling the mask over her eyes.

He slept next to the blonde noblewoman as he had never slept before. But when he awoke, she was gone. He looked around in concern and confusion. *After you've gone, and left me cryin'...* He felt blue, but then he saw her coming back to her seat looking combed and fresh. He couldn't hold back the adoring smile that spread over his face at the sight of her.

. . .

Perhaps the greatest single reason that Charles Smithers was on this flight from New York was his gradual discovery that decorating interiors of privates houses is like being a ghostwriter. Once he'd done the job, he was expected to evaporate. The more the clients liked Char's work, the more they didn't want him spooking around afterward. He had always disappeared, though it pained him to depart like a herd dog, driving the painters, the carpenters, the seamstresses, and so on, ahead of him. Many times he'd wanted to go back, more precisely, to be *invited* back, to revel in his own creations, but at the beginning he had not been a famous maestro whose name and presence gave an added cachet, and no matter how good his work, he had never been able to translate himself into one. So he'd made a strategic retreat into commercial interiors, and made a name for himself in that field. He'd also made a lot of money. Now he was ready to try again on the private house circuit, but this time as a rising star, a household name. This holiday was going to be, in fact, a long preparatory tour, starting in Venice because it was the southernmost point where he had a well-placed contact. He would get to see inside the great houses, but above all he would hobnob with the *haut monde.* When he returned he would have an address book worth forgetting beside someone's telephone. Back to window dressing, he smiled. But this time it was his own window he was dressing. All those *nouveaux* around New York, they would be humbled by the aristocrats of Europe, the Real Society of the world; those who had more than mere money, who had enjoyed money as well as status for centuries, those for whom being careless of their underlings was as natural as being born. Let them eat cake! These were the serene, confident people who no more hesitated to talk of private matters in front of their retainers than in front of their dogs. And they were free from the prejudices of the *nouveaux*. These were the people who understood that talent was another kind of nobility, who took up talented people. They had taken up Dante, and Leonardo da Vinci, and Shakespeare and Titian. They would take up Charles Smithers. Charles Smithers smiled at the seat back in the row ahead, which was practically prostrate before him.

As they waited for their breakfast, his neighbor opened her magazine and showed him an article, one of a series, on fashionable people in Venice. This one was about a couple called Barone and Baronessa Patristi and Trudi Gotham, whom they called Lady Trudi. It was written in Italian and he couldn't read it. His companion explained to him that her younger sister had gone to school with Sofia Patristi. Edmondo had inherited a most wonderful palace, but hadn't very much money. His parents had wisely chosen to have only one child so as not to divide what they had, and then he was lucky enough to fall in love with an heiress of the rich Fierazzo family, so everything had turned out beautifully. They had even bought back the family villa in the country near Verona. They needed two properties, because they had a son and a daughter. The villa would go to the daughter and the palace would go to the son. They were just restoring the palace and redoing it all inside. In fact, she said, if you looked closely at the photographs, you could see that it was practically falling to pieces. Char looked at the photographs with longing and wondered if he would ever be able to get a commission like that. She put the magazine away and began to pick at her breakfast. He addressed his breakfast but monitored her comportment out of the corner of his eye as she drank her juice and took a few bites of fruit. She took a sip of coffee, then put it down and said she would wait and have a proper coffee in the airport. He did the same. She opened a yellow paperback with Poirot on the cover, and became instantly engrossed in the story. She didn't speak another word until the end of the journey.

As the ramp rolled against the airplane with a thump, she turned to him as though the impact had activated a programmed response.

"As you are going to Venice, perhaps you wouldn't mind taking this magazine to my aunt. If it's no trouble, of course. She'd be amused by the article I showed you."

"Oh, no trouble at all. I'd be delighted," exclaimed Char, reaching for the magazine which she had not yet offered. She appeared to be unaware of his gesture, but he caught on and yanked back the hands like wayward brats and trapped them between his knees to signal his own disapproval of their grasping nature.

"How nice of you," she smiled, tilting her head a little to one side in the kindest possible attitude of condescension. "I'll write down her address for you."

He watched as she sent her jeweled hand scurrying about inside her copious Gucci handbag, but averted his gaze to feign an interest in the inscrutable activity of the workmen darting about under the plane like ants discovering a windfall pear. Well aware he was that a lady's handbag was among her most intimate appurtenances. Once, as a child, he had ventured to creep away to his room with his mother's handbag so he could clean it for her. How many times he had heard her sigh to her friends as she churned through its contents, "What this bag needs is a good housecleaning!" He could still see the tangled jumble spilling out onto his bed. First he had washed it all over the inside with his facecloth and then dried it with his towel; they had both turned brownish red from the leather and the stain had never quite faded away. He had sorted everything into little packets with rubber bands and paper clips and replaced it all in a tidy way. With what innocent pleasure he had sneaked it back downstairs to the table in the hall before she missed it.

He could still feel inside himself the shining childish face he wore as he pursued his mother through the house waiting for her to discover his wonderful surprise. When she finally discovered it, she had shrieked with dismay. "Charles," she had gasped, "this is something you must never, *never* do— go into a woman's handbag. I had no *idea* you would ever do such a thing!" Thanks to that little incident, he had a phobia about those damned objects which had given him many uncomfortable hours in theaters and restaurants, where he was morbidly distracted by the fear that the woman seated next to him was getting ready to walk off without her handbag and leave him to run after her, dangling the insinuating vessel at arm's length.

His fellow traveler drew from the handbag a silver card case engraved with a coronet. She reached in again and brought forth a gold pen. "No," she murmured, dropping the card case back into the handbag, "I'll do it this way." She wrote across the top of the magazine in large, lasso loops: Contessa Dicadoro, Palazzo Dicadoro-Leoni, tel. 29937.

"If you telephone her and tell her that you have a magazine for her from her niece, Silla—Bellaforte," she wrote under the address, *per Laetitia da Silla—ti telefonerò,* "I'm sure she will invite you to come and see her *palazzo,* which I know you will like very much. And when you see Pat Mayer, tell him I said hello—and I didn't know that he'd been *trudicato.* I knew him when he lived in Rome. Goodbye." She had gathered her book and handbag as she spoke, and stood up with an attitude of finality that rooted him to his seat. She was gone.

Defeated, he slumped over the magazine, now in his grasp. He read the inscription: *Contessa Dicadoro.* Contessa Dicadoro . . . Contessa Dicadoro: the name was reviving his spirits. A gorgeous double-page spread fell open in his brain. There was Cole Porter on a balcony with a beautiful woman whose blonde hair was swept back to emphasize the classic beauty of her profile. She was wearing diamond earrings and chains of diamonds around her neck that made glints in the photograph. Behind them, through the Gothic arches, was a ballroom with massive glass chandeliers that made profusions of glints. Cole Porter and the woman were looking at each other and laughing, sharing a joke on common mortals. Across the bottom of the balcony was the article's title written in thick letters cut out of ripply blue water: "Cole Porter's Venice: My Ritzy Little Corner." The woman was Contessa Dicadoro, a Canadian married into a famous family, who was quoted saying how much everyone liked the Porters and how much *fun* they were.

Where had he seen it? He was sitting in the library stacks back in college. It wasn't a recent magazine even then. He was writing a term paper for an English course called "Society and Literature in the Twentieth Century: An Investigation of Class in American Culture since 1918," taught by the Marxist professor. His paper was called "Paper Palaces: An Analysis of Upper-Class Representations in Popular

Literature, Screenplays, and Song Lyrics." The last chapter was called "Dull Glitter" to show the professor that he had the right—being in this case the left—slant on things. He had put on the cover:

> *Not all that tempts your wand'ring eyes*
> *And heedless hearts is lawful prize*
> *Nor all that glisters gold.*

He'd got an A on it—and saved his grade-point average.

With the magazine for Contessa Dicadoro in his briefcase, Charles Smithers entered Venice a New Man. Even the sniffer dogs seemed pleased with him as he breezed through customs and through the automatic doors into the expectant gaze of the waiting crowd. The CIGA representative was waiting to take him to the motor launch for the Gritti, holding up a card bearing the name *Ciarls Smitters,* but never mind. Life was moving on apace. "Onward and upward! Excelsior!" cried the voice in his brain, making fun of him. He had to find a way to silence that awful patter commenting on every waking thought—sometimes romping right into his conversations.

The passage down the Grand Canal with him standing at the back of the water taxi couldn't have felt more like a royal progress. It built his confidence to the point that when they sidled up to the landing stage at the Gritti, he felt equal to the imminent encounter with *Ricevimento* and the famous figureheads of the *Portineria*. Transported to his room on a Mexican wave of deference, he found himself proffering a tip to a bellboy backing toward the door like Blackrod at the opening of Parliament. Respect for the queen, quipped the voice in his head. But he shunned its suggestion that he look over the lad's shoulder, widen his eyes, and drop his jaw as if to signal impending disaster. He was determined to turn off the comic band and tune in to glorious dignity.

Late the next morning, he rang Patrick Mayer at the Gotham Library, who invited him to come straight over for coffee. The prospect gave him the courage to ring Contessa Dicadoro. He was surprised that she was expecting his call and she too invited him to come over at once. Char was both pleased and dismayed to say that he already had an engagement for the next hour or two, but he offered to come later. They agreed on four o'clock.

Char had not seen Patrick Mayer since his departure for Europe nearly ten years ago. After leaving New York, Patrick had lived in a succession of cities, first Rome, then Paris, then London, and had specialized in society. He seemed to know something about everybody. He had extended his limited funds working for friends who owned art galleries and bookstores, more as charming accomplice than employee, but his great chance had come when he met Ermintrude Gotham, who eventually invited him to collaborate in her thriving hobby, the Gotham Library of Autobiographical Materials, now housed in a tall *palazzo* near San Marco and open to the public six days a week: like her father before her, Trudi Gotham didn't do things in half measures. The wrought-iron gates were open. Charles crossed the garden to the *androne,* where he was met by the porter.

"Mr. Mayer is expecting me," said Charles with the careful courtesy due to a man performing a service.

The porter stared at him, then screwed his features into a hideous gargoyle. Charles took this to mean that he didn't speak English. The porter motioned toward the stairs and walked back into his office.

The two flights of stairs led directly into the grand salon, which was lined with bookshelves and card file cabinets, and furnished with long tables flanked with upholstered chairs like the library in a good club. Patrick was seated at a massive walnut desk at the end of the room. He waved and indicated that he would join Charles in a second and that he should look around while he waited. Charles opened a file drawer and leafed through the cards. There were a lot of classic names mixed in with famous contemporary names, along with some names he had heard of and others he felt he ought to know. How many there were! He stepped back and counted how many drawers there were and made a rough calculation—huge. He remembered that someone had written that "reading through the card file of the Gotham Library of Autobiographical Materials (GLAM) is like running down the roster of some imaginary institute of twentieth-century culture and its heritage." So there it was: Miss Gotham had made a GLAM slam. He closed the drawer as Patrick appeared beside him. Charles followed him back to the stairs.

"The houseboy is taking my place for a minute," whispered Patrick as they left the reading room. "Let's go down to the watergate for a quick smoke. We can pick up a coffee in the readers' lounge as we go by."

Patrick opened the doors onto the Grand Canal. "Oh damn. The outer gate's locked. We'll just have to stand here inside; I don't feel like getting the porter to open it." Patrick rested his cup on the crossbar of the gate and lit a cigarette. Charles did the same.

"I'm so glad to see you," said Patrick. "Not just in Venice, but here today, right now. The readers drive me mad. I can't keep them quiet. I've asked Trudi a hundred times to make a rule that they can't share diaries, but she won't do it. She hates rules. So all day they sit around pointing out passages to each other and whispering and snickering. Have you ever thought how infuriating it would be to sit every day in a room where people whisper and snicker?"

"I was impressed by the glamorous names in the card file of the G-L-A-M." replied Charles. "In fact, I think it's a GLAM slam."

"That's a pun or something, isn't it? Don't explain it," said Patrick. "I'll work it out tonight while I'm counting sheep. I'll sing it to the rattle of the radiators, chachacha. Miss Gotham made a grand slam, grand slam."

"*GLAM* slam, don't you get it?" said Charles.

"Oh yeah. What did I say?"

"Grand slam. You have no ear for language at all, Pat. I can't understand how you learned Italian."

"Not many people can understand it the way I learned it, but I can make the servants come and go. That's enough."

"How? *Vieni qui, Lorenzo, vieni qui, grazie, basta*—like that? Even I can do that," said Charles.

"*Sì.* But look, I've got to get back to the nursery. Someone might need his diary changed."

"Someone with diary-a—what do you call it? The insatiable desire to—"

"Stop it, Char."

"That's right. The insatiable desire to stop it."

"Char, you're incorrigible."

"So encourage me."

"Look. I'm freezing. You came in a jacket, but I'm in my shirtsleeves. And February is not spring."

"Okay, but—" Char looked around the *androne* waving

his cigarette. "Where should I put my butt? I mean, what do you do with yours in this place?"

"There's an ashtray on the window ledge."

"You want I should keep my ash on the shelf? *On the shelf,*" he sang, "*my ash is on the shelf.*"

"Bye-bye, Char. See you tonight for dinner. And don't be late because Momma Trudi worries when people don't show up on time. It's like a wedding."

"And you're the groom? Always currying?"

"Go, Char. Go sweep the Piazza or something. The grandest drawing room in Europe is a mess. Get busy."

"It's full of riffraff. I don't do the streets. I've turned over a new leaf: I'm going to start writing diaries."

Patrick looked at an island of discarded fruit and flowers floating by. "Aren't you going to hate it here, a tidy person like you?"

"Penance. It's my purgatory," said Charles. "I came to Venice as a last resort."

Patrick was pulling the door closed. "I have to get inside. Oh hell. I mean, permit me to return into the house and go back to work."

"Get inside? Hell?"

"*Goodbye Char.* Go away."

"*Au revoir,* oh reever. I'm off to Dicadoro with my diary on my knee."

"Just don't have Dicadoro on your knee when you come

tonight," smiled Patrick as he started up the staircase. "Miss Momma wouldn't be flattered. Ciao."

"Ciao," Charles waved as he turned to go. "Till chow," he muttered under his breath.

Charles walked slowly along the *fondamenta* to Palazzo Dicadoro-Leoni; he wanted to be five minutes late. He had been working on his dignity since that ridiculous schoolboy conversation with Pat. He would have to make up for it tonight. Out in the Canal a small barge fitted with a wire scoop on the front was cruising along collecting the islands of garbage floating on the water. When the basket was full, the operator would push a lever causing it to rise and empty itself into the bin in the middle of the barge. Char noted that the machine was leaving a trail of garbage in its wake and the operator was eating a sandwich.

As Charles approached the great door of Palazzo Dicadoro-Leoni, he struck a casual, aloof manner in case anyone was looking. He rang the bell and was about to devise a waiting posture when a movement above attracted his attention. *Yikes!* he recoiled: two gargoyles in one day. A maid in a gray uniform was leaning from a window glowering at him. She disappeared and the door clicked open. As he walked through the *androne* he saw that there was another door to a garden walkway that opened onto a *calle* at the rear. He wondered if he should have entered by that door instead. The concierge who gave him directions had had some doubts about the entrance and now he saw what they meant. Maybe that explained why the maid was scowling. He waited at the top of the stairs without knocking until the maid saw fit to open the door. She was no more pleased to see him there than she was at the other door. She stood in the doorway and removed her apron before stepping aside to let him in. He followed her into the drawing room.

Contessa Dicadoro rose and walked unhurriedly across the room. She was blonde, but no longer the blonde in the picture. In fact, he could hardly find the ghost of that young woman in her ravaged features. The room was large and during her leisurely crossing he had time to register that it too was the worse for wear. It filled him with wonder that a person could be so grand as not to bother about such things.

"Hello," she put out her hand. "I'm so glad you could come."

From the way she proffered her hand he thought for a second she expected him to kiss it, but he made a split-second battlefield decision not to risk going over the top, and made do with an American handshake. He presented the magazine in the envelope which the concierge had supplied. She glanced inside. "Oh yes. The magazine. My niece told me there's an article about some people here. Thank you. Please sit down. Would you like some tea? I don't know how busy Barbara is in the kitchen . . ."

"No, no thank you. Unless you would like some."

"So you have just come from America?"

"Yes. I live in New York. I'm a decorator."

"And have you seen many Venetian interiors?"

"No. In fact this is almost the first private house I've seen here. It's my first visit to Venice."

"I remember the first time I came as a girl, from Canada. We brought a car with us. In those days you couldn't get near Venice with a car. You had to come by boat or train, so we took a villa in the country where we could leave the car and go for weekends. Then we took a suite at the Grand for the summer. Some people took villas at the Lido, but we didn't like the beach here. We were spoiled by having a house in Florida with our own beach and tropical gardens. Delius used to come down. He used to hunt alligators with my father. All around us it was wilderness; Florida was beautiful in those days. Here everything's been settled for a thousand years at least. Some people say it's a wilderness anyhow," she laughed, and he could see, now, the fun-loving woman in the photograph, "but they're just being wicked."

The maid reappeared, but this time looking less fierce. *"Il Reverendo,"* she murmured. A middle-aged man followed her. He was tall and slender, with gray hair and a square jaw that made him look like a soldier.

Contessa Dicadoro was surprised, but clearly pleased to see him. She rose and went to give him her hand, over which he bowed and feigned a kiss. Charles took note.

"Laetitia, forgive me for interrupting," said the *Reverendo.* "Our telephone is down again and we wanted to let you know that we're giving a little dinner for Edmondo before he goes back to the country; Sofi said she'd come too. Are you free tomorrow?"

She indicated Charles. "Bart, this is Charles Smithers, who's visiting Venice. He brought me something from Silla. Mr. Smithers, Reverend Sir Bartholomew Barton." They shook hands.

"Yes," the Contessa continued, turning to Reverend Sir Bartholomew Barton, "tell Nancy that would be very nice. I would love to come. Let me get you a cup of tea."

Charles realized that he was *de trop.* He shook the *Reverendo*'s hand again and murmured that he was just leaving, addressing a hint of a bow toward his hostess. Contessa Dicadoro smiled assent and he found himself leaving the drawing room, heading for the stairs. His great moment was already over.

As he descended, the words *de trop* came back, but this time as *de tropp,* and swung into *Baby, if I'm the bottom, You're the top.* "Oh shit," he muttered. "I don't want to be the bottom." For once the little voice was silent. He was in bad sorts as he trudged over the last bridge to the Gritti, when a gondolier approached him.

"Sir, good sir, would you like to see the real Venice? My Venice? I would like to take you. I will show you my house."

"*Sì,*" said Charles.

. . .

As the gondolier pushed off, he began his discourse: "We are here near to San Marco and a very old part of Venice."

"Never mind the travelogue," said Charles. "I just want to ride. Maybe I'll ask questions later."

The gondolier rowed into the Grand Canal. Charles recognized, with bitterness, Dicadoro's palace and imagined that the Reverend Sir was probably still up there swilling tea, but he cheered up, as they passed the Gotham palace, with the thought that tonight's dinner would give him a second chance to launch himself. As the Rialto Bridge came into sight, the gondola crossed over and entered a side canal.

"Where are we going?" asked Charles. "Anyplace in particular? I was enjoying the Grand Canal."

"I am taking you to the real Venice," said the gondolier, "to show you my house. Here on the right is the famous San Rocco with many paintings by our famous Tintoretto." He turned into a broader *rio*. "And there on the right above is my house."

Charles turned his head just in time to see a giant tin can whistle past the gondolier's head and land in the water with a splash. "Did you tell your wife we were coming?" he asked.

"*Porca Madonna!*" shouted the gondolier, scanning the windows opposite his house. "This is very dangerous," he insisted as he tied up the gondola next to a landing. "I must call the police." He ran up the steps and over the bridge in the direction of his house. A few minutes later he was back, carrying a bag and a bottle of wine with some plastic cups.

"What's that you brought back with you?" asked Charles as they resumed their tour, hoping he wasn't going to offer him any.

"It's my dinner. I have to work tonight."

Charles was himself again; he was looking forward to the Gotham party; he'd had his new suit pressed by the Gritti and he knew he looked swell. In his head the voice sang, *Heaven, I'm in heaven, And my heart beats so that I can hardly speak.* It sang with a swing that made him step out like Fred Astaire. *And I seem to find the happiness I seek, When we're—* The words were becoming irrelevant, Charles demurred. *Cheek to cheek,* the voice carried on. Oh no you don't, thought Charles as he crossed a bridge, how about *Drifting with the current down a moonlit stream, While above the heavens in their glory gleam. . . .* He approached the gate of Palazzo Gotham, savoring the privilege of ringing the discreet private doorbell of Miss Ermintrude Gotham as opposed to the one on the large brass plaque of the library. While he waited for someone to answer, he cobbled together a joke for Pat: *Knock, knock. Who's there? Ermintrude.* "*Chi é?*" said the porter through the intercom. "Charles Smithers," he answered. *Ermintrude who?* The gate opened. *Ermintrud-*

ing? drawled Charles in his Lord Snooty manner, as he stepped into the garden.

The butler met him at the elevator and showed him the seating plan. There was a Contessa, a Baronessa, a Count, and that Reverend Sir Bart Barton, Bart. and his wife. *Bart, bart, bart,* thought Charles, still annoyed with him: *woof, woof, woof.* Charles was seated between Lady Barton and Contessa Bonlin. The butler showed him into the *salone.* Patrick met him at the door.

"Good for you, Charles; perfect timing. I'll introduce you around, but first, come meet Trudi." She was across the room talking to the butler. Charles recognized her willowy figure and gray bobbed hair from her photographs.

Trudi Gotham dropped her conversation and turned to Charles the instant Patrick brought him up to her, giving him a broad but shy smile that swept away any doubts he might have had about liking her. "Thank you for the flowers," she said, indicating a large bouquet of flamingos. "They're my favorites; all the florists know, but I don't usually get such a generous bunch. Aren't they beautiful? And they last. I hope you'll be able to enjoy them more than once while you're here."

Charles smiled and nodded and murmured banalities as he shook her hand. He was always tongue-tied when he was falling in love. But he trusted that a woman as wonderful as she would understand.

"I'll introduce him around," said Patrick. "Well," he said

sotto voce as they moved away, "that's Momma. What do you think?"

Charles put his hand on his heart and rolled his eyes. Patrick took him around the room introducing him to each of the guests. At the end, Charles found himself planted once again in front of *il Reverendo,* who reached out to shake his hand.

"I'm so sorry that I interrupted your visit this afternoon. I didn't mean to, but Laetitia is completely frivolous. We love her, but she hasn't a practical bone in her body. I gathered you didn't even have time to look over the house. Has she been in touch with you about coming back? I know she's very keen that you should rent it."

Charles's emotions ricocheted like a racquetball. He didn't know what to say. "I've hardly been back to the hotel, in fact; there could be a message. Of course I'd be happy to see her again. And I'm glad to have the chance to see you here tonight. Is this an amazing coincidence, or is Venice a very small town?"

"Woofie," Lady Barton came up, "could I borrow your pen, darling? I want to give Bona the name of that catmint that makes the soporific tea."

Charles's emotions took another dizzying wham: did she say "Woofie"?

Sir Bartholomew read Charles's thoughts. "School nickname. Bart-Barton-Bart, bark-bark-bark, had to become Woofie; inevitable at that age. You were asking whether

Venice is a small town. The answer is, if you stay here a month, you'll know everybody."

The butler announced dinner, and the guests followed Trudi to the small winter dining room, since they were only eight.

Charles bowed to Contessa Bonlin on his left and to Baronessa Bonome, who was next to Patrick across the table, and helped Lady Barton on his right with her chair. She turned to him.

"My husband met you today at Laetitia's. He couldn't believe she'd let you slip away like that, and then after you left she talked about nothing except how much she hoped you'd rent the place. So I hope you won't be put off. She'd do anything for you—let you give a big party there before you moved in so she could introduce you to all her friends, give you people to call on in Rome. She's very generous and good-hearted. Her only problem is that she has big draws on her finances and she's not very adept at managing her affairs. We all try to help discreetly in the background."

"What does she do," asked Charles, "when she rents her apartment? Where does she live? Does she have another apartment in the palace?"

"No, no. Those are all rented, unfortunately for tiny rents

that she can't change. And she even has to make repairs when things go wrong. She goes to stay with her sister, or her daughter, or friends. She counts on Barbara, her maid, to look after things when she's away. Barbara's included in the rent."

"Now that," said Charles, "in my case could be a decisive factor."

"Very wise," agreed Lady Barton. "A good maid is like gold. Laetitia wouldn't part with Barbara for anything. I have a friend in London who says that her advice to anyone buying a house is first to find a good maid, then find out where she lives and buy the house next door."

The whole table laughed. Trudi Gotham never bothered at small dinner parties to enforce the right-left principle, so table talk tended to follow the Venetian convention and become general.

"That's been a big change in our lives," said Conte Vio from his place on Trudi's right. "I remember years ago the telephone would ring and we never paid the slightest attention. It was the maid's job to answer it. Nowadays, when the telephone rings," he looked sheepish, "I have to go answer it. And half the time it's for the maid."

"At Lievedon," said Trudi, speaking of her former husband's country seat in England, "we had servants that William had grown up with, the children of his parents's servants, and a good many of his parents' servants were still there as well. Of course the staff now cost ten, even twenty times what they cost a few decades ago, which puts the whole show on the road to ruin. That way of life is virtually over, everywhere."

"Trudi," said Baronessa Bonome, leaning forward, "I've always wondered, was your husband's family descended from the Roman Cato?"

"That's a very good question," said Trudi, with delight, "and one I asked, myself. The answer seems to be that they don't know, but would like to think so. And one can't blame them. Imagine the pleasure of descending from someone who could report information like *the Celts devoted themselves to warfare and witty conversation.*"

Charles was fascinated with what he was hearing, but a little disappointed that the general talk kept him from making friends with anyone; he certainly hadn't the courage to jump into the arena and take on the lions. Even Patrick wasn't saying much. Conversation moved to a court case out in the Veneto, reported in the newspaper: a man had forced his neighbor to cut back an extension he had built from three meters to one meter because it came too near the property line. The newspaper maintained that the extension had not damaged the man, but in forcing its destruction by two thirds, the man had ruined the neighbor's house, purely on the age-old Venetian principle of hate-thy-neighbor.

"I think Sidney Smith was right," said Sir Bartholomew, "that the reason neighbors can never agree is that they argue from different premises. But I try to avoid theorizing about Venetian ways. I say nobody understands the Venetian for the same reason that nobody owns a cat: he doesn't want it. So I don't try." He turned to Baronessa Bonome. "Am I right, Bona?"

"I'm afraid you are," she said sadly. "Nobody owns a cat."

When Charles got back to the Gritti, there was a message from Contessa Dicadoro, asking him to telephone. The concierge told him that she had been worried he might be about to leave, but the concierge had reassured her that Mr. Smithers hadn't indicated his departure was imminent. "I suppose," he added, "she'll be offering to rent you her apartment. Frankly, you're better off here where the plumbing works and the fuses don't blow." As Charles went up in the elevator to the tune of *What a difference a day made, Twenty-four little hours,* he was thinking that he could fill up his address book by going around Europe looking for expensive places to rent from greedy ex-grandees. But the thought didn't make him happy.

Over coffee Contessa Bonlin had told him that Contessa Dicadoro's son lived in Venice and depended on her for money. Conte Bonlin, her husband, who wasn't at the dinner because nowadays business had to come before pleasure, had known the son since he was born. There were rumors about why he needed so much money, but no one knew for sure. The received wisdom was that Laetitia was barely keeping one step ahead of the banks. But she was not alone: many of the old families were in similar straits. The whole idea made Charles want to kick something and swear. He'd been lured over here on false pretenses.

He started to go out on the balcony for a last look at the Grand Canal before going to bed but the maid had closed the shutters, so he gave up. He crawled into bed dispirited, brooding about decline and fall, dreams and grandeur buried in the sands. *I met a traveler from an antique land* Here with the past so close, evanescence whispered in the walls. He turned off the light and looked into the dense blackness of the shuttered room that closed around him like the grave. He could hear in the stillness, echoing over the town, the mournful tenor of the *Marangon* tolling from its tower in the Piazza the end of the day. Florian's and Quadri's would be stacking up their tables and chairs where Venetians no longer passed the time. *Now night descending, the proud scene was o'er* He longed for sleep and summoned from the folds of memory, to count, one loss, followed by another, and another, gamboling down the ages; he reckoned them, now here, now there, Atlantis   Eden   Ark   Roanoke   Shangri-La   Crystal Palace   Pharos   Colossus at   Rhodes   something at Halicarnassus   Babylon   great roc   dodo tyrannosaurus   missing link   lost tribes   King Solomon's Temple   Camelot

grail   Golden Book   *able was I take but*
degree away   *great Anarch*   *untune that*
string   *seated one day at the organ*
curtain fall   *universal darkness*
see darkly *greatest* aristocracy
crown   unicorn   *Now*
that we have seen *each*
other   *if you'll*
believe inme
I'llbelieve
inyou

•

MAYOR

Casa Bullo had a magnificent terrace with a romantic view over rooftops toward the Rialto that the Bullo family would not have traded for anything—perhaps not even for Ivo Bullo himself, who occasionally, as he descended the ninety-seven steps each morning and ascended them every evening, entertained unorthodox thoughts on the matter. The fact was never allowed to escape him, since every person who scaled those ninety-seven steps planted it like a flag at his feet, that he ought, as Mayor, to have enough influence to get a permit to install an elevator. But for him the problem was always the imbroglio. First, since he lived on the top floor, he would be asking the other residents in the building to agree to a project more in his interest than theirs, a proposal which they would grasp as an opportunity second only to being given the winning numbers for Lotto, and would cash in at once with a list of little favors that he would thenceforth be bound to perform, simply because he could and it wouldn't be sporting not to, even if he threw up the whole idea of having an elevator. He was better off avoiding the issue. It was like Michele Ardo always said: "Frogs shouldn't even talk to scorpions." And then forcing the permission through the different departments would be the same thing all over again. His wife made the best of the situation and used the stairs as a fitness facility, a home stepping machine, holding herself firmly to a minimum of five round trips a day, sometimes having to go down and up one more time before going to bed, to meet her quota. Similarly, his son set his stopwatch before leaping from the top step like an Olympic skier, timing his descents and ascents; he had a note of his best records on his bedroom wall. So Ivo had long since stopped thinking about an elevator as he negotiated this part of his daily journey; he dwelled instead on the discomforts of a life of compromise.

Venetians on the whole were satisfied that Ivo Bullo was well cast as Mayor. He was good-looking, having that noble head and irresolute profile of the Italian penny (circa 1912), which dignified his small, sturdy Venetian build. Turned out in a dark suit, with a rich yet modest tie, no one looked worthier than he. It was true that people didn't altogether trust him. Too often his eyes had that faraway look of the window cleaner. But politics have a logic of their own, and it was precisely this enigmatic mien that first attracted his most rigorous partisans, those who claimed from the moment they met him that they recognized the sine qua non of political success, that common ground between them of superior wisdom and *furbezza,* that is to say, guile.

In reality, Ivo Bullo could lay claim to none of the above; he was a dreamer, pure and simple, with a taste for romance. But that fact, as it went unrecognized, did nothing to inhibit his being drawn young into the front row of the political class, where for a time his performance corresponded perfectly to his backers' mistaken idea of his character.

The truth is: had he not played hooky from the Marchiori cocktail party, a crime he committed for the singular motive of sitting on a white silk cloud of a sofa, next to Isabella, his wife of thirty years, to watch a television rerun of *Roman Holiday,* his political career should have turned out differently. The irony of it was that they had sat on that same sofa watching earlier reruns of that same film probably ten times, and on a lesser, previous sofa, probably ten times before that. On this occasion their teenage son had written them off as infantile and retired to his room to watch something less silly. But for Ivo and Isabella, *Roman Holiday* never lost its power to communicate directly to themselves. Isabella was Audrey Hepburn, pert and slim like she was when they first met, with the smile that hooked Ivo in an instant. On the other hand, Ivo was not Gregory Peck. And as far as Ivo knew, Isabella had never known a Gregory Peck in her real life; she had never had a romantic, idealistic, self-sacrificing lover—except in the film. Instead, Ivo was the suitable man from her real life that the Audrey Hepburn character presumably married, probably a prince, when she went back to her homeland, sadder but wiser, after the film was over. Since becoming Mayor of Venice, Ivo discovered that he enjoyed the film more, almost as much as Isabella did, and he attributed to this new perspective his rash decision to skip the Marchiori party on the eve of the most momentous vote of his political career.

As a result, when Ivo Bullo, Mayor of Venice, made his usual entrance the next morning at Ca' Farsetti, with a crowd of clamoring assistants treading sole to sole with their images in the netherworld of the shimmering terrazzo, accompanied by echoing footfalls resounding like distant applause, with cleaners along the way resting to look at the entourage, and staff clutching documents bursting from their offices like shopkeepers saluting a royal passage, he found himself feeling much less like the Doge of Venice than he normally did, when his glory wasn't groaning under a *sumo* press of dread about the Council meeting that afternoon. This time, *Roman Holiday* had not only diverted him, it had thrown him right off course.

Last night at Dino Marchiori's there would have been tense talk about strategy and what-if scenarios. Carlo Volo, lighting one cigarette after another, would have been laying down the law about negotiating positions, and warning about statements that, although true, absolutely must not be uttered. When Carlo wanted to make a point, he took a deep drag on his cigarette and then talked with smoke pouring from his mouth and nose. Looming, fat, Michele Ardo would have been silent as a bodyguard looking from one to the other in a shrewd, threatening way, as though getting ready for someone to make a false move. He was the one who divined the political undertones among the opposition and decided which conflicts to play off to advantage. He saved his observations for the end of a meeting so he had the effect of a doctor writing a prescription. Ivo had been drilled so many times on so many issues in the past six months that he was fed up with the whole imbroglio. But it would soon be over: at two o'clock that afternoon, the Council would have the fate of the proposal on the table. The vote would be close. In the case of a tie, it would force him, as Mayor, to the test.

Ten years earlier, even a year earlier, the proposal for a subway system in Venice would have seemed to him as preposterous as putting a helicopter pad on San Marco. He could not remember how the idea became commonplace. What he knew was that he was in the middle of it with a vengeance. He had a share in the consortium that had surreptitiously—he could think of no other word for it—bought tracts of mainland real estate all along the shore of the lagoon, land which would serve for stations on the subway system or other commercial purposes and which would appreciate in value exponentially from the minute the project was approved—this afternoon. The idea made him wince. It was not his idea, but he had become, because he was Mayor, an essential part of it, and the four of them who were members of the City Council were relied on by the bankers and industrialists who were funding the lion's share to look after their interests. Even with his minor share, Ivo Bullo was up to his ears in debt. The others had used their influence to persuade the banks to lend him far more than he could afford. In fact, for him, the whole *faccenda* had become such a matter of financial life and death that he could hardly bear to focus on it. Of course Isabella knew about it, but only up to a point. She didn't understand the full extent of the political danger and practically nothing of the financial danger. He had at least been able to provide for that.

As his assistants dispersed to their offices, he paused to greet his secretary. In reality, Alessia was more a civil servant than a secretary, and she had never been chosen by him. On the contrary: at the time he became Mayor she had been drawn out of the secretarial pool as someone due for promotion and presented to him as the only possible candidate. He hated to think how often he'd wished that he'd put his foot down and insisted on someone more suitable. He had never wished it more poignantly than he did today. For one thing, she was a shocking sight, wearing her hair in the current just-out-of-bed style, which only accentuated in Ivo's mind the fact that for all the interest she showed in her work, she might as well have stayed in bed. Her pride and joy seemed to be the dark red talons at her fingertips, the preservation of which demanded a singular stiff-fingered typing technique which, to be fair, she performed with an amazing virtuoso skill. Being young and cool, she showed no loyalty or enthusiasm and indicated her level of engagement by chewing gum with intensity or slack-jawed indifference. In short, she was the kind of secretary wives simultaneously value and deplore, as having no designs on, but also no respect for, their husbands. Only once had Mayor Bullo ever seen her outside the office, when Isabella had pointed her out to him getting on a bus with some friends in Piazzale Roma. Mixed in with a group of analogous companions, she looked so animated and normal that he hardly recognized her.

Today, as he approached her desk, she smiled without quite looking at him and busied herself with the sole item on her desk, a paper handkerchief, which she folded briskly into a small square and then dropped into the wastepaper basket.

"*Buongiorno,* Alessia," the Mayor feigned saccharine goodwill to hide the rue he felt that notwithstanding his strenuous efforts to the contrary she had somehow managed to become privy to heaven only knew how much of this business, despite having the brain of a bird. As far as he could see she was a roving predator of anything exciting, with a terrier's delight in adventure and a bloodhound's tenacity for holding on to its scent. On the monitor beside her, a cartoon screensaver careened through hair-raising scenarios of a large-headed child in breathtaking sequence pursued by an avalanche, trapped in the path of a train, chased over a cliff, pushed from an airplane, cornered in a lion's den: this screen was one of the perils of addressing her at her desk. With an animation as arresting as a scream in the street, its fascination was irresistible, like a coiled snake to a rabbit. The Mayor mustered the fortitude to drag his gaze away and marched into his office. One of his assistants had told him that this screensaver was in fact a game and that Alessia played it with dazzling panache, hardly ever getting smashed or eaten. Today this served as one more example of the anarchy loose in the world.

He had hardly the time to stifle a groan and put down his briefcase before the Notary Paolo Grandi, rushing in and slamming the door, made him jump. Without pausing to say hello, Grandi started laying out documents on the Mayor's desk.

"We have to do a few more signatures for the last piece of property. Grillo held out until the last minute and got himself double what anyone else got, but we had to pay it. The minute the newspapers started discussing the subway project, it became a seller's market. As I told Michele and Carlo last night—sorry you weren't there; we rang and your son said you were indisposed—if we had to do it over again,

I would favor bringing the newspapers in on the deal. The good part is that we managed to buy up seventy-five percent of the land before anyone twigged about the project."

Ivo could hardly bear to look at the documents. "Just show me where to sign."

"Here." Grandi pointed to a blank line under a block of gray illegible type. "This is the purchase contract; it's just like all the others." Grandi removed the signed contract and pulled forward two more papers side by side. "Sign here. These are for your part of the mortgage, and for the bank."

Ivo looked at them. The sums on the loan made him dizzy.

Grandi read the expression on his face. "It's a lot of money, but don't worry: the bank form is to let you overdraw your account to make the mortgage payments until the resale. It's only a temporary debt."

Ivo sat down and scrawled his name with a sigh as the feeble hope flickered that in a desperate moment he might be able to deny this scribble was his true signature. But Grandi wasn't the only witness. As he looked up, Alessia was standing at the half-open door, watching.

"And it's not like you're alone," continued Grandi with his back to the door. "Volo, Marchiori, Ardo, and I all have the same portion of the debt as you and we all signed these same papers last night."

"Oh I wouldn't say that," replied Bullo, looking meaningfully beyond him to the door. "Yes, Alessia, what is it?"

"I'm sorry to bother you," she began, then paused.

"The first part of the work," continued Grandi, without taking any notice of Bullo's efforts to signal the extraneous presence of his secretary, "will be excavation, and that will be the first contract awarded. The excavating firm can give you a little something in a plain white envelope."

"I beg your pardon!" Ivo jumped to his feet and fairly shouted at Grandi, who stared with disbelief. "Tell me," urged Bullo to his secretary fixed in the half-open door. "What is it?"

"Your wife says that Marchiori and Ardo have been ringing you at home, and would you ring her, and they've also been ringing here, but I've told them you have meetings right up until the Council meeting."

Grandi turned and addressed the space halfway between her and the Mayor. "Oh, they probably want to talk about what we discussed last night; you can tell them if they ring back that I've been here."

Dismissed, the secretary started to close the door, but she was still visible when Grandi resumed his discourse.

"I've already had a discreet conversation with the head of the excavating firm set to get the job. He knows all about how it's done and it's completely safe. All they have to do is to quantify the costs per meter, calculate and charge on the basis of going deeper than they need to, but carry out only the work that's necessary. Who's going to go down and measure how deep they've gone? Those of us who are carrying more than we can afford will get the difference in a plain envelope, left anonymously on our secretary's desk, to help tide us over." As Grandi spoke, he was gathering up the papers and putting them in his briefcase.

"Oh dear," sighed Ivo, "I never thought—"

Grandi was at the door, ready to leave: "Think of it as a concession to the environmentalists, the *Verdi;* you're going to help keep the excavation from going down a meter more than necessary. I'll come back at two to watch the vote." He opened the door and came face-to-face with the leader of the *Verdi* group of councilors. He threw a "speak of the Devil!" look over his shoulder and stepped aside to let Alfonso Delmuro have his go at the Mayor.

The phone on the Mayor's desk rang. It was Alessia saying that Delmuro had just barged his way in without asking her whether he was free.

"Oh that's fine, Alessia. I'm happy to see Mr. Delmuro." He turned to Delmuro. "Tell me."

"Listen, Mr. Mayor, I know you're going to be pushing to get this vote through with all your little bits and pieces of coalition partners and that you're not paying any attention to us because you know we're small and that we won't budge. But I just want to warn you: yesterday we got the results of the study we commissioned on the certain damage and probable damage that your project will cause to the fabric and environment of the city—short, medium, and long term." He placed a heavy black binder on the Mayor's desk.

"This report is hot, believe me. Even if you get the vote through today, the newspapers, when they get hold of this, will turn public opinion completely against it. I'm leaving my copy for you to look at before you cast your deciding vote—as I am sure you will have to do. I'll pass by and pick it up on my way into the meeting." He walked back to the door. As he opened it he gave the Mayor a wry smile: "Have a nice read, Mayor Bullo."

The Mayor picked up the phone. "Alessia, please either stay at your desk or have someone cover it until the Council meeting. I don't want to see anyone at all and I don't want to receive any phone calls. Please ring my wife and tell her that if anyone rings, to say that I have seen Grandi. Thank you." He opened the book that Delmuro had placed before him. He couldn't help being interested in it because he suspected that he probably agreed with every word of it. He turned to the Table of Contents.

Two hours later, he was still gazing at the Table of Contents when the phone rang and he knew it was time to go.

"It's time, Mr. Mayor, for the Council meeting. Everyone is waiting for you to go in."

Ivo Bullo opened the door and came face-to-face with Delmuro, who was waiting for his report. Over Delmuro's shoulder he could see Marchiori and Ardo behind Alessia's desk, waiting for him. Then he noticed something that made his knees weak: on Alessia's desk there was a plain white envelope planted on the desk's outer edge where he could pick it up in passing. Through the door to the meeting room he could see Carlo Volo standing in a cloud of smoke like a soul in Hell.

"I guess by now you've got the pitch," said Delmuro, looking at the book under the Mayor's arm.

Pitch, thought Bullo, that's it. Pitch. In his mind's eye, he could see his old teacher Mrs. Rossi at the Liceo Classico frowning down at him. Circle eight: Graft. He would never forget it again. Then it dawned on him: no one would dare come near him if he walked in with Delmuro.

"It's very true what you say," proffered the Mayor to his companion. "I was interested by the scope of the study, though I couldn't examine it in detail."

Delmuro was not expecting such a friendly response and found himself unable to leave the Mayor's side. "The important thing is that it should influence your actions."

"It could," said the Mayor, as Marchiori and Ardo fell in behind them, "have an effect on the outcome." He had to keep Delmuro from leaving his side until he was safely at his post in the meeting hall. "There are several important things that are not very clear." Only a few more steps and he was there. "But perhaps there will be time to clarify them," he concluded as he stepped into his place. Looking down at the councilors he could see that several of them in the vicinity of Marchiori and Ardo were staring at him with powerful emotion, but he couldn't make out what it was. Did they know what he was thinking? At that moment, Alessia hurried toward him with the plain white envelope, which she dropped on the table in front of him in plain sight of the whole City Council. Was she out of her mind? Then he realized that he still had Delmuro's report under his arm and that Delmuro had gone to his seat. He looked out over the room and placed the black binder on the envelope as though unaware of its presence. Volo and Marchiori and Ardo continued to stare at him. He could feel the corrosive intensity of their looks, but he didn't let his glance cross with theirs. Instead, he looked down the hall at the crowd of journalists and spectators. The hall was full, but journalists and photographers were still coming in. Everyone was here for the debate and vote on the subway system. The President started working his way through the agenda. No one was making any move to slow things down, so the cards were falling fast.

Nevertheless, when the moment came, Ivo Bullo was in another world. He was aware that the bizarre project was being discussed and he could hear Marchiori and Ardo and Volo arguing in favor of the scheme, but in a strange, detached way. He was aware that they were trying to catch his eye, trying to tell him something, and he guessed that they must have sensed something had changed between them, that he was drifting away. He recalled the face of Gregory Peck making his heroic sacrifice in the service of a higher good. It hovered in his memory right up until the vote. He watched Marchiori looking around as he slowly raised his hand in favor, then Ardo put his hand up in the same cautious way, then Volo scanned the room and slowly raised his hand halfway. It was a tie. But Bullo didn't respond.

The counters were walking up and down tallying the vote. Then Ivo noticed that they were counting Volo, and him too, because the outcome had been so analyzed that it was a foregone conclusion how the vote would go. The teller announced the measure as passed with the Mayor's deciding vote, but Marchiori, in a fury, jumped up, followed by Ardo and Volo and Calmar, Russo, Delmuro, and others as well, all shouting that the Mayor had not cast his vote. The counters looked confused. One came up to him.

"Mr. Mayor, did you vote?"

The room was still.

Ivo Bullo shook his head. "No, I didn't."

"Do you want to?"

"No."

His answer fell like a firecracker in a flock of pigeons. Journalists rushed in all directions. Some crowded through the door, running down the steps and shouting into the street. Some ran into the offices to use the telephones, then raced back into the hall to get some interviews. They rushed toward the Mayor, but were flagged down by Marchiori and Ardo and Volo, who each took on a group of four or five. Ivo wondered what they were saying about him. Delmuro came up to take his book. He shook the Mayor's hand and pointed to the envelope.

"It's to throw away," said Ivo.

Ivo Bullo walked back to his office. As he passed Alessia, he sensed that she was giving him one of her stop-chew, slack-jawed, what-the-hell-are-you-playing-at expressions. He rarely walked alone to his office after a meeting. She would find out soon enough. But worse, so would Isabella.

He closed the door and sat down behind his desk, wondering if he would ever sit there again or if his undoing would come so fast. He gazed out the window at the pigeons, which everyone hated and wanted to exterminate, flying erratically this way and that, as though they perceived opposition wherever they turned. Though he hated them as much as anyone, at this moment he felt like one of them. Only the *Verdi* thought well of them. He remembered Delmuro's handshake at the end. Some people called them flying rats.

From now on, life would be hard; harder even than if he'd been caught doing the wrong thing. No lawyer could protect him from what was about to happen. No one would want to help him; better a crook than a cad was almost the law. In the end, he would be exposed as a crook because he had been a cad, and no one would understand about the change of heart, about sacrificing his own interests for the sake of doing the right thing. He could see now that there was no provision for that kind of behavior in real life; it was a thing of romance. At best it was a thing for bachelors and people without responsibility. He wondered whether he would drag Marchiori and Volo and Ardo and Grandi down with him, or whether they would manage to save themselves. Grandi's saying that "lawyers, having no principles, have no enemies" was true, and would save him, and enable him to save the others. They would isolate their former colleague and put as much blame on him as they could make stick. Pitch. There it was again. He couldn't escape it.

The sure thing was that he would drag his family down with him. They wouldn't have a chance to save themselves. They would all be pariahs: his married daughter, his teenage son, his eventual grandchildren. None of the Bullos would ever be seen again at the grand public events, not even at the private ones like cocktails at the Panfilis', and the Patristis'. None. And on top of it all, he would be ruined. Bankrupt. To put it in plain terms, he would have to sell out at a loss. They would lose their house. His children would end up with nothing. He would never get another job. He could even go to jail. And Isabella, after all, was not a princess; she had no place to go back to, and she would never understand why he had done such a thing, even if he tried to explain. The contradictions in his life that loomed up and disappeared like mirages in a desert had no context in the world they shared. True, it was a world they had built together, but the plans were Isabella's. They were a normal couple; she was the pragmatist. In all these years Isabella had never even noticed the problem of his role in *Roman Holiday.*

The thought of how clearly she would see their present predicament made his stomach churn. He too had a saying in his mind, "Virtue is its own reward," but unlike Grandi's, as he now perceived, his wasn't true. He did not feel good about what he'd done; far from it. All it amounted to was that he'd ruined his family and tricked his friends for the sake of a pious gesture that no one expected of him, not even the definitive point of political reference, the man in the street.

His remorse was tireless, scanning his memory and illuminating, like a torch in a cave, swarming horrors everywhere he looked. He was trying to grasp the hatred that the others in the consortium must feel for him, imagining the ecstatic terror of those fleeing stags and foxes that the *Verdi* were always defending, when the door banged open like a shot and Ardo, Volo, and Marchiori pushed and jostled through it nearly falling over one another in their eagerness to get to him first. Instinctively, Ivo Bullo stood up to defend himself. Behind them, outside, he could see Alessia wearing an alarmed oh-my-God face that he'd never seen before. A confused thought that she might have been able to save him from a train or a lion glimmered and was gone. The first to get to him was Ardo, who grabbed him by the lapels.

"I—I—" Ivo couldn't think of anything to say. Words wouldn't help. His son knew karate. Ivo Bullo saw in that instant that he had wasted much of his time on earth.

"You were brilliant!" growled Ardo, shaking him and hugging him like a soccer player who's made a goal. "How did you know to do that?" He handed him on to Volo, who nearly suffocated him in his smoke-filled jersey, and Marchiori, who kept slapping him on the back as though he were choking, so he could hardly hear Ardo going on about how his tame journalist Granchio had just got back from Rome and found out on his way here that the newspapers were ready to expose their consortium's interest as soon as the vote passed.

"I heard some rumors this morning," said Ardo, "but he didn't get the word to me until just as we were about to go in and I was trying to speak to you, to send you a note—he waved the plain white envelope—to pass you the message by telepathy. I was trying everything. I found out afterward, the newspaper articles were already written. They've had to pull everything. Granchio's just been on the phone to me outside here on your secretary's phone. They're convinced we've got a better offer, and guess what? They're looking for a piece of the action. They want to broker a different kind of deal."

Carlo Volo exploded in a fit of laughing and coughing. "We—we only had a few minutes to decide what to do," he managed to say between spasms. "We decided to vote in favor up to the point of a tie, so we could rebuild the deal if we had the chance."

"In fact," said Ardo, "it's the deal we should have made

in the first place. I was afraid we'd been too ambitious. We talked about it last night. Granchio says the newspapers are in a position to bring a larger group of industrialists into the consortium, which they think should be more representative. And quite right they are. We'll take what we paid for it as a down payment with the understanding that they don't have to pay us another lira until there's a decision on the subway and the property is sold. Then we'll share out the sale price among all of us. In fact, Grandi was here for the vote and got the picture at once. He's already gone to start erasing our companies and restructuring everything with the newspaper groups."

"Come on," said Marchiori, "this calls for a celebration. Let's go down to the Monaco and have a sandwich and a *prosecco.*"

"Do you mind if we put it off and do it properly later on?" asked the Mayor. "I'm still not quite right after last night."

"No. Come along," said Volo. "This is a great day. We're all safe and solvent again. We'll go down and get a taxi while you get your things together. Then you can go home and rest."

Ivo Bullo looked around the office. He couldn't see anything he needed to take home, since he was coming back in the morning. As he passed Alessia's desk, he saw that she was hunched over, painting her nails a deep shade of blood.

She didn't even notice him. For a change, the child was not facing violent death many times a minute on her monitor; instead, there was a certificate with a score of several thousand and the message "Congratulations! Champion Alessia." He decided not to summon her attention just to tell her he was leaving for the day. She would figure it out eventually.

As he went down the stairs he noted for the first time that there was something satisfactory about Alessia, and that was her total artlessness. She was what she was. It was a virtue he rarely had occasion to ponder.

So take a lesson from the champion defender against all perils, he murmured to himself: I am not Gregory Peck, and I was never meant to be. I am what I was, what I have always been: I am the man who gets the princess after the story's over, and who on her behalf meets and vanquishes morning and evening, day after day, ninety-seven ineluctable challenges to his strength and honesty.

INTERPRETER

Baronessa Bonome believed that a person could tune in to universal truth, to the secrets of life, and she was always turning the dial, searching for the band. She collected old recipes for traditional cures and assimilated superstitions so thoroughly that if someone explained to her that to place the image of an elephant with its trunk toward the door was to invite bad luck, she would, henceforth, be mindful not only of elephants but also of teapots, coffeepots, and watering cans.

Everyone liked Bona Bonome and trusted her good nature, but no one took her seriously: for one thing, her credulity was more than childlike, it verged on the simple-minded. Everyone said so, especially the men, who had to be disciplined by their wives to take their turns sitting next to her at dinner parties. But she caught them all on the hop, and at the same time *made* Contessa Bonlin's cocktail party, when she dropped the news that she had up and bought the most notorious of the *bad luck* palaces on the

Grand Canal. Of course the fact that the price she paid for the palace was absurdly low caused a ripple of jealousy to pass through the town—it was after all a nice piece of real estate—and for a time Venetian society busied itself regaling the shade of La Rochefoucauld. But this soon gave way, when she actually packed her worldly goods and went to live there, to a rapt anticipation of *Schadenfreude.*

In the period leading up to this stunning acquisition, Bona had lived alone for several years in a small palace in Cannaregio not far from the Casinò. The *palazzetto* was pretty enough, but after living her entire married life in a spacious *piano nobile* near Sant'Angelo, she found it difficult to settle down on a different scale in a strange part of town. The choice had not been hers. When her husband died, their children, Enrico and Serena, both married, insisted that she simplify her life and her estate by selling the larger of their two properties and moving to the smaller one. That their parents had taken great care to ensure that they should each inherit a respectable residence in Venice didn't interest them at all. Neither of them envisaged living in Venice ever again.

In consequence, though she would have done anything to hide the fact, most poignantly from herself, Bona was lonely, and in a way that social life couldn't remedy. Toward confrontation with this horrible truth she was inexorably sliding one evening as she climbed into bed after another of those cocktail parties cloned, each one on the one preceding, for people who couldn't endure sitting at home alone of an evening. But she was saved by a miracle. As she lay in bed wondering whether to seek distraction in Agatha Christie or oblivion in sleep, she heard a strange voice floating on the night air from the *rio* beneath her window, venturing a melody that she could almost grasp, but not quite. It was such a curious sound that she rose and went onto the balcony. There, bathed in moonlight on the balustrade of the bridge, a lone cat serenaded the empty night. Judging from its size, and the sweetness of its voice, Bona surmised it to be a eunuch. As she listened, the tune came to her.

"'La Bergamasca'!" she whispered in a voice so small that it barely amounted to a petal wafting down to the troubadour, but it was enough. With a spectacular leap from the balustrade over the water he gained the *fondamenta,* stalked to Bona's front door, and sat down to wait, without giving her so much as a glance. Looking down from the balcony, Bona felt unaccountably giddy, as though she were being drawn into a vortex. She held on to the window as she stepped inside. Something was happening at last. She put on her dressing gown and went downstairs.

She took such a long time turning off the burglar alarm and unlocking the four-way bolting system that she feared he might have wandered away, but she had hardly opened the door when he pushed through and trotted up the stairs like he lived there, leaving her to bolt the door again—but unable to reset the alarm, because she had no idea where in the house he might be. As she climbed the stairs and started searching for him room by room, she wondered if she hadn't been foolish to let him in. By the time she arrived at the last room, her bedroom, from which she was sure she was going to have to begin the search all over again, she had resolved to take him down to the kitchen, give him a bowl of milk, and then turn him out. But when she came into her bedroom and saw him hunkered down on the end of her bed, his golden eyes glimmering like moons in a broad tabby face and addressing her with a frank unwinking gaze, she recognized him as just the friend she needed.

"Do you mind if I call you Musci?" she asked, smoothing the stripes of his back. "Let me know if you need anything." With that she took off her dressing gown, crawled into bed, and fell into a sleep of transfiguring dreams in which she sat in a palatial room at a writing desk turning the pages of something resembling an outsize calendar, putting circles around dates on every page. It was a happy dream, and it turned out to be a recurring dream, but it was a dream that took her some time to understand.

For many years, when her family was young, Bona Bonome worked as a simultaneous translator for public speakers, in the days before interpreters were consigned to soundproof boxes from which to relay their renderings to earphones.

Instead, Bona would stand at the lectern beside the speaker and translate phrase by phrase. It was strenuous work, requiring perfect concentration. She found that standing very close to the speaker, even touching, helped her to intuit the direction of the discourse. In those days, when she was slim and decorative, and most of the speakers were men, her method was highly regarded. But in the course of time, it became outmoded and she was consigned to the translation boxes. Closed in with the electronic equipment, her intuition didn't work at all; she even found it hard to concentrate. Soon she was dispatched from the boxes. Nowadays, she accompanied tour groups visiting private houses. The work did nothing to exercise her intuition, and was not well paid. In fact, she worried about money a good deal and she was becoming suspect among her friends, who noted telltale economies, as an emerging poor person. Oddly enough, at the time of Musci's arrival it never even entered her head that she could not afford the care and feeding of a large cat, and as Musci disdained to appear at social occasions, her friends never had the chance to remind her.

Nevertheless, from the first moment, Musci not only slept at the foot of Baronessa Bonome's bed, but he became her constant daytime companion, accompanying her everywhere, even to places where pets were forbidden, exactly like a spoiled lapdog. At least that was how it appeared. In truth, a good part of the time it was Bona who was accompanying Musci and never so much as when they started popping into tobacconists. For her part Bona hadn't been inside a tobacconist since they lost the monopoly on salt, so she was somewhat at a loss the first time Musci led her into the one nearest her house. But the telepathy between them was such that she understood there was something she was meant to see. Under a shelf where people filled out forms and addressed their postcards, Musci curled up to watch Bona try to divine the purpose of their visit. Bona looked here and there, casting about as though it was a game of "I Spy with My Little Eye" they were playing. Over the ledge, under which Musci sat watching with his unwinking gaze but doing nothing to indicate whether she was getting hotter or colder in her search, there were papers posted on the wall covered with results for games of chance. Bona was about to look away when she realized that the numbers, many of them, seemed familiar. What a strange feeling of *déjà vu* crept over her. The dreams—these were numbers from her dreams. Of course the dreams weren't about a ninety-day calendar; how stupid she felt: they were about the numbers of Lotto. She looked around and found a rack full of Lotto forms on the ledge. She took one, and with trembling fingers picked up the pen on a string, and then felt very stupid indeed: she couldn't remember the numbers she'd dreamed only the night before. Eventually she conjured up three of the five and guessed at the others, so her first win was very small.

From that day onward, she always wrote down her numbers on waking, and followed Musci to a new tobacconist after every dream, because, she supposed, she shouldn't become known as someone who won several times a month. Strange people might begin to take an interest in her. It was bad enough having to invent a story for her bank manager, whose curiosity as to why her account had suddenly begun to grow was becoming ever more difficult for him to control. She decided she had better organize a logical explanation and put her affairs in order. She found an accountant who had no trouble at all understanding that she had a little real estate business for which people gave her cash commissions, though he grasped a little less readily that she wanted to pay any tax that might fall due. In her pusillanimous way, Bona thought the tranquillity worth the expense.

But that was only the beginning. Just as spring gave way to summer, hardly a month later, Bona had a big win and had to go to Rome to claim it. On the train with Musci it occurred to her that she should open an account at a Rome bank and share the secret of her new riches with a Roman bank manager rather than her Venetian one. When she spoke to Dott. Benedetto at Banca Romana, he understood perfectly and was delighted that she had chosen to put her money in his bank: he had never seen such a check in his life. She spent the rest of the day being advised about investments, and spent the next afternoon in her accountant's office back in Venice preparing the way for the evidence of wealth that would soon show itself in her affairs. She stuck to her story about having discovered a talent for selling and renting property. Her success story was compelling. The accountant started referring his clients to her as a person of genius in the field. To her intense amusement, no sooner would she be asked to sell a Palladian villa or a working farm than she would receive a call from a prospective buyer asking for a Palladian villa or a working farm. A travel agent would ring her and ask for five very special apartments on the Grand Canal for five VIP clients to rent for a short period. Within the week five friends or acquaintances would ring, in confidence, offering to rent for a short period, to people of the right sort—purely as a precaution against burglary, she was given to understand—their Grand Canal apartments. These latter clients, being friends and knowing Bona to be somewhat needy, were generous enough to pay her, like anyone else, the full fee for her services—a fee which, for fear of giving offense, she couldn't refuse. So just as her dreams came true, her fiction became fact. And Musci purred in the background like a finely tuned machine.

Then one day her accountant rang and asked her to come and look at a palace he had long been trying to sell with no success. The owner was getting desperate; she had suddenly arrived in town and was pressing him to get some results. Could Baronessa Bonome come at once to meet the owner and help him somehow to sell it? He named the palace; she was about to cut him off short—she wouldn't even name the place for fear of the bad luck it could bring—but Musci was already on his way down the stairs. So she agreed to meet the accountant. But with what trepidation! All the way across town she laid down the law to Musci with uncharacteristic asperity about the peril of getting involved with this particular piece of property, but all she got in response was an occasional sympathetic gaze. She was so worked up by her diatribe that she arrived at the palace fifteen minutes before her appointment. Musci trotted up to the door and pushed his face into the corner. The door opened. He walked in; Bona followed. Perhaps out of ceremony, Musci meowed, so Bona hallooed. But no one replied. Musci started up the stairs, and Bona followed. She felt as if she were in a play. In a minute they were standing in the room of her dreams, beside the writing table. A more positive view of the palace began to assert itself: it didn't feel half as bad as she'd expected. In fact it was pleasant. A window was open; she walked over and stepped up on the strange little platform leading up to the windows and stood looking down the Grand Canal. Musci jumped up and perched on the sill beside her. They stood daydreaming together exactly where they would one night watch two Renaissance friends glide away into eternity. But for the moment her intuition informed her only that something important awaited her here. Nevertheless, all the way home she confided to Musci her long-entrenched fears about the house. For his part, he trotted along beside her with a distinct air of *allegria.*

"It's nice, isn't it." One of the moving men waved his arm in an expansive gesture around the *androne.* He was paying a compliment to the new owner. Baronessa Bonome had told the two men to rest until the next boatload arrived because they had worked so hard getting the furniture up to the second *piano nobile.*

He went on: "I've always wanted to have a look inside this place. There used to be stories about it. Did you ever hear any of them?"

"Oh yes. Probably all of them." Baronessa Bonome was standing at the watergate of their new home with Musci seated at her feet, enjoying the September breeze from the Grand Canal. "In fact I believe some of them; maybe all of them."

"Well aren't you afraid then," said the young man with a ponytail seated on the crate next to him, "with only a fat old pussins to protect you?"

Bona suppressed a smile and looked down at Musci, who had jumped up as if he'd heard a shot and walked slowly toward the perpetrator of this gratuitous insult. At times like this Musci adopted the manner of a sulky female with a wanton saunter.

Dangerous talk, thought Bona; he's in for it.

Musci stopped, looked hard at the young man, then trotted back to Bona.

"They act like they understand, don't they," he went on, "but in reality there's nothing stupider than a cat."

"Oh my goodness," cried Bona. "You really mustn't talk like that. This cat is smarter than the three of us combined. You should apologize."

The older man reached in his rucksack and pulled out a tuna fish sandwich. He broke off a corner and offered it to Musci, who devoured it with exaggerated relish as a mark of favor.

A barge laden to the point of unsteadiness eased up to the watergate. While the men set up the gangway, Bona's son-in-law, Alberto, jumped from the prow and turned to take Serena's hand as she jumped after him.

"You hitched a ride," laughed Bona when she saw them. "You young moderns are equal to anything."

"It was the quickest way," said Alberto, "and they didn't mind. Anyhow, we've locked up over there. They've got all they can deal with today, so they're going to come back to finish tomorrow morning. Before we go back to Padua I want to get your bedroom and the kitchen set up so you can survive. We'll come back first thing in the morning and go over there to meet them and finish clearing out. I'll run up and get them started on your bedroom. I hope Gilda can remember where she put the sheets so she can make your bed."

"She's down here working on the kitchen, but I'll send her up. She knows where she packed everything." Bona turned to her daughter. "He's a sterling son-in-law; you did very well from my point of view."

"Oh he's great. And the children adore him. He was saying how they're going to love visiting here with the garden and the fireplaces and the balconies; all he thinks about is making them happy. To tell the truth, we're surprised by the atmosphere; we expected it to feel like Count Dracula's castle. But I still think you're a bit foolhardy. The legends about this place have been going on for centuries. They can't be completely baseless."

This consideration remained a sensitive point with Bona; it was the reason she hadn't consulted anyone about the move and it was her least favorite topic. "On the whole, the positives outweigh the negatives, and after all I'm not alone. I have Musci with me, and Gilda and Luigino downstairs."

A train of chairs, tables, rugs, headboards, mattresses, baldachinos, and packing crates passed continuously en route to the first *piano nobile.*

"What are you going to do with the third floor?" asked Serena. "It's a pity Enrico and I made you sell all that furniture from the big house. You shouldn't have listened to us."

"I'll leave it empty and see what happens," said Bona. "I don't need the space; I've got more now than we had at Sant'Angelo when there were four of us."

They walked over to the watergate to see how much was left to unload. The young man with the ponytail was standing on the prow smoking a cigarette, waiting for his companions to come back from upstairs. They had just started walking up the gangway when the young man vaulted into the canal.

"What happened?" cried Serena to the men.

"Dunno. It must have been a wave or something." The men ran onto the barge and looked over the edge. "Hey! This is no time for a swim!" They were hooting with laughter. "We've got work to do, Sandro. Come on. You can't leave all the work to us while you play."

Sandro came splashing around the side of the boat in a fury.

"Somebody pushed me, dammit. Who did that?"

"Oh come off it. We weren't even near you."

"I'm telling you, someone pushed me."

"Okay. It was a ghost. Satisfied?" The men were annoyed now. The boss said, "Go get yourself dried off so you don't get water on everything."

Bona looked around and spotted Musci sitting in the shadows examining his forepaw as though pondering whether to polish his nails on his chest fur.

"Satisfied?" asked Bona, and then whispered, "I don't blame you; I used to hate being taken for stupid."

Alberto came down the stairs. "Bona, I'm wondering whether we should get the exterminator in here tomorrow.

I think Musci saw a mouse or a rat up there. A while ago I saw him coming from that sitting room fluffed out like a porcupine."

Bona shook her head. "It's something to do with that room. I haven't figured it out yet. He goes in there all the time and, as you saw, comes out looking like he's stepped on a live wire."

Bona's life in her new palace took on a simplicity and calm that she had never before enjoyed. She stopped dreaming and spent her days sitting on the balcony watching the life on the Grand Canal, reading on the terrace and working in the garden with Musci. Together they were creating a herb garden for the kitchen with parsley, basil, rosemary, thyme, lovage, oregano, a patch of rocket, and chili peppers along the edge, with special plants like borage for cheerfulness and a whole corner of silvery catnips with yellow, lavender, and blue flowers, *Nepeta cataria, Nepeta mussinii, nepeta faassenii* and *Nepeta sibirica,* for Musci's pleasure and her evening tea.

While she was packing up and moving, she had forsaken even the diminished social life she had maintained after Musci's arrival. Settled in her new house, she discovered she still had no urge to throw herself back into the social swim. She chatted to her friends on the telephone but made excuses when they proffered invitations or hinted that

people were eager to be invited to see her new house. For
one thing, she had concluded that everyone was waiting for
the worst—on the evidence of their disappointment when
she reported that her dwelling was full of beautiful rooms,
with windows opening onto views that made her feel like
the luckiest person in the world, first for being born Venetian and second for having the chance to savor it in such an
enchanting house. It was a sure means of getting a caller to
ring off.

But the longer she lived in the house, the more she realized that there was in fact another kind of enchantment loi-
tering in the fringes, but creeping nearer all the time. There
was the room that Musci frequented and that she, thus far,
had avoided. It was clear that he wanted her to keep him
company there, so she had a television from one of the guest
bedrooms installed and made it into a sitting room where
she could take her catnip tea after dinner and watch a film
or read a book. The first evening she used the room, Musci
came in after she had already started a film, so she wasn't
actually looking at him, but she had the feeling that his fur
had shot out in all directions as though he'd seen a dog. The
same thing happened again as he walked out of the room.
She perceived that it occurred when he walked through a
particular area. And although the phenomenon didn't buzz
like a short circuit, it looked like it should. Some evenings
he walked up and down like an expectant father, making

his fur stand up again and again as though he liked it. It was a terrible distraction when she was trying to read or watch television or even sip her tea in peace; anyhow, Bona decided it wasn't good for him. She put a chair there to make him take a different route. The next evening she sat down in the chair to read and fell instantly asleep.

"What's happened to you? Can I help you up?" Bona was talking to a young woman who seemed to be sunk in the floor up to her knees.

"Oh no. It's fine. I'm in a different *palazzo,* the one that was here before the one you're in. When they rebuilt it, they got the floors wrong—thanks to my son—but that's another story." The young woman was speaking a Tuscan Italian that fell on Bona's ear with a charming sweetness. In fact the woman seemed *dolcissima,* and not much more than twenty.

"Are you dead, then, and a ghost?" asked Bona with dismay.

"Yes," she sighed, "I died when my son was born and I stayed here in the nursery to be with him. I couldn't bear to leave. But it didn't do any good. I couldn't help him."

"What happened? Can you come up and sit down? Who are you?" Bona was rapt with sympathy and interest.

"I'm fine here. My name's Bianca and I've been here for

centuries. If it makes you more comfortable I can come up, but for me it makes no difference. We don't have your problem of getting tired. Our problem is that we have no sense of time: we lose track of what's happening on your side. That's why I couldn't help my son. When Alvise was tiny, we had a harmony and I never left him, but once he started to talk and took up with life, I couldn't stay in tune with him. I would be distracted by a memory and when I came back whole years would have flown by. When I came back the first time, Alvise was already an outsider in the family because his stepmother was jealous for her own children, so I appealed to his father, who adored him. The second time, I found Alvise in love and happy, so I thought the worst was over. But on the eve of his marriage, they poisoned him and his half brother took his bride. I'd never grasped how bad it was for him until he'd already arrived on this side. They're all on this side now, but in proper eternity, not here on the fringe of time like us."

"Like us?" asked Bona.

"Alvise's here too. We don't communicate very much. I'm rather displeased with him; he stayed behind for revenge. He says he's achieved more than I did. But I don't call what he's done an achievement. He says that hate is a harder spur than love. But even he didn't do what he meant to do. You can find him. He's up in the dining room. He sits down. He had his portrait painted just before his marriage, seated in a *poltrona* with a book, and for some reason he likes to hold that pose."

When Bona woke up in the armchair, she was exhausted. Musci, who had wedged himself in beside her, jumped down and headed for the bedroom. As Bona moved through the house turning off lights and gathering up the newpaper, her book, and her glasses, she could feel around her the neighboring world of Bianca and Alvise. So it was all true. There were ghosts in this house. But Bianca was not a troublemaker. It must be Alvise. Her heart ached for Bianca: how sad it must be to have a son gone to the bad.

The autumn evenings were turning cool, so one rainy afternoon Luigino suggested that he should begin serving her dinner in the garden room instead of on the terrace. Bona thought it sounded like a lovely idea until she walked by the dining room and saw Musci's plate in front of the fireplace. She asked Gilda to pass the message to Luigino: dinner in the dining room—and a small fire, please.

That evening as she sat eating her dinner alone at the long table with Musci hunkered down on the hearth watching her, she wondered what she was supposed to do. Bianca had said that she could find Alvise here, but Musci seemed not to have located his electrical charge or whatever it was that had made his fur stand up in the sitting room where he found Bianca. Musci was staring at her, inscrutable, and the fire behind him looked as if it was trying to go out. She was about to say to Musci, "How ill this fire burns," when he stood up and jumped into the chair beside her. He looked at the far wall and meowed.

"Alvise," called Bona, watching the wall, "Alvise."

Out of the light pattern from the chandelier, an image hovering about a foot from the floor slowly formed of a young man about the same age as Bianca, sitting in a carved armchair with a book. Without so much as a greeting, he leaned toward her.

"Get this." He held up his book and read:

> *Between the idea*
> *And the reality*
> *Between the motion*
> *And the act*
> *Falls the Shadow.*

"This poet's got the story of my life, rather, afterlife. I waited for that murdering wife-stealer Marcantonio to move in here so I could get him but I drifted off. So when I grabbed my chance to cut off his life, I found out I was a couple of hundred years too late: I'd cut off some other poor sap. You know what I said? 'Doubledamn, I missed!' I used to be a marksman. Talk about wide of the mark—and I couldn't try again. The target was long gone. It didn't half put me in a bad mood. Then the same thing happened when I was tearing down the house. I drifted off and they started rebuilding it before I knew it. The best I could do was mess up the plans so they got the floors in the wrong place. That's why I'm up so high here, or rather, you're down so low. My mother says I've ruined the house with my evil temper, and made everyone who came here miserable. But how would you like it? You lose your life, so you go for revenge, and then you lose that too! 'Falls the Shadow.' It's a curse. In fact, I'm a curse. I'm sorry you came to live here. I remember now. My mother said you're a good person and I should try to be good with you. When was it she said that? Anyhow, you're better off with her. I'm bad news." He disappeared.

Bona was aghast. For one thing she had hardly expected a ghost to be so spirited, and for another thing, he had spoken in the most beautiful Venetian she had ever heard. Could this young man be the locus of the miseries of this house?

The gentle presence of Bianca in the sitting room became a feature of Bona's evenings as the after-dinner naps, which gave the occasion for their meetings, became routine. Bona was mindful that the conversations that ensued never strained the delicate rapport between their two worlds but touched upon universal subjects like the joys of memory and the problems of grown-up children. During these visits, Musci sat beside her, pressed right up against her side.

One evening Bianca lamented to Bona that she would like to take Alvise away. She wanted to be with her family, but because she had stayed behind to be with him, she couldn't go without him. She felt that Bona could help her to escape because Bona helped her to focus. She thought that Bona might be her last chance.

That evening after dinner Bona told Musci that she wanted to talk to Alvise about going with his mother. Musci jumped into her chair. First he called and then she called. Slowly Alvise appeared exactly as he was the first time.

"I need to talk to you," said Alvise.

"I need to talk to *you*," said Bona.

"Yes but this is urgent; you mustn't let me forget about it. I've found a picture that you have to go buy. I don't care how much it costs or anything about it, you just have to get it and bring it here. I can make it up somehow. Your friend will take you." He disappeared.

"Alvise! Come back!" She wondered that she dared be peremptory with a ghost. She was treating him like a son.

"What do you want?"

"If I do this for you, will you do something for me?"

"We'll talk when I see the picture." He was gone again.

Bona and Musci were wandering separately through the viewing rooms of the auction house. Musci had slipped by the guard and was keeping out of sight while Bona waited for her mission to manifest itself. She found Musci hiding in a small corridor next to a stack of paintings leaning against the wall. Musci put his nose on the largest one at the back. Bona pulled it out and saw nothing but a dirty black canvas with frayed edges. A custodian appeared.

"Does this 'painting' have a catalog number?" asked Bona.

"No. It's part of that lot. Do you want it? Give me a fifty and it's yours; you won't have to come to the auction."

Twenty minutes later, Bona and Musci were in a water taxi heading home with a large black canvas.

In the *androne* Bona leaned the painting against the wall. It was as tall as she was. She got a wet cloth from the kitchen and started to wash away the dust. Suddenly she jumped back. There was the face of Alvise. This must be the famous portrait. She stopped washing it, and rang a picture restorer that someone had once recommended, Dr. Sartor, and asked him if he could come over as soon as possible to look at a painting which needed major restoration. She asked Luigino to take it up to the dining room.

That same afternoon she took Dr. Sartor to the dining room to see it. He took a damp cloth from his bag and wiped the canvas here and there with elaborate care, revealing a piece of carving on the chair and the book.

"This could come up quite well, but it's an onerous task. For one thing it needs to be relined."

"How long would it take?"

"Several months at least. We could start work on it now, but we have other things in the laboratory that we have to keep working on. If you like I can take it now and at least get started on it." He picked it up and maneuvered it through the doorway. He was nearing the stairway when Alvise came running from the dining room.

"Where's he going with my painting? Stop him!"

For Dr. Sartor, Alvise was not there, so he continued toward the stairs unaware of the onslaught closing in from the rear.

"Stop him! Stop him!"

Dr. Sartor started down the steps. Alvise ran up behind him, gave him a vicious shove, and grabbed the painting as the restorer took a pair of quick steps down, then a long step down, then a very long, soaring step encompassing about half the flight, after which he lost his balance and plunged down the stairs headfirst, landing in a heap at the bottom. Bona was horrified.

"Gilda, Gilda, call an ambulance!" she screamed, then turned on the ghost full force: "Alvise, your wickedness is beyond all bounds. How could you do that? Not only is the man hurt, I'll end up paying a huge settlement for what's happened to him here. I could even lose the palace."

Given the *vis viva,* Alvise would have paled at the thought: it was an eventuality not to be countenanced. He had to work fast: "No. Go look. He's as drunk as a lord. He'll be all right. You can't kill a drunk."

The ambulance attendants rushed in with the stretcher. The paramedic bent over Dr. Sartor.

"He's hit his head." The paramedic sniffed the air. "Has he been drinking?"

"No," said Bona, mystified. "He came a few minutes ago to look at a picture."

Dr. Sartor opened his eyes and looked around. He tried to roll over to get up.

"You've had too much to drink," said the paramedic.

"Me?" said Dr. Sartor. "I haven't had a drop." He started to get up. "Good heavens. I feel like I'm drunk. But I can't remember drinking anything. What is going on? I knew I never should have come to this dreadful palace. Now I remember: I was pushed down the stairs."

The ambulance men helped him up and steadied him as they walked out the door.

Bona sighed with relief. "But Alvise, why did you do that? He was going to restore the painting."

"I want you to do it. Go buy a book. I don't want it ever to leave the palace again. Don't you understand? It's the only trace of me left in the world."

Bona and her daughter were sitting on stools in front of an easel in the garden room. "I'd love to learn how to restore paintings," said Serena. "You've made amazing progress. This house has really given you a renaissance."

"Believe me, I've had help at every step. Especially with

the relining. Anyhow it's almost finished. When it's done, I'll call the Belle Arti and have them list it as a national treasure so it never gets lost again. A friend gave me a note of the documentation which identifies it in the State Archives."

"Mamma, there's something I've been wanting to talk to you about, but not on the telephone. Alberto and I have been thinking about coming back to Venice. We've decided we want the children to grow up the way we did. Alberto says that commuting to Padua is no problem since he did it all through university. We wondered if you thought it was a good idea."

"You mean," smiled Bona, "you'd like to have the third floor?"

"Well . . . yes. We would. It's such a nice house and we'd like to be with you."

"It's a deal," said Bona. "It's what I was hoping would happen. When would you like to come?"

"Should we try to get in by Christmas?"

"That's only six weeks away," said Bona, biting her lip with uncertainty. "I guess I can be ready for you by then."

"What do you have to do, Mamma? Alberto and I can get the place ready."

"Oh, it's not that. For that matter Gilda and Luigino can clean it for you. It's just that the house has a few eccentricities I'd like to take care of before you move in, but I'm already working on it. So go ahead with your plans."

. . .

That evening after dinner, when Bona and Musci walked into the sitting room, they discovered Alvise and Bianca waiting for them.

"Bianca," exclaimed Bona, "I'm surprised to find you here like this."

"She could come anytime she wants to, like I do, but she's too shy on her own," said Alvise. "But she wanted me to come with her to talk to you. We're thinking of leaving."

"Alvise is so pleased with what you've done with his portrait," said Bianca, "and the way you're going to protect it, that he feels he can go away now."

"I put the documentation in the Archives at some point," said Alvise, "and I asked your friend here," nodding at Musci, "to keep my mind on helping you restore the portrait. But there's one more thing I want to do before we go. There's another painting I want you to buy. When you see it, you won't be sorry."

The next morning Musci took Bona to an antique shop. As soon as she walked in the door, she recognized on the floor, leaning against a chair, the little portrait of Bianca she was meant to buy.

"What is that portrait?" asked Bona.

"Ah," said the dealer, clasping his hands. "That is a wonderful piece which arrived yesterday. It is almost certainly a

Giorgione. Notice that it is a similar size to the old woman in the Accademia."

"What would be its price, then?" asked Bona.

"Well, I can sell it for much less than its actual value, because I was able to buy it quite cheaply. The attribution to Giorgione was unfortunately withdrawn in a recent book. Of course these attributions come and go, but it takes time."

"Fine. I'm seriously interested. Not because it's a putative Giorgione, but because I fancy it. I would like to buy it now, if you're ready to sell it," said Bona, opening her handbag and taking out her checkbook.

The dealer didn't hesitate for a second to ask triple what he paid for it.

As she wrote the check, she asked him to wrap the painting so she could safely carry it. She wanted to take it home at once. Alvise was right. There should be a trace of Bianca in the house as well.

Not long after this second acquisition, she received a letter from a British scholar who had come across the documentation concerning Alvise's portrait in an archive he thought he knew frontward and backward. He wondered whether the painting was still in the palace and whether he could come and see it. The portrait was now a documented Giulio Campagnola. The scholar had long been searching for the lost paintings of Campagnola's illustrious career of which nothing remained. He was doubly rewarded for his visit when Bona showed him the portrait of Bianca with the signature on the back.

In the evening fog of that same November day, Bona heard a boat hitting against the watergate and opened the window to look. She hadn't had time even to lean out to see, when Musci leaped onto the sill. Together they looked down and saw a gondolier in a dark coat, helping a young woman and a young man into his gondola, then pushing swiftly away. From the window they watched the gondola slide into the mist and slowly disappear. Neither of them moved until Gilda came in to see what was causing the draft. As Bona closed the window and turned back into the house, she found herself regretting their departure. In the end it had happened so suddenly. There were so many things she would have liked to ask them. She wondered whether Alvise would be held responsible in some way for the things he did after he was already dead. But now they were gone. She wondered if she would ever find them again.

It was cold and the movers didn't bother to close the door of the watergate between loads so Luigino had to stay downstairs and close it after them every time. Bona had put on her coat and come down to see how things were going. The door was open and the mist floated in from the canal as a train of chairs, tables, wardrobes, beds, cribs, small chairs, small tables, boxes, and toy boxes passed continuously en route to the third floor. Musci was nowhere to be seen.

During the arrival of Serena and her family, Musci had made himself scarce, but he was known to be a snob, so Bona wasn't worried until she went to bed and Musci had still not returned. She looked out into the garden from her bedroom window and thought she could see him. She called and he replied, but with a meow that was hardly more than a grunt. She wondered if he had found something. In all the time they had been together he had never behaved like this, but Bona knew that he had a mind of his own, so she went to bed. As she lay reading, she heard Musci singing, venturing an elusive, haunting melody that she knew but couldn't place. She went to the window. He was now outside the garden on the adjacent bridge, sitting on the parapet in the lamplight. What was he singing? She listened; it was a sad melody. "*Danny Boy*"!

" 'Tis you, 'tis you must go, and I must bide,' " Bona sang softly. At the sound of her voice, Musci jumped from the parapet into the darkness of the *calle* and was gone.

The abruptness of his departure spun her back to the evening when she was so lonely and he appeared. Now she was left with the identical loneliness and he was gone, possibly forever. She went to bed thinking of how empty her life would be without Musci; she would even miss Alvise and Bianca, but Musci had become practically an extension of herself. As she lay wondering what to do about the terrible ache in her heart, and in her throat, and the tears welling up getting ready to spill, the door opened slowly. At first Bona couldn't see anyone, but looking down, she saw a little girl in a nightdress coming toward her with a book.

"Can I read my book in your bed, *Nonna*?" She climbed in without waiting for an answer. "Mamma is getting Giovanni ready for bed while Nanny unpacks, and Papa's looking for a screwdriver because Giovanni's bed wobbles."

"You know, Carlina," Bona said gently, "your mamma was never allowed in my bed."

"I know," said Carlina, arranging her pillow. "Mamma told me. But I can go in her bed. She says we're modern. Now that we live here you can be modern too. It's much nicer." She opened her book to the first page. "Could you read it to me, *Nonna*?"

Bona put her arm around her granddaughter and reached for her glasses. She read *The Town Singers of Bremen* all the way through to the happy ending, doing all the lovely voices.

GONDOLIER

*B*rrrrriiiiiiiinnnnnngbrrinngbrrinngbrrinngbrrrrriinnng bringbringbringbrrrrrrrring!

Sometimes Bruno Scarpa wondered whether he should start carrying keys to his house so he didn't have to wait for his wife to get around to answering the door.

"*Chi è?*"

"It's me, Amalia," he shouted into the intercom. "Open the door, open the door, open the door! I'm in a hurry!"

He burst into the hall as soon as he heard the buzz and started to run up the stairs, pulling himself on the banister and stamping his feet to emphasize that he was in a tearing rush. That way maybe Amalia would catch on and have the apartment door open when he got up there and have his supper ready in a bag waiting for him.

The drawback of making such a racket was that when he began to slow down after the first three flights, everyone in the building noticed. It bothered him, because he should have been in good form after rowing a gondola for almost forty years, but he'd given up the racing, and the tourist work wasn't strenuous. Also he was not very long in the leg and at fifty-plus he was getting somewhat thick in the midriff.

Amalia, wearing a flowered smock and wooden clogs, was standing in the doorway smoking a cigarette. "What's got into you?"

She handed him a bag and a bottle of wine with some plastic cups balanced over the neck. Her curly hair was an improbable auburn, cut mannishly short, but her face still showed some of the sullen beauty that had staggered the boys at the *scuola media*. Bruno liked to brag about how cruel she was in those days, especially how she walked all over that bookworm who kept on asking her out even after she'd left school to work in the travel agency and he went on to the *liceo*. The night before he crawled off to university in Milan, she finally told him she was going to marry Bruno, who'd quit school when he was sixteen and already had a good job. So there! Squashed! Hahaha! Bruno annoyed her when he crowed like that. She hadn't thrown over Massimo to be mean, and not exactly for Bruno either. It was more because her mother was against Massimo, for the same reason she herself had been against her own daughter's boyfriend Carlo: someone who goes away to university will never come back to live in Venice. To keep her at home Amalia's whole family had wanted her to marry Bruno, and they were right: a gondolier doesn't get lured away by better opportunities in Milan. Now Silvia was married to her own gondolier, Silvano. She was living the life she'd grown up with in Venice, and her children were Venetian.

"I've got an American down there paying me to fetch my dinner, you'll be pleased to know," panted Bruno. "I told him I was coming up here to ring the *vigili.* Somebody threw a tin can out the window and almost hit me in the head. I think it was those *meridionali* across the way. You've got to ring the *vigili* and report them." He turned and started running back down the stairs, holding his dinner and his bottle in one arm so he could keep his other hand on the railing.

"Get your gondola in line, Volpòn, we're loading this group right now," Ciapate called to Bruno from the pier.

Bruno, or Volpòn as he was known, was sitting in the hut at the gondola station, enjoying his dinner. He placed some plastic cups around the table and poured wine for the others sitting in the hut with him, who weren't rowing tonight because the group had turned out smaller than they expected. In February business was unpredictable.

"I'll pick up last," called Bruno. "My motor can't run without fuel."

The pier was crowded with Australians jockeying themselves into cliques to go together in the same gondola, while Ciapate struggled to distribute them evenly.

When Bruno finally came out, impenitent, wiping his mouth with his handkerchief, Ciapate was bristling.

"You're not working, Volpòn. I've already got two more gondolas lined up, and only these people here to load."

Bruno was drawing a deep breath, ready to start a furious shouting match, when two good-looking women in long leather coats walked up to Ciapate and asked in English if they could take a gondola.

Bruno stepped forward with a smile. "I am here at your service," he bowed. This was better than working on a group serenade, which was a fixed-price deal. "Please wait here with my friend," he continued, indicating Ciapate, "while I bring my gondola to the steps."

Bruno stood in his gondola helping the ladies to step down and guiding them to the double seat with brocade cushions. He opened an afghan to put over their knees if they got cold. He placed it on the side chair in front of them and bowed, then climbed up on the edge and stepped along the poop. He picked up his oar and with a graceful flourish swung them around to face the Grand Canal. In front of them, the group's gondolas were gathered around a gondola rigged out with an amplifying system and a canopy festooned with Christmas lights in Japanese lanterns, which transported the accordionist and the singer.

Bruno threw a smirk over his shoulder at Ciapate as he

leaned on his oar. "I am Volpòn, the big fox," he began. He liked to introduce himself as he rowed so his passengers would turn around and see him silhouetted against the sky like a cowboy hero up on his horse. "My real name is Bruno, but they call me Volpòn, because I'm a clever one. We gondoliers have nicknames: sometimes they call me Avvocato, the lawyer, because I argue with the politicians, but my real nickname, from when I was young, is Volpòn. So please call me Volpòn. The big fox." He had a winning smile which he turned on from time to time like an LED message. He knew he was still attractive, and he was fairly certain that his middle-age spread was virtually imperceptible.

The two women exchanged incredulous smiles at the news of their being in the charge of a clever one. Bruno thought they were equally pretty and well dressed, with silk scarves and little leather hats, one a bit younger than the other. But he focused on the older one, who was about fifty and seemed to be the boss. She wasn't very tall, but she was slender and graceful with short blonde hair. The other was a little larger with long dark hair, but with less *presenza*, less class. Afterward, he congratulated himself on his perception. They were business partners, but the Blonde was the real owner. She had started buying fashions in the Veneto, leather goods and shoes. She had decided to buy a house in Venice. They were staying at the Hotel Gritti, dividing their time between their suppliers and real estate agents. Bruno was exhilarated by the way she had appeared before Ciapate at the moment he was about to lose his temper. Something told him she was special, and he wanted to make a good impression.

"Where would you like to go?" asked Bruno, getting down on one knee behind them to make the exchange more intimate. "Would you like to see the small canals?"

"No, not this time," said the Blonde, turning to speak and pulling back in surprise to find him so near. "Why don't we just follow along after the other gondolas so we can hear the music. But not too close, because we'd like to hear what you have to tell us."

So far so good, thought Bruno. The remark was encouraging, starting with the suggestion that this might not be a unique occasion. He put his best foot forward.

"Is this your first visit to our beautiful city?"

"No," said the Blonde. "I come often, but it's the first time for Betsy, my business partner."

Bruno started his discourse. "Here on the Grand Canal are many old palaces, but very few with old families inside. The palaces are still beautiful, but the life has changed."

"Where is the Gotham Library?" asked the Blonde. "I can never recognize it from the Canal."

Bruno paused. Americans always wanted to know which palace was the Gotham Library. *Pazienza.* "You see there where there's a boat out in front? That's it. And you see: not lived in by Venetians."

Bruno started again. "You may be surprised, but of the

Venetian people we gondoliers are most pure in original blood, because no one comes into this work from outside. See those gondoliers in the serenade? All have some family connection to a gondolier; it goes in families. See the young man on the left? That handsome one? He is my son-in-law, Silvano, and—" He paused a second considering whether to go on; he decided to risk it: "I have to watch that no American girl steals him. American women love gondoliers." The two women looked at each other and giggled. So far so good, he thought, and went on:

"If you like gondoliers, I can tell you my story."

"Oh yes, please." They both nodded.

"But after this song," said Betsy. "I love 'O Sole Mio.'" The singer stood in the prow of the music gondola singing with his arms outstretched.

"You may change your mind after this," teased the Blonde as a vulgar vibrato wobbled across the water like yards and yards of Day-Glo rickrack.

"It is not Venetian music," sniffed Volpòn. He decided to withhold his discourse until the Blonde asked him to continue—a tactic which obliged him to listen to "Arrivederci Roma" and "Ciao Venezia" before he was invited to speak again.

"When I had only eight years," he began, reversing their direction to leave the other gondolas behind so he could have the stage to himself and also so he wouldn't have to queue up behind the group when they came back to land,

"I used to visit the ferry where my uncle worked and got the idea to row before I could manage the oar. You would say like riding a bicycle when your feet don't touch the pedals. You see how to do it, but you can't. I never rode a bicycle; when I was a boy they were against the law. Well," he laughed, "they still are, but it's different now. Before, it was wrong to break the law; now it's wrong to get caught. Now we say if you don't get caught, you're not a criminal. I tell the politicians the old way was better, but today there's no justice, so it's all the same. I tell them: this is Italy, not Venice. Anyhow, when the oar's too big, you keep trying for the height and the force you need, trying to push yourself to grow. And somehow, one day you've done it. That's the way for a gondolier. We measure ourselves on the oar and how we work it. Anyway Venetians are not tall like Americans and we have the character for short men: smart and determined. When you see some tall *conte* or *barone* with a Venetian name, you know he's got strange blood mixed in. My brother says that in a crowd you can swing a club over your head and never have to worry about hitting a pure Venetian."

The two women gasped and laughed. The older one said, "That's true; the Venetians I know are not like Texans."

"What are their names?" asked Bruno. "I can tell you if they are true Venetian names."

The younger woman looked at her expectantly, but the

older woman shrugged. "They haven't lived in Venice for years and years. And believe me, the Venetians I know, here or in America, have never told me the things you're explaining. Please tell us more."

Bruno could see that she admired him, but it was too near the end of the trip to start on any of his other dissertations. He decided to have a go. "If you're looking for a house and have to go around, why don't you let me be your gondolier? I could help you to find a good place; I know plenty of people and I could maybe save you from being cheated or making a mistake. And I could explain more of Venice."

As they were pulling up to the pier, Volpòn had to make a quick decision whether to try to win her over with a discount price, or just fleece her in the normal way and trust that she was expecting it anyhow. He decided on the second course, since it would mean he could charge more if she decided to accept his proposition.

The Blonde paid what he asked without even blinking and gave him a reasonable tip as well for his "fascinating discourse." As she was about to walk away, she turned and handed him a card. "If you hear of any nice apartments on the Grand Canal—not a huge *piano nobile* or anything like that—but something nice, in good condition, let me know. I've heard that the agents don't always know about the best things."

Volpòn recognized the gesture as an invitation, so when she extended her hand, instead of shaking it, he raised it to his lips and kissed it. When her companion followed suit, he thought he'd better kiss her hand too, but he made it decidedly mechanical, to send the right message: the Blonde was the one he liked.

When they were gone he looked at the card: Heather Smith, President, Fashion Design Group Ltd. He put the card in his pocket. Eder Smit, he murmured to himself: beautiful name, president of a fashion company, buying a house in Venice. He wanted to see her again. He got busy asking around for apartments on the Grand Canal.

The next afternoon he stepped into the Gritti and asked one of the assistant concierges whether Signora Smith was in. The young man looked at the keys and said she didn't seem to be, but that she might be sitting on the terrace. He would check and get a message to her, at the first opportunity, that Volpòn was looking for her. The hotel didn't encourage gondoliers to loiter in the lobby, so Bruno left, saying that he would wait for a while at the gondoliers' station just outside before going back to his own station.

He was appropriating a chair from behind the arbor so he could sit pretending to be petting the gondoliers' dog

Orso while watching to see if she came out, when he saw her with her friend almost running out the door looking up and down the *campo* for him.

"Oh, there you are," she said. "They said you were looking for us. Do you have some news?"

"Yes. I've found some apartments you might like to see. I can arrange appointments and take you around."

"Great! We were going to stop by the gondoliers' place later and look for you anyway. We decided to take you up on your offer to be our gondolier. Could we go and look tomorrow morning? And could you leave word with the concierge this afternoon what time and pick us up here? Bye. See you tomorrow. *Grazie.*" They both waved and went back into the hotel.

The effect on Bruno was seismic. He went on a diet effective instanter; he went shopping for a new gabardine gondolier's shirt, and for the rest of the day he tried to keep his face in the sun even though he knew, in his rational self, that its tanning power in February was derisory. But the rational world was no longer his. Instead, he dwelt in the clouds and meditated on this run of good luck: first, she had materialized like an angel when he needed her; then, she had entertained his transparent message; and now, she had sent him a clear response. There was only one problem: how were they going to get rid of that bothersome Brunette?

. . .

He worked all his contacts to find apartments. He checked with the concierge of the big hotels, and at the bars where the barmen picked up gossip; he telephoned friends who knew agents. He hadn't been so busy since he'd done his year of military service. By late afternoon he had found two properties, not listed with the big agencies, but at opposite ends of the Grand Canal. They would have to set out at nine in the morning. That was early for him. But his sentiments, along with the chance to earn a sizable commission, prevailed. The agents were giving him a hard time because he wanted a share of the seller's commission as well as what he would collect from her. They were being stubborn, but they would wake up when they saw her: she was one swanky dame.

When he went into the Gritti to leave word, the concierge said, "We have a message for you from Mrs. Smith." Bruno held his breath while the concierge leafed through his stack of papers, pausing from time to time to deal with guests. He wondered if the concierge was teasing him. "Let's see. We rang your station and left a message. They have a reservation at Da Ivo and would like you to pick them up at seven-thirty."

Fantastic! Luck was still with him! Bruno could hardly believe it. Just to be sure, he went to the souvenir shop and bought a tiny plastic hand making horns and put it on the ring with the keys to his gondola covers and chains which he always carried with him.

When Bruno pulled up to the *pontile* at the Gritti, the two women were waiting. They made a big fuss over him. He felt a little sorry for the Brunette, who was probably as taken with him as the Blonde was, and would soon have to face the bitter truth. He was in high spirits as he rowed through the gondola station at San Moise, winking and saluting his friends, so they would take a good look at his favorite passenger. They registered their approval with grins and nods.

In the *campo* before the Church of San Moise and down the streets on both sides of the canal, shops were turning out their lights and pulling down their shutters. Apart from a few couples, the streets were deserted.

"Venice has changed," said Bruno, making a sweeping gesture as they approached the bridge at Via XXII Marzo. "At this time there used to be many men around in the streets talking and having drinks in bars, while the women and children were at home. Only gondoliers keep up the old traditions and have fun together as men."

On the landing at the restaurant, Heather Smith offered to pay, saying that they would walk home, but he shrugged as though money didn't concern him, saying they could settle it all later. Once they were inside, he rowed down to the kitchen window and asked the cook to get word to the waiter to signal him when Mrs. Smith and her friend were ready to leave because he was waiting for them outside. He sat in the cold, starving, and listening to the radio. But it was worth it. When she discovered that he had sat out in the cold waiting for her, she was all giggles like a schoolgirl. And when they got back to the hotel she let him give her a kiss on the cheek. True, she made him kiss the Brunette as well, but that was just a ploy. She had to be kind to her business partner.

Waiting beside the *pontile* at the Gritti the next morning at nine o'clock, Bruno started to make a note of his hours, but his passengers appeared almost immediately. When he had settled his precious cargo, plus the Brunette, Bruno set out down the Grand Canal explaining that he had booked only two appointments for the morning because the houses were so distant from each other. In any case, her reaction to these would give him an idea of what she liked. The first was a palace near the railway station with a garden in front. It was for sale as a whole or as three separate apartments. Bruno had set this one up first because it was far enough away that he would have time to do his talk about gondoliers and school and marriage, which he thought would have a good effect on her.

"Now," began Bruno, "what would you like to hear? Would you like me to tell about the life of a gondolier, or about palaces?"

"Can we have both?" asked Betsy.

"Oh yes!" agreed Mrs. Smith. "If we see something interesting, we'll ask, but otherwise you can tell us whatever you want to." As she said this, she pulled out of her handbag a pad of paper and a pen. "In case I want to remember something you say."

Bruno's ego rose and grew like an inflating zeppelin.

"On the way we will pass the Casinò, which is where the great composer Wagner died, and you can see right here the Palazzo Rezzonico where a famous English poet died. Not Shakespeare. The other one." He laughed. "As you can see, we gondoliers are not students. I am telling you history as it is passed down through gondoliers. Of course we go to school, but today they teach less Venice, more Italy, and I never liked school. We gondoliers get free as soon as we can, when we're sixteen, because our school is very hard. They make you do more at home than at school. My mother got tired of arguing and did my homework to keep me out of trouble with the teachers, and she did it for my brother too. If the teacher shouted at us our mother had to go down to the school and shout back to defend us. She was practically going to school with us. She even did some of my sister's homework when she had hard teachers. My mother became an educated woman. We used to tease her about it. But when we got to be sixteen, she was ready to let us quit. My wife"—he shrugged and stole a look to see if she reacted—"helped my daughter in the same way, but girls are better at school, so it wasn't so much work. I was sorry not to have a son, but a girl is less trouble and we gondoliers work unsocial hours. You think when you choose a wife it's such an important choice, but in the end you probably spend less time with your wife and children than you spent with your mother and your brothers and sisters when you were growing up. I suppose that's why our mothers are so important, more than the wife. Our real family is when we're growing up. Our fathers are not very important either." There, he thought, that ought to take care of any misgivings she might have about his wife and family.

"See the trees up on the left?" He pointed ahead. "That's the garden of the palace we're going to see."

"Look, the railway station is right there," said Betsy. "That could be handy."

"Oh by the way," said Mrs. Smith, "seeing the station reminds me. Betsy has to leave early tomorrow morning. We thought it might be fun to go to the airport in a gondola. Would it take a long time?"

Bruno nearly fainted with happiness. She was getting rid of the Brunette. He tried to sound businesslike. "I usually say an hour and a half. What time is the flight? Would you both be going to the airport? It would be very lonely for me to come back by myself." He flashed Heather an eloquent smile. This was just what he was looking for—a chance to be alone with her.

"I wouldn't dream of making you come back alone," she

smiled back at him. "If we decide on the gondola, of course I'll go too. I wouldn't miss it for anything. I'll have the concierge leave you a message later today." She looked at the garden he had pointed out. "I don't really know this part of town. What's it like?"

"Very Venetian," he said, turning down the side canal that flanked the palace. He knew this was the standard euphemism for the less fashionable areas, but he couldn't think of a better answer.

Looking up, they could see a strange eclectic facade, like a patchwork of odd pieces. It was the width of a single room and gave onto a large neglected garden.

A woman awaited them beside the landing. "How do you do."

"*Buongiorno,*" said Mrs. Smith as she climbed the steps. "We don't know this part of Venice, but isn't the Henry James story *The Aspern Papers* set somewhere around here?

They shook hands and walked through the garden toward the entrance. "I'm not sure," said the agent. "It could be this palace. It is historic from the nineteenth century."

"The tangled garden made me think of it."

Bruno had found his radio station and was getting comfortable when they reappeared at the landing. He guessed he wouldn't be getting a commission on this one.

As they pulled away, Mrs. Smith turned to him. "Have you ever seen inside that palace?"

Bruno confessed that he had not.

"It's arranged in the oddest way. The big rooms are down the side looking at that modern building and the rooms that look on the garden toward the Grand Canal are bathrooms and dressing rooms and a kind of utility room. It would take a lot of work to make it nice, if you could even get permission. Is the next one like this?"

Bruno was a little worried because he didn't know. He decided to evade: "It's in a very picturesque location and better than this. It's at the other end of Venice, but we have plenty of time because you were so quick." He had planned to take a nice rest while they looked through the palace and was a little sorry that he had to row all the way down to the Public Gardens.

He suggested that they cut through to the Grand Canal and see some minor Venice on the way. For him it would be less strenuous than rowing in the Grand Canal. He was wondering about rowing to the airport. He hadn't rowed that far for years. And then to turn straight around and come back. But it was his chance. Somehow he was going to have to manage it. He set off down the *rio* heading away from the railway station and toward the Accademia.

"Look Betsy, I'm sure that's the palace of *The Aspern Papers* over there," said Heather, pointing to a house they were passing. "I remember that garden on the side."

Bruno didn't know what they were talking about. He was worried that she might not like the next place either.

He couldn't wait to get rid of that Brunette; he didn't like dealing with two women at once.

Maneuvering through the small canals occupied Bruno's attention. His passengers lapsed into conversation about what Betsy should do between the time she got back to New York and Heather's return the following week. There were certain details to be confirmed about their orders, which Betsy would have to convey to her.

They had come back into the Grand Canal and were approaching the Gritti. Heather turned to Bruno. "Would you mind stopping for a few minutes at the hotel, so we can have a coffee? Do we have time?"

In fact Bruno didn't mind stopping at all. He was dreading the row through the basin where the water was in a constant squall from the motor traffic.

When they rejoined him, they each had a notebook and spent the rest of the trip working and taking notes. At last Bruno swung the gondola under a bridge and pulled up beside a neo-Gothic house with a large canopied terrace and views over the basin. Heather thought it had possibilities and they stayed inside for nearly an hour. When they came out, they were in good spirits.

"That was interesting," said Heather to Bruno. "I might like to see it again. It's rather modern, but the views and the terraces are wonderful."

They talked about their work all the way back to the

hotel. When they got out, Heather thanked him and said she'd be in touch about the airport. He could see that the Brunette had got her thinking about her work. He left feeling disgruntled.

That afternoon, as Bruno was lounging on the bench at the gondoliers' station daydreaming about Heather and wondering when he was going to see her again, Ciapate came out of the hut and walked up to him. Bruno sensed he was still trying to get even for the other night when Heather rolled up on a wave of good luck.

"Hey Volpòn. Here's a message for you from your girlfriend. They've decided not to go by gondola to the airport."

Bruno could have hit him. "Very good," he said. "I was hoping they would change their minds." He was furious. He walked down the *fondamenta* until he was out of sight. He grabbed his key ring from his pocket and wrenched off the little hand. He threw it on the pavement and stamped on it again and again until it was broken into small pieces. Then he realized that he was doing something foolish, practically insane. He ran over to the souvenir stand and bought another one. He sat on the wall overlooking the basin, putting the charm on his key ring and worrying about how he was going to get to see Heather Smith again. After tomorrow she would be alone and free to spend as much time with him as she liked. He was sure he could get something going, even if it was only being her regular gondolier. She had told him not to look for any more apartments. He wondered if he could prevail on the concierge at the Gritti to encourage her to keep calling on him. He walked over to the public telephone and called the hotel.

"Volpòn," said the concierge. "You got our message about the airport? And about the railway station?"

When Bruno went back he had a bone to pick with Ciapate about giving him only half the message. Heather had to meet someone at the railway station tomorrow afternoon and she wanted him to take her. From what he understood of her conversation with Betsy in the gondola, she was staying on to do some more work. It occurred to him that for her to pick up a supplier in a gondola was a sure way of inviting him to quote her the highest possible prices for his goods, but Bruno wouldn't have warned her off for anything.

The following afternoon when he picked her up, he thought she looked exceptionally pretty. He couldn't imagine that she would turn herself out like that for a business contact, so it was a good sign. He helped her in with the greatest tenderness and many smiles.

Without Betsy, she wasn't so lighthearted. All the way to the station, she seemed to be thinking about something else and she didn't ask any questions. He imagined that she was thinking about her business and how she was going to deal with her supplier. He wished that she would tell him about the business because he was sure that he, Volpòn, could help her get a better deal. In fact, he decided to try to get involved if he could. He could be her agent in Venice.

At the landing stage, she asked him if he would be allowed to wait where he was until she came back. She set out toward the station, and when she reached the steps she suddenly perked up and started to run. He wondered what had made her do that. Was it a sudden burst of happiness? He smiled.

In minutes she reappeared with an Italian carrying a briefcase in one hand and a large Vuitton suitcase in the other. To Bruno that case screamed Fancy Shoe Samples. He wanted to catch her eye as she came along to establish their rapport so this salesman would know his place. He concentrated his gaze to try to force her to look at him, but she continued to talk animatedly to the man as they drew closer and closer. Businesswomen, thought Bruno; they think they're so smart when they're talking business. If she'd been his wife, she'd have been put in line by now. She was refusing to look, being important and executive. As she came up to the gondola, she gave him a huge smile as though she'd come upon him by surprise. He gave her a deep significant look and squeezed her hand hard.

"Oh!" she squeaked and pulled her hand away, still

smiling as she stepped into the gondola. Bruno continued to look hard at her, while the man put his foot on the gondola. As he shifted his weight forward to step in, Bruno gave the oar a twitch and sent the man leaping into the gondola, hurling his suitcase ahead and grabbing for the edge to keep from falling.

The man still had his back to Bruno when he said, "If you do that again, Volpòn, I'll throw you out and row myself."

This was not a claim that Bruno normally would have given much credit, but as the man knew his name and spoke Venetian, he took it at face value and passed it off as a joke.

"Sorry," he winked at Heather. "I was distracted for a minute."

As the man turned, Heather beamed at Bruno. "Volpòn, Betsy and I planned this as a surprise for you. This is my husband."

The man Bruno saw before him was none other than that groveling bookworm Massimo Bon.

"How's Amalia? You haven't changed much." Massimo sat down beside Heather and turned to talk to Volpòn. "I'm surprised you didn't recognize me. I guess I've changed after thirty years in New York. You know I went there straight from Milan."

Bruno didn't reply. He was trying to decide which would be the shortest, ugliest route back to the Gritti.

"Would it be too much work for you to stay on the Grand Canal?" Massimo Bon was going out of his way to make himself agreeable.

Bruno shrugged. "For me it's the same."

Massimo looked around. "Talk about change: every time I come back I can't believe how this place changes—the most protected city in the world. It looks whiter and whiter, every time I see it. What happened to all the reds and pinks? Is it just my rosy memories?"

Bruno couldn't believe what was happening to him. It was as if the wheel of fortune had been slowly turning to get even with him for stealing the beautiful Amalia. Or was it the charm he'd stamped to pieces when Ciapate had tricked him by giving him only the bad part of the message. He rowed without speaking, lost in his own thoughts, and they eventually lapsed into their own conversation. They seemed to have a son who had just moved to Rome. As they were pulling up to the Gritti, he decided to make the best of it.

"Volpòn," said Heather, "the concierge will pay for all the trips we made when Betsy was here. Thank you so much for helping to make her first visit to Venice so special."

"But this trip," said Massimo, "is on me."

Bruno turned on the smile and announced his fee: double what it should have been. Now, he thought, we will see what kind of *Grand Signore* is Mr. Massimo Bon.

Massimo blinked. "I see my wife's been spoiling you."

He reached into his jacket for his wallet. "I heard a funny remark from a colleague when I was in Milan just now. He told me, 'If Islamic law were introduced in Venice, the glove merchants would go out of business.' Well, there you are." He handed him a stack of banknotes. "I suppose it's nice to know that at least some things in Venice never change."

LORD

B lair Nolesworthy—Lord Nolesworthy to you—preened himself on being self-made. He was only fifty when he and his new wife sailed into Venetian life, but such was the weight of his presence that everyone mistook him for a much older man. To his laughing, girlish wife of thirty-eight, the Venetians, in their first rash effort to pigeonhole the pair, gave an overgenerous forty-five—*però* a well-husbanded forty-five.

The landing of Lord and Lady Nolesworthy in the Serenissima was a sensation from the instant their water taxi tied up at the Gritti Palace Hotel, so precarious under a ziggurat of suitcases that the young porter panicked and ran for reinforcements—leaving Milord and Milady to address the lurching platform like a pair of intrepid cats. The Nolesworthys being as yet unknown, it was this mountain of luggage that struck also the Venetian ladies taking their morning coffee on the terrace. What they saw made them sit up and strain for a better look at these new arrivals who didn't scruple to heap Gucci on Vuitton like Pelion on Ossa. *Formidabile.*

Contessa Zecchino leaned toward Contessa Bonome and growled in her ear. "It looks as though they mean to stay awhile; I'll ask Franco at the concierge who they are."

So before the letters of introduction had even dropped through the letterboxes, the news was rampant, and the Venetian ladies in full cry after it. From Venice's Grand Canal to London's West End the telephone lines sang.

Baronessa Patristi rang the Consul General's wife in London.

"Hello darling, it's Sofi. I was sending some of Edmondo's things down to the country for him and it made me wonder when you're coming back to Longa. Oh perfect. You'll be here for my party; I'll send the invitation to Longa. Oh, before I ring off, do you know some people called Lord and Lady Norsworthy, Nollsworthy?"

"The Nolesworthys! Haven't you had my letter? They've bought Ninni's grandmother's palace; the whole thing. You'll get a letter from me any day now, and I'll tell you the rest when I get there. *Ciao, ciao.*"

Contessa Zecchino rang Lady Trotter (the former Giulietta Dario), who knew everyone in London *and* in the country, not to mention everyone in Italy: "Lord and Lady Nolesworthy? Indeed! She's part Italian. Her name was Luisa

Button. They say she's related to the Umbrian family that makes pasta, but they changed the name when they came to England. Anyhow, I've written to Amelia and Moceniga. And Chiara has just been here. Ring her. I'm coming to stay with her next week. *A presto!*"

Contessa Bonome got onto Lady Boodle, who had just put down the phone from talking to Luisa Nolesworthy herself.

"My dear," exclaimed Lady Boodle, "everyone is ringing me; none of my letters have got through; it's just like it was in the war. The important thing to know is that Lady Nolesworthy is the second wife, but she's Blair's first *Lady* Nolesworthy, because his title arrived only seconds before she did. Anyhow, you'll like them. They give wonderful parties. There are a dozen letters from me and everyone else on the way. Just be patient. All will be revealed."

It was from Blair Nolesworthy himself that they learned how, when his father denied him a literary education and put him to work at seventeen, he thought his prospects as wretched as a Bonsai's. But after a few weeks in the family business, he recognized that the *vita attiva* knocked the *vita contemplativa* for six, and that his brain was not after all a slow-devouring academic power but a roaring furnace voracious for fuel.

The merest acquaintance was soon able to confirm that

he bolted fresh ideas as hungrily as dragons bolted virgins and as fast as they could scamper into range. He ruled over a vast domain of information and opinion: his advice would flash out first in one direction and then another like a beacon from the rocks; his judgments seared like passing rockets; he was peremptory, and dangerous as a wounded animal.

But his asperity had its attractive side. More often than not, it bannered forth in aphorisms. He became the lion of the Sunday papers, padded after by journalists smitten with sound and fury.

Spinning at the inmost core of his being was the need to turn a profit, to compete. It was his greatest pleasure to be a billionaire, having started life meanly with scarcely a million pounds to his name. His father's business, one of the oldest of the ceramic manufacturers in Staffordshire, had, under the scourge of this firebrand son, clambered onto the rails of progress and gained such momentum over its competitors that several were hooked aboard as it shot past with not so much as a click in the cadence to mark the event.

His father, Humphrey Nolesworthy, Chairman, plucked the first plum from the new growth by setting up and endowing a Ceramics Museum for the nation, a celebration of a great British industry newly revitalized, which, coupled with other munificent gestures, entitled him to a life peerage.

With serene pleasure, he chose to style himself Baron Nolesworthy of Stoke on Trent. A functionary at the College of Arms, however, wrote to him on behalf of the Garter King suggesting that he might, as he had gone to school in Dorset, like to use the name Trent as it pertained not only to the Staffordshire river but also to a Dorset town.

Humphrey Nolesworthy read the communication and whiffed a note of condescension. Moreover, he discerned the odor of politics in a ploy to save the name of the principal pottery town for his chief business rival, who had raced him to the Lords and lost, but only by a nose. By the time he put down the letter, he appeared to have swollen to half again his normal stature. With eyes bulging and an expression black as Vulcan, he rose and started to pace. At the third lap, he thundered for his faithful secretary, who slipped into step beside him, pad and pencil poised.

He was a large man with a barrel chest, a domed head, and a mustache cut so short that it stuck straight out from his upper lip, like a weapon of last reserve. It was said that his wife, mother of his only son, was more assertive even than he.

Together they paced, man and secretary, for a full minute before he spoke.

"Take a letter, Miss Cowdray, to the College of Arms:"

I have before me yours of the twenty-fourth instant and concur with your request to drop "of Stoke,"

*reducing the geographical reference to Trent. Please
have the kindness to indicate your concurrence by
initialing the enclosed copy of this letter.*

I remain, Sir, your most obedient servant,

*H. M. V. Nolesworthy, President and Founder
The National Ceramics Institute of Great Britain*

P.S. My messenger will await your reply.

The next day he had in his hands the authority to style himself Lord Nolesworthy on Trent; he knew that the Heralds had understood "*of* Trent," and he would likely hear from them again, but he regarded the matter as closed.

His son, Blair, was of a less robust appearance than he, but taking after his mother had an unexpected wiry strength of body and character both. He was tall and lean with the stiff, eccentric movements of a Monsieur Hulot, which caused many, on first meeting, to attribute to him a whimsical and harmless nature.

By the time he was forty, Blair owned almost half of his father's business. He decided to move on to something else. When his father mooted the idea of financing the ceramics museum, Blair offered to set it up for him. He gathered a pack of specialists and turned them loose in search of museum-worthy pieces, then himself joined the hunt. But he owed his success, and his own peerage, to an evening at the Beefsteak Club.

Holding forth to an old geezer one evening about his shopping adventures, he was surprised to find that his auditor had something to teach him.

"Young man," said the old geezer, "I've been collecting since before you were born. To most people collecting is a treasure hunt, but from what you've told me, you really need a collection. So buy one. It's cheaper than making one. In the modern market the only way is to buy bulk."

"That's all very well," said Blair with finality, "but the collection I need doesn't exist."

"If you interrupt me," said the old man, "I will lose my train of thought. The only way is to buy in bulk, I think I said. To furnish a house, a clever man will buy out an antique shop, sell off what doesn't suit, buy another stock, and so on. It takes time; it ties up capital; but it's the only way to beat the market. It's the supermarket method. Remember the parable of the fisherman."

"Yes I remember," said Blair, glancing about for someone to interrupt them.

"I told you not to interrupt me," said the old man. "I will teach you the lesson: the fisherman throws out his nets and they catch all sorts of things he doesn't want. What's he do? He uses a bigger net and finds a way to profit on everything he catches—even to the point of taking the things he can't sell and giving them to someone who might do him a favor someday."

Blair stared like a toad. But he was not absent: he had licked in the idea before it had even spread its wings.

The next time he found a shop with a fine collection of ceramics and porcelain, he made it his business to find out about the rest of the catch in the net—the silver, the glass, the furniture, the pictures.

One morning he wandered into the shop, a familiar visitor, and drawled to the proprietor, "What would you take for your stock? I've looked it over, and I'm ready to buy if the price is right. I'll be back at eleven."

When he came back, he found his adversary reduced from connoisseur to barrow merchant. For Blair Nolesworthy, this was an unexpected bonus. In a few hours the haggling was over; the goods were in his warehouse being sorted by experts, and the former dealer was having lunch in a smart restaurant bragging to his friends. After buying up several shops in this manner, Blair Nolesworthy laughed to learn that the dealers were having a hard time getting back into business. He could have given them a word of advice.

In this way he brought together a fine collection of British ceramics for his father's museum, and was able to pass the pieces on at not a penny more than the tagged prices. From the remaining goods he selected the best and used them to buy a half share in a friend's antique business. The rest of the stock he kept in a warehouse and called it My Collection. After a few years he created out of this stock a vast and quite good collection which he donated to the nation for the purpose of furnishing national monuments and important public buildings.

No one had ever thought to do such a practical thing before, and in due course, following ample proof that his munificence more than matched his father's, a grateful nation rewarded him with a life peerage of his own.

He chose to style himself Baron Nolesworthy of the Five Towns. The Heralds, when they got the word, looked at one another and let it pass.

While he was thus trimming his sails, his wife of twenty years drifted away. Her absence went virtually unnoticed until someone mentioned to him, in tones of commiseration, that she was being seen with the Earl of Dartford's brother, whose wife had died the year before. This news focused his mind. That same afternoon Blair Nolesworthy had his lawyer write to the truant Mrs. Nolesworthy offering an immediate and handsome divorce settlement. For the first time he noticed with regret that they had no children to link them: he wouldn't have minded figuring in the margins of the Dartford family.

Once seated in the House of Lords, he set about organizing a new and better life. First he needed a collaborator.

Within a week he had a new secretary in Miss Luisa Button. She was tall and slender, full of fun, with a mind as strong and supple as an anaconda. She turned out to be his ideal woman. Within a month they knew that they were going to marry. Together they chose her replacement, an earnest and efficient niece of his father's secretary: another Miss Cowdray.

On their honeymoon they toured Italy, entertaining a vague idea about trying life in another country. One afternoon they sat chatting in their suite in the Grand Hotel in Rome. This seat of ancient empire had plenty to offer, but somehow it was not enough. And so, like Alexander, they unrolled the map to see what else they fancied. Their sights fell on Venice. The next day they decamped, turning northward.

They stayed in Venice for a week to get its measure, to look at houses, and to try to fathom what kind of a life they could fashion for themselves in this flickering legend. It took Lord Nolesworthy only a day to divine that the sole power a foreigner could wield in Venice was social power. However, he saw it for what it was: the devastating power of the invitation, the introduction, the window on the real world. He had plenty of those commodities, and thought the setup had prospects.

Today it would be lunch for twenty. In the long *salone* which reached all the way from the Grand Canal to the balcony over the garden, Lady Nolesworthy sat at her desk with place cards arranged in a circle before her.

Before the broad windows giving onto the Canal, Flûte, the paragon of the standard French poodle, sat very still on a small Persian rug. He sat still for two reasons. One, he was leering at the maids going back and forth with trays and linen, the unmistakable signs of an invasion. The other was that the floor had just been waxed and polished, and was dangerous.

Luisa looked up from her desk, and seeing Flûte so seated, rigid and staring, laughed.

"Oh, what's wrong, Flûte? Do you disapprove?"

Flûte gave a wide, moaning yawn, licked his lips with emphasis, and without rising marched in place for two or three steps with his front paws. To Luisa, this conveyed disapproval with a capital *D*.

Flûte was the ideal pet for Lady Nolesworthy. He was elegant, intelligent, and reluctant to trust anyone too far. Blair had given him to Luisa on their first anniversary. It was Flûte who made them a family, and they adored him.

The Venetian maids thought it was a scandal the fuss the Nolesworthys made over that animal. When the maids were alone with him, they loved to polish the floor of the *salone* until it shone like glass, and then put out his dinner, an hour late, at the far end. The hilarity of watching him negotiate the slick passage, like a drunken sailor on a heaving deck, made it worth all the work. The Nolesworthys were pleased with their maids for bringing their terrazzo floors to such a glorious state, and ascribed their diligence to some romance between Venetians and their native pavement. They never learned the true motive. It was one of the few occasions when someone succeeded in putting something over on the Nolesworthys, and it sealed their relationship with their Venetian maids in a way that otherwise would never have been possible.

"Don't worry, Flûte," said Luisa. "We'll stay downstairs. Hardly anyone will come up to bother you, and not until the very end."

They would use the marble table that dominated like a shining pool the garden end of the entrance hall. The *androne,* to give the room its proper name, was beautiful in summer, the most Venetian place in the world. And yet no Venetian would dream of offering lunch in this great hall, perhaps because it was on the ground floor and in principle unfit for living. The *androne* was paved in russet marbles, with cool *marmorino* walls, and roofed with ancient beams painted over with *millefiori* and golden ribbons. It terminated in a stately colonnade on a quaint garden bounded by brick walls, with iron gates giving onto a sleepy *rio.* The land entrance came through a corridor at the side of this room and was reached along a small *calle* flanked by palaces which gave onto either the Grand Canal or the *rio,* but not both. In this palace, as it pleased Lord Nolesworthy to point out, they had achieved the near-impossible in Venice: a watergate at the front and at the back. He couldn't think of another palace like it.

It was not a difficult placement today. They were all English-speaking, mostly people passing through, with a few representatives of the Anglo-American community in Venice. There were Tom and Batty Browne, an old baronet and his wife—she in a wheelchair with a broken ankle—who were staying with them in the garden flat. She made a note to have the butler put the little ramp by the lift. The ladies would have coffee upstairs if they liked, and the gentlemen could smoke in the garden, where everyone would have a glass of *prosecco* before.

She put the cards for Blair and herself in place and began experimenting. There were Trudy Gotham and her house guests the Duke and Duchess of Dorset. They, since there were no Venetians today, would take pride of place. There were an American senator and his wife, Tim and Kitty Brond; a young Canadian art dealer, Elmo Carlton, with his client, Mrs. Albert Donahue, a recent widow; and an American artist, Tom Grackle, a bit rough to add texture. There were the American Consul, Peter Schuldt, and his wife, Nancy; the head of the British Universities Centre, Professor Sir Roger Lodge, and Lady Lodge; the Acting Director of UNESCO, Monsieur Arnaud; and an architectural historian writing on British restorations, Dr. Freddie Cole, and his young photographer, Ms. Darlene Hills.

Lady Nolesworthy yawned. She was glad she had had the last-minute inspiration to invite Fanny Rider, the French Canadian potter. She kept things lively. A prodigy of self-promotion, she lived by selling her works to friends, and friends of friends as they wove in and out of Venice ad infinitum, carrying away with them virtually her entire production. In a way it was as though she wasn't in Venice at all. After thirty years she had made no mark and might have been anywhere. Yet the merest hint that her fame might be less than monumental revealed in her a brooding menace like something set aside, forgotten, on a shelf: a jar of rhubarb counting down. A careless knock, a chance remark, and there it was: the warning gasp that tickled Lord Nolesworthy more than anything else about her. As for the droll insights on life and art and Venetian ways which she gave in trade for meals and patronage, he didn't need them.

The ideal place for Fanny Rider was next to a man of bland self-confidence, impervious to affront. She would put Sir Roger there. On Fanny's other side, she would put Elmo Carlton, the art dealer whose client would then inevitably go with him to Miss Rider's studio and buy a bowl, such as the one Lady Nolesworthy made a note to place in the center of the table filled with roses.

The drinks in the garden were cut short by the appearance of the butler, who murmured to Lady Nolesworthy, with the cook's apologies, that the twenty small soufflés were already at their zeniths and should be served at once. Lady Nolesworthy had no choice but to hurry her guests to table.

M. Arnaud had no sooner sat down than he began regretting that the Nolesworthys weren't more French about their table, letting conversation flow naturally in any direction, instead of being so strict and British about who spoke to whom. He would have liked to spend the whole time talking to the Duchess, even sharing her with the host if necessary. Most of all he would have liked for her to hear his story about de Gaulle, which he had never used in Venice, but it needed a large audience, the whole table listening, and you couldn't have that here. He didn't much fancy the old Englishwoman in the wheelchair on his right who had just been rolled up from the guest apartment. He was afraid she might tell him about why she couldn't walk.

"Luisa tells me," said the voice from the wheelchair, "that you are with UNESCO."

"Yes," he replied, "I'll own up. But first tell me how you ended up in that cast." It was out before he had time to think.

"If you insist," said Lady Browne. "It's a strange story, but not everyone wants to hear about such things."

"Oh," insisted M. Arnaud, "I do very much."

"Very well. I had an accident almost as amazing as Von Horváth's accident on the Champs-Élysées. Do you know that story?"

"Wasn't he struck by lightning?"

"Virtually—killed by a limb falling from a tree in a storm. Canceled from above."

"The hand of fate."

"That's exactly how it struck me," nodded Batty. "The day it happened—I was just a young woman strolling along Avenue Foch with my mother when we ran into Von Horváth. She'd met him at a party somewhere. He stopped to talk and I remember that he went on and on like he wanted to talk all evening. After a while, we all stepped under an awning to get out of the rain, but I was trapped just at the edge so a rivulet from the awning poured straight into my boot. My mother was a very focused person so I hesitated to interrupt her; it was just the sort of thing that would embarrass her and make her cross. It's strange to remember. I stood there and let it fill up and when the boot was full my leg felt the way it does now in plaster; it was the same ankle. Eventually Von Horváth went his way and we went ours. The next day we learned how he died. I never forgot it and I think that incident convinced me that there's a destiny that shapes our ends. So all the time Tom was in the Navy and I was raising the children, I felt there was this implicit order in the universe."

"Nothing you could do, so why worry."

"Exactly. Until I had this peculiar accident which changed my mind completely." She stopped. From the other side of M. Arnaud, the Duchess caught her eye. M. Arnaud turned to meet Lord Nolesworthy's summons. He sneaked a quick glance back at Lady Browne to see if she could quickly summarize, but she was already learning about restorations from the man on her right.

As Lady Nolesworthy drew her conversation with Senator Brond to a close, she glanced in Blair's direction and smiled to see that he had already moved on.

Trudy Gotham saw Luisa turn to the Duke of Dorset and remembered that there was something Luisa had asked her to talk to Sir Thomas about, but she had forgotten what it was. For all Trudy Gotham's reputation for shrewdness, her manner of conversation tended almost exclusively to simple and spontaneous candor. *Tant pis,* she thought, and turned to Lord Nolesworthy.

"You've made this house so beautiful; you must have spent millions. And you never seem to get tired of giving these lovely parties. Why did your first wife leave you?"

Blair Nolesworthy entertained the innocent question with the same genuine amusement he felt when parrying with a hostile journalist trying to catch him on the hop. He paused a second before leaning toward her: "She left me to find happiness," he confided. "And I have."

The Duke of Dorset was genuinely interested in hearing Lady Nolesworthy's opinion about Venetian politics. He was thinking of writing a book on modern Italy.

"It's quite surprising," she laughed. "But that's what they tell me."

"I get it," the Duke laughed with her. "So what we have here is soft communism amongst the counts, residual fascism amongst the middle classes, anarchism amongst the shopkeepers, confused radicalism amongst the workers, and a general consensus to let sleeping dogs lie."

Kitty Brond was not so interested in her grilled fish nor her neighbor on the right as in the conversation that her new friend the Duke of Dorset was having with Lady Nolesworthy. She had tried twice to join in, when Luisa leaned forward and summoned Elmo Carlton from his San Pietro.

"My dear," she smiled, "Mrs. Brond has been trying to get your attention."

As the senator's wife turned her chastened face toward the art dealer, Lady Nolesworthy glanced around for other stragglers.

"I was going to ask you," said Kitty Brond, "how you happen to know these people. The Nolesworthys."

Elmo Carlton grinned with pleasure. "Luisa and I went

to school together in England. She was one of the first girls when the school went co-ed; she was running the place by the end." He smiled at Luisa, who was half listening to him. She found herself emulating Mrs. Brond, hankering after a conversation that didn't belong to her.

Fanny Rider turned with energy toward Sir Roger Lodge. "Do you remember the last time I sat next to you?"

"I certainly do. I couldn't forget a thing like that. Just remind me. Was it here in Venice?"

"Yes. It was two years ago when you were setting up the British Universities Fine Arts Course. I offered to teach a course in pottery and you said that you wanted me to do it the next time."

"Oh yes. We came to your studio. I do remember very well.

> *Shapes of all Sorts and Sizes, great and small,*
> *That stood along the floor and by the wall.*

Most interesting. Tell me. What are you working on now?"

"I'm doing a series of owls. It's called 'Tribute to Pallas Athena.' The owl is her symbol. She's the goddess of wisdom."

"A tribute to the gods. *Who is the Potter, pray, and who the Pot?*" The Professor smiled engagingly.

"What? I'm the potter," said Miss Rider.

"I guess Athena's not the goddess of potters, is she."

"Who?" queried the potter in disbelief. "Pallas Athena? She's the Greek goddess of wisdom. The Romans called her Minerva. I don't know who's the goddess of pottery. I suppose I should. It's one of the fine arts, I know that much."

"Do you know this verse about a piece of pottery?" He held up his glass:

> *My clay with long Oblivion is gone dry:*
> *But fill me with the old familiar Juice,*
> *Methinks I might recover by and by.*

He emptied his glass and beamed at her.

"No," she said coldly. "As I was saying, pottery is one of the fine arts."

"Poetry," sighed Sir Roger. "That's Omar Khayyám. Wonderful verses. Poetry is one of the highest arts, isn't it. People always listen to what a poet says. Enviable position, really."

"As a potter, I express myself with my hands, not with words."

"Very wise. Words have been known to fail. Did you ever read Samuel Beckett's *Watt*? There's a very amusing failure of words, and about a pot, too, as it happens: 'It was not a pot of which one could say, pot, pot, and be comforted." He leaned toward her confidentially. "Being Beckett, I suppose it was the kind of pot you'd call a *po*'. What's the French for potter, do you know? Not a *po'er*, I don't suppose. We'll ask my wife after lunch. She knows all that sort of thing."

"As I was saying, my latest pottery is a tribute to wisdom. I mentioned it thinking that being a professor, wisdom might somehow interest you."

"It does indeed. It's my business. My line of country. It is indeed." Sir Roger turned toward her with a smile of good cheer.

"Perhaps then," she offered icily, "you would like to see the owls in my latest series."

"Owls!" he exclaimed. "I like owls. They're humorous-looking, aren't they. And yet they stand for wisdom. In Italian they call them *gufi*. Goofies. But I guess I don't have to tell you that, do I. You live in Italy. They have seven bones in their necks and can turn their heads right around and look the other way."

"It would be," said Miss Rider, "a great advantage in certain social situations."

"Oh, isn't that the truth," he caroled. "You can get so stuck having to face the way you're turned."

Peter Schuldt made a silent wish for the Nolesworthys' lemon mousse with ginger crust to appear and took a gulp of wine before returning to the "blue rinse" on his right. She was nice enough, even somewhat evasive, but he felt he'd seen her before. That usually meant some nuisance at the public counter in the Consulate. She was with that Canadian art dealer. Canadians sometimes came in thinking they had some sort of neighborly rights. Few made the mistake twice. His assistant was *bravissima* for getting rid of people who thought they had rights. He took another gulp of wine and looked again at her place card.

"Now then, Mrs. Donahue, you said you'd seen all these galleries. Is your tour guide wearing out your shoes?"

"Oh no. I've just been looking around with Elmo. I suppose I should take a guided tour. I should think the Doge's Palace needs a guide. What do you think?"

"Oh yes. I haven't been there myself. You see, running a consulate as I do, I have no time. It's a heavy job. I often work late doing the work that they should be doing in Rome. The buck stops here."

"So true." Mrs. Donahue was all sympathy. "You consuls are the unsung heroes of the diplomatic service. I know that. But it's too bad if you don't get to indulge in the pleasures of lying abroad for your country."

"It's not a lying-down job, unfortunately. But that's enough about me; I shouldn't complain. Tell me more about yourself. You said you've come over with that young man to look at pictures. Are you on a buying junket?"

"Almost the opposite. We're thinking about what to do with my late husband's collection. According to his will, I'm to give some pictures to the National Gallery, but it's up to me to divide it all into three collections—one to give away and two for the children. It's his way of getting me to learn about something I didn't really have time for when he was alive. I suppose it's also to keep me busy and stop me feeling so alone."

"I suppose it's the tax question, is it? Couldn't you make more money selling them?"

"I'm not sure I could, when you calculate the taxes and so on. But I like the idea of giving pictures to the National Gallery. You see, my husband worked for the government and through his work he got the chance to buy art."

"How did he get a chance to make an art collection working for the government? Did he work in a museum?"

"No, no. He was a diplomat, like you."

"Oh. Were you ever here in Italy?"

"Yes. Several times. The last time he was Ambassador. That was only a few years ago. I couldn't swear to it, but I think you may have come to the Embassy when we were there."

"Oh sure! Now I remember. Gosh, I'm so sorry. Your husband was a really nice guy. I remember him really well."

"I guess you've been here for quite a long time. Do you have a lot of tourist problems in Venice?"

"Kind of you to ask. We manage to keep it to a minimum."

Lady Lodge looked across the table at her husband. What could Luisa have been thinking of to put Roger between that potty potter and the nubile photographer. Oh dear,

Miss Rider seemed to be refusing to talk to him over dessert. She practically had her back to him. Ah, good girl: Luisa was rising to her feet—not a minute too soon.

Luisa let Flûte trot by, then closed the bedroom door behind her. The lunch had been less boring than she'd expected, and they'd been quite decent about not staying too late. She kicked off her shoes and stretched out on the chaise longue for a little siesta. Blair was still down in the garden talking to Dr. Cole, who had asked for a tour of the palace. She could hear Blair's voice through the open window.

"I was telling the Duchess at lunch how much I like my *altana*. Of course I don't suppose any Venetian man would be caught dead up there—it's where the ladies used to bleach their hair. They had these crownless hats with broad brims so they could pull their hair through and spread it out in the sun, without sunburning their faces. Then, when they got blonde enough, they would go off and get themselves painted by Maestro Tiziano. I go up there every morning after breakfast with the *Gazzettino* and a cup of coffee. At about eight o'clock it's the perfect temperature, clear and quiet, with a nice breeze even in dead summer. Five stories above the world: it's marvelous. The next time you come, I'll take you up there. It has no architectural interest—except that you look out over the whole town. You know Venice lies so flat that you can see its shape, the interlocking boxing gloves. That might interest you. And you can see a lot of architecture, actually, roof details and relative heights of buildings, like a very detailed relief map. Next time we'll do that."

Luisa smiled to herself. That was an exit line, but she was sure that Dr. Cole would not take his cue. Professors rarely did. He would leave when his glass was empty, or the decanter, if it was still in sight. But Blair was wise to that, so it probably wasn't. Sure enough, there was Dr. Cole's voice, starting up a new line of conversation.

"I'm sure everyone asks you this, but I always wonder what it's like to live in Venice. It's one of those beautiful places where you think life must be improved by the architecture. I used to wonder about Edinburgh that way, too."

"Well, I can tell you about both," said Blair. "In some ways Venice is a lot like Edinburgh. I lived there for two years when I was setting up a factory near Glasgow. Edinburgh is where society is, like Venice, but Glasgow is where the action is, like Milan. But most important for living there, if you're not born a Scot you never become a Scot. 'Scots are born not sworn, sir,' that's what my old butler used to say; he felt he could say that to me because I carry my mother's name. But that's the sort of thing you hear in Venice all the time, not about foreigners so much—they expect foreigners not to have to be told—but about other Italians."

"That chimes true," said Dr. Cole. "When I was young I thought Scotland would suit me—beautiful buildings, fishing, shooting—so I answered an ad in *The Scotsman* for the National Buildings Registry. I was called for an interview, but I think they were just curious to see what kind of Englishman would put himself in for a Scottish job. Naturally I didn't get it."

"It's the same here. You can live here for years but you're never 'one of us.' If you die here, they think it strange you didn't go home to do it. And if you're buried here, you'll come forth at the last trump a *foresto,* still an interloper. And you have to be careful: the Venetians have special side agreements with God that let them do things their own way. They always have had." Blair was laughing. Now he was taking them inside to the door; she could hear the small voice of Ms. Darlene Hills among the echoes.

His laughter made Luisa smile; he was in such a happy mood these days. Blair was right of course. The Venetians had a way of holding off the people who wished them well, people who could help them. But they let in the enemy. She remembered the other evening at the Bonlins' saying goodbye to Annalisa. Someone had been teasing Alvise about his birthday. She had asked Annalisa when it was, and offered to give him a party.

Annalisa had hugged her and said, "Oh Luisa, you're an angel. But I think he'll want to let it go by quietly. It's such a *big* birthday. He can't bear it! Giulia says she might do something discreet and tactful. But it all depends."

Luisa sensed that it was an excuse, that Giulia Panfili

was going to leave her out. She wondered why. Then it dawned on her that it must be the work of Sofi Patristi, because of the time she didn't invite her architect boyfriend after she'd begun to be seen with him in Venetian houses. Well, that was something Lady Nolesworthy felt strongly about. Sofi ought to have a better sense of her own heritage. She had married into one of the best Venetian families and she shouldn't be allowed to sully its name by having a liaison with a person of no name at all. Of course the divorce hadn't been her fault, but that didn't give her carte blanche. How could the Venetians let her do it? Luisa felt outraged that she should be the one to defend the ramparts of Venetian nobility. She wondered if she was becoming dynastic-minded. She would ring Giulia tomorrow. There was no point today: she would be at the Italian Heritage meeting at Malcontenta. But Luisa really wanted to find out what she thought of that architect. Giulia was no fool and would understand that Luisa Nolesworthy knew why she wasn't being invited to Alvise's birthday party. Maybe she would decide not to play along with Sofi, since there was no doubt about who was *right*.

Then there was another thing. The *Parroco* at San Stefano had rung her about raising funds to restore his *pietra dura* altar. She would mention that too—it was Giulia's own parish church—and offer her ten or fifteen million lire as a friendly gesture to get the ball rolling.

Content, she curled up and fell asleep.

When she woke up Blair was sitting on the bed reading *The Times.*

"Something historic has happened," he said.

"What on earth?" she queried, sitting up and rubbing her face.

"Something's happened to Flûte."

Luisa looked at Flûte in his basket and then at Blair.

"When I came in he was asleep on his back, like a dead beetle. They say when animals expose their bellies like that, they trust you. How'd you manage that?"

"How wonderful! I can't imagine. This morning he was in a major huff. He set up a terrible howl when they brought out the floor polisher. I had to take him with me when I ran out to the hairdresser. When we came back, he crept onto his rug and wouldn't get off. Maybe he was listening when I told the maids after lunch that they could ease up on waxing and polishing for a while: I'd rather not take a flying leap these days."

"Oh well, that's a relief," he laughed. "I've been feeling a bit too mellow lately. I was afraid maybe he'd sensed it."

The morning air was soothing, soft as a warm bath. Blair Nolesworthy took another sip of coffee and looked down from his *altana* on the Serenissima.

I am monarch of all I survey,
My right there is none to dispute;
From the center all round to the sea
I am Lord of the fowl and the brute.

It was curious how that poem had popped into his head the first time he ever looked out over Venice. It did capture the feeling one got from this position. How did it go on?

Oh, solitude! Where are the charms
That sages have seen in thy face?
Better dwell in the midst of alarms,
Than reign in this terrible place.

He chuckled: there was something in that too.

He wondered why he felt this restlessness. Did it have anything to do with Luisa's little secret? It was too soon to tell, but he knew that he was going to get a son. The mere idea made him want to play the fool, slap people on the back and do caprioles. He had to keep pushing it out of his mind.

The boy will send me back to work, he smiled to himself, just as I was beginning to favor the lazy life. His mind ranged over the British scene. The ceramics industry was done; the ceramics museum was done; furnishing the national monuments was done. Where, oh where, was something interesting that would suit him, that needed doing? Nothing came to mind, and his eyes slowly registered on the scene below.

All those towers pointing hither and yon, at strange angles. *Giacomo, Giacomo*—that's what Venetians say when their legs are unsteady. Daydreaming spires—worse than Oxford really. In places like this, the past banquets on the present. People offer themselves to the feast. It surprised him to think that he'd already been here for three years. No, he wouldn't linger in its slow-chapped power.

Somewhere in his brain there was a furnace roaring, far away. An idea was coming. Was it to do with ceramics? Was his old self coming back? *Fornasa da veri.* That was Venetian for glass furnace, he thought, and sat up straight. *Glass.* The British glass industry—tableware; stodgy and dull it was, with a shrinking market. As far as he was concerned, the glassware industry had sat down by the roadside to die. The Venetian glass industry was another one dead as a dodo. But they hadn't sat down by the road. No sirree! They'd taken to the road like a band of gypsies. Blue elephants; street vendors' rubbish; that was their specialty now. Still, what there was left that was good had the old virtues: light, refined, beautiful colors: there were lessons to be learned from Venetian glass.

During the last Parliament there had been talk: Britain needed to build up its manufacturing base. The Minister was inspirational; the traditional mode for addressing venture capital. Glass tableware: it went well with the ceramics;

yes, he would "complete the service." Ha! There it was! Just the line to drop on the PM when he made his annual offering. He glanced at the newspaper that lay folded on his lap: *Gazzett.* Yes! He would be gazetted *Lord Stoke:* he would insist on it. Could it be an earldom? No, better be realistic; hereditary titles were hard to get. A viscountcy might be the limit. The lad would have to wait for his title.

As he stood up, the newspaper fell from his lap. He picked it up, and on an impulse he flung it out over the roof toward the Grand Canal. He would never have to struggle with Italian again. The morning breeze caught it and separated the pages into a flock of wild shapes. The effect was pleasing and Lord Nolesworthy descended to his study with a light heart. He phoned down to the gondolier; from his window he could hear the telephone at the watergate ringing out over the Grand Canal.

"Bepi. Do me a favor and get in touch with some of your friends over at Murano. I want to go to all the reputable glass factories in the next day or two and see, at each one, the whole glassmaking process from start to finish. Do you have a pencil? Make a list: Salviati, Cenedese, Venini, Pauly, Barovier . . . Okay, sure, Moretti's a good one, too. I'm ready to go at five minutes' notice."

As he put down the phone, he wondered whether Bepi would have any trouble getting the *via libera* for him to witness the process. In the old days it was a state secret. They used to kill people for revealing it. He didn't imagine there were many secrets left in the Venetian glass business, except possibly how much of the junk came from China. At that end of the market the bigger business was probably in printing the *Murano Glass* stickers they put on the stuff when it arrived.

Once in Girolamo Barbaro's house he'd seen a portrait of an ancestor handing his small son a book the size of a pocket diary containing the secrets of Venetian glass. He remembered asking if he could see the book, just out of curiosity, but Girolamo said he'd never seen it himself. His family had climbed out of the glass business centuries ago, long before it sank into the bogus zone. Well, if there were any secrets left to discover, he rubbed his palms, if there were any, he should know them by dinnertime tomorrow.

He could have them bound into a little book and hand them on to his son; they could have a portrait painted. The boy would look like his mother, with snappy black Button eyes and a bright expression. And when he was a bit older, he would present him with The Great British Glassware Industry. And maybe a viscountcy, if he got an earldom. After all, you should never give up.

Never give up. It always made him think of that last Doge surrendering to save the past. What an unseemly, un-Venetian gesture *that* was: the beginning of the precious rot that afflicts this place. Napoleon was a one-man show; anyone could see that. Without him, the army would have gone home—or, being French, come over to the Venetians like they did for the Germans. The Doge should have invited the General to dinner to discuss terms, and sent over to Murano for some ground glass. It seemed such a Venetian solution: perhaps he *had* done that. And the only consequence was the famous heartburn. So Murano failed the Republic? Well, he grinned, clicking his heels, *retribution is nigh.*

The phone rang. He jumped like a cricket and put out his hand as if to calm the squealing instrument just long enough to warn the future with a jubilant whisper— "*Almanach de Gotha,* Here We Come!"

MOTHER

Rosa's old legs sagged outward at the knee, causing her to rock when she walked like a doll on an inclined plane. Her daughter-in-law Sabrina said it must be some kind of deficiency and she should go to the doctor, but Rosa said it was normal for her age; her mother had been the same. Nevertheless, she didn't like walking, and that was another reason she didn't like Venice. In any normal city a person could run about on a motor scooter; a child could have a bicycle; a family could have a car. But Sabrina was Venetian. So Rosa had to live in Venice and sleep in the living room with her seven-year-old grandson.

The Espositos' apartment was up six flights of stairs on the top floor of a narrow building put up for the parish poor a century or so before. Their entrance shared a blind alley with another similar building whose entrance had greater dignity by virtue of having a stoop leading up to it. Their entrance, at pavement level, might have been taken for the door to a storeroom, except for the five odd doorbells, each declaring its independence from the others, scattered on the wall beside it.

On a Sunday, Rosa gave herself a rest from her morning expeditions to the *magazzino* with her shopping cart and rarely went farther than the church next door, but today she had to go to the Rialto. As she came out she was surprised that despite its being a cold June the sad little alley had got hold of a beam of sunlight. Instinctively she went and stood in it while she checked her handbag that she'd left nothing behind, and straightened her jacket before setting off through the underpass that led into Campo San Pantalon. In her pocket she fingered Sabrina's wedding band and the engagement ring with the little diamond that she had bought for Luigi when he was madly in love. Sabrina had swollen fingers now because of the baby so she couldn't wear them. That much was understandable; what confounded Rosa was Sabrina's way of leaving valuables in plain sight where any passing antenna man or roofer could pop in the window and help himself. Rosa had given up telling her that if she had come down to live in Naples she would have learned better habits in a hurry. So when Rosa went in the bedroom to comb her hair and saw the rings on the dresser, she didn't think twice about scooping them up for safekeeping, along with a pair of earrings and a nice-looking pen she thought might be worth taking.

She paused at the gate beside the row of ticking gas meters. Not long after she moved in she had stood down there surveying the pipes, convinced that one of the neighbors must be feeding air into their gas line because the pasta water took an age to come to the boil. When she couldn't find anything on the neighbors, she fathomed that the air had to be coming in farther up the line, which meant that they were part of a big scam like you'd find in Naples or Sicily. This gave her and Luigi a good laugh, but it annoyed Sabrina, who stuck to the view that there was an absolute, fundamental difference between Venetians and Southerners. Today the ticking set Rosa thinking about whether she should stop in church. She had planned to stop, but she was worried about the time. She took such small steps and it was such a long way to the Rialto. She decided to play it safe: after all, it was Sunday.

From the back of the sanctuary she scanned the congregation and picked out Sabrina exactly where she thought she'd be, over near the sacristy talking to her friend the priest, Don Giuseppe. The Mass was about to begin, but Paolo wasn't anywhere to be seen. Then Rosa found him, practically under her nose, sitting in the last pew with his head bowed, lost in the *folle capricci di Paperino,* the mad escapades of Donald Duck. She almost laughed right there in church at how he took after his father.

On the way out she bought a candle and followed her special ritual of lighting it from the tallest of the burning candles, then placing it in the highest position on the rack, even if it meant occasionally demoting another one to make way. She crossed herself and was about to ask God to help Luigi get them a better place to live and to help Sabrina get over being Venetian, when the candle guttered, causing her heart to leap with alarm. But the flame didn't go out; it took hold and spread into a fat, strong flame of promise. What a fright! But what a relief! All her life she had felt close to God, but since she'd been in Venice, she'd had some misgivings that being farther apart their rapport might flag. The sign kindled her faith. She set out again, down the steps and around the corner, this time as fast as her legs could carry her. She was determined to get back before the Mass was over. Today was going to be her lucky day: the first time since she'd come to live with her son's family that she'd been allowed to cook, and she'd been given permission to make Sunday lunch. This in itself was an answer to her prayers.

Rosa Maria Rosario. Rosa passed the time musing as she swayed along. One son. Widow Esposito. Displaced person. That was the story so far. She walked on for a while in a reverie of Naples and then in a fantasy of Sabrina loving the *terra firma,* which in her mind resembled Naples, until she reached the vaporetto stop at San Tomà. As she hunkered down on the bench to wait, her soft girth eased comfortably around her so that with her broad, disapproving face, the suggestion of a placid frog belied the tenacity of mind and body that had many times scored over the devils of adversity. She waited with her back to the Grand Canal but turned on purpose to scorn it: spinach water; a common drain; and this was the best that Venice had to offer. Ha. As for living up three stories so you could lean out the window and see a dirty green *rio,* Sabrina had to be missing a few gears in her pretty little red-blonde head. In Naples it was worth climbing stairs to catch even a glimpse of the great blue bay. And even if you couldn't see the water from your house, you could feel it shining down from the sky because the bay and the sky blended together like a sail over the land. But she had promised herself that she would give up mooning about Naples, which she might never see again, and try to settle in better with her son's family. It wasn't going to be easy. For the nine months she had been in Venice, she hadn't been allowed to do more in the kitchen than make a pot of coffee before anyone was up in the morning. Never mind; today was the beginning of a better life.

This morning Sabrina had come in while she was having her coffee and taken a rabbit out of the freezer.

"Today," said Rosa, "I could make lunch, if it would be any help."

"I thought I'd cook this rabbit," said Sabrina. "Paolo doesn't much like it, but I think it's been in the freezer long enough."

"I can do that," said Rosa. "The thing is I have a taste for fried potatoes like the way we used to do them at home;

I bought the oil and the potatoes yesterday. It's all out in the hall cupboard."

Actually, those things had been hidden in the back of the cupboard behind her clothes for over a week, but at first she hadn't been ready, and then she hadn't felt up to it. Today she could tell that the time was right. Sabrina hadn't objected at all. The baby was getting so big, it took all her energy just to do a few chores like make up their bed and keep Paolo in clean clothes for school. This week she even let Rosa do the shopping, something she had forbidden when Rosa first came to live with them. But things were changing. In two months the baby would be there, which meant five people in a one-bedroom apartment.

"*Impossibile!*" The exclamation croaked unexpectedly from Rosa's throat.

"*Sì,*" concurred the man waiting on the bench opposite, happy to pass the time, "on Sunday the vaporettos are impossible. They've just skipped two in a row."

At that moment the vaporetto slammed against the *pontile* with a growl, and the stranger added, "Someone told me that they train new drivers on Sundays."

But Rosa wasn't out to make friends with Venetians. She got on the vaporetto and sat down in the cabin on the low bench next to the door where she could get out quickly. She tapped on her watch as she calculated: it would take about ten minutes to get to the Rialto, ten minutes to find Luigi at the bar and give him the message, and twenty minutes to

get back to San Tomà, then the walk, another twenty minutes, which could make it twelve-ish when she got back to
the church.

On Sundays Luigi slipped away before anyone except
his mother was up. Even on Sundays she was an early riser,
because she liked to get her bedclothes off the sofa before
everyone else was up. But on weekdays she got up at dawn
to clean out cupboards and take things over to their storeroom at San Samuele to get ready for the new baby. Sabrina didn't appreciate her efforts, but Luigi didn't see
anything wrong with it, and he liked having coffee with
her on a Sunday morning before drifting out to the bar
near the central post office. It was the same place he went
every day to play cards and watch television when he finished his work in the sorting room. He was the only post-
man who spent his free time in the neighborhood of the
post office, but he didn't come there because he liked his
job; not at all; it was convenient and he'd got so he felt at
home there. In fact, more than anything, it was a place to
pass the time away from home, where there weren't enough
chairs, there weren't enough beds, and according to his
wife there were twice the number of women there should
be. But only one of them understood a man's need to get out
of the house. Every Sunday his mother sneaked his wallet
from his jacket and put some money from her pension into
it so Sabrina couldn't complain about the expense. But
today Rosa hadn't put the wallet back in his pocket, so she

had to take it to him. It would give her the chance to tell him that she was making her special fried potatoes so he should be sure to be home by one o'clock. She wanted him to be on time.

Before going to Mass, Sabrina got down on her hands and knees and dragged the deep fryer out from under the bed and put it on the stove because she couldn't stand the idea of her mother-in-law prowling around in her bedroom. So there it sat ready and waiting when Rosa lugged the bag of potatoes and the oil into the kitchen from the hall cupboard. She went straight to work. She opened the two cans of oil, emptied them into the deep fryer, and turned the knob, but she was dismayed at how big the pot was, because the oil wasn't enough. On the counter she saw the open can Sabrina kept there, nearly full, so she poured that in too. She had learned from her brother's restaurant that the secret of perfect results was plenty of oil. She picked up the salad cruet from the table; there was about a cup of oil in it. She poured that in as well. If Sabrina could have seen her, she would have laid down the law, but what she didn't know wouldn't hurt her. Rosa would replace everything, and more. She picked three potatoes and then added another two: it wouldn't do to have someone saying that there wasn't enough for four after she'd put in so much oil. She peeled them and started to cut them one by one into her thin little strips that made the hot fat go *whisssssssssh* when the basket went in and cooked the potatoes to a beautiful toast color in a minute. But the fat had to be very hot to get it right. She stopped cutting and wondered for a minute whether anybody was going to appreciate all this work, whether ordinary fat chips wouldn't be just as good, but she shook her head and kept on cutting the thin little sticks that were her specialty, until she'd finished the five potatoes. She washed them all together and put them on a towel on the side to dry near the window. Across the *rio,* the snoopy wife of the gondolier was leaning from the window hanging out her Sunday wash and sneaking little looks at the way Rosa was cutting the potatoes, so Rosa pulled the shutters together and hooked them in a way that blocked the view but left enough gap for a good draft. She looked again at the oil and shook her head. Then she remembered that down in the bottom of the cleaning cupboard she had seen another jar of oil. She took it out and held it up to the light. It was thick and heavy, but she dumped it in anyway; she had to be sure that the oil came right up to the line. That last little bit did it. Rosa knew that her "no holds barred" determination was the trait that most got on Sabrina's nerves, so she prayed under her breath as she surveyed everything laid out in readiness for lunch: the drying potatoes, the thawing rabbit, the oil. "Please God keep Sabrina busy in church today." She placed a pan on the stove ready for the rabbit, then went in the bedroom to comb her hair and get ready to deliver Luigi's wallet.

Pushing through the door into the dim atmosphere of smoke and drink, Rosa felt like she'd been swept back in time to Bar Sport in Naples, looking for Babbo. But in this bar there was no good old Nando looking after his regulars. Here there was a redheaded Venetian who didn't like having an old lady in a black dress coming into his establishment.

"*Prego?* Yes, please?" His voice accosted her passing figure, but she rocked past him without even looking. She could see Luigi in the corner, biting his thumbnail and frowning at his cards. She had laid the wallet on the table and was already on her way back to the door when he noticed. For one thing she didn't want to hear his protests about how it wasn't his fault the wallet got left behind, which he would have trotted out given half a chance.

"*Grazie! Ciao, Mamma!*" he called after her.

But she just waved without turning and kept moving. At the door she remembered to turn and call to him: "Luigi, be home at one o'clock; I'm making my fried potatoes." Had she been back in Naples, a word with Nando would have been enough, but here she couldn't count on anybody.

Back on the vaporetto Rosa tapped her watch and

looked at the pale clouds gathering in the northern sky. She hoped it wouldn't rain. June should be sunny, but here it often wasn't: God lived in Naples.

The walk back seemed shorter than the walk out. It was, she decided, a case of life getting easier as the future got brighter. When she was so miserable about leaving Naples, Don Gennaro had told her that she must brighten the corner wherever she was, and that if she did that, God would light her way. Before she knew it, she had arrived at the corner of Calle San Pantalon, only a minute from the *campo.* As she rested, looking in the window of the *pasticcerìa,* she realized that even against her will, the neighborhood had begun to give her the familiar feeling of home. Then she saw some *sfogliatelle napoletane,* which struck her as another good omen on this important day, so she went in and bought a dozen of them to celebrate. As she walked down the *calle* beside the church, she could hear singing, so she still had plenty of time. Nonetheless, she was eager to get to the *campo,* where she would be sure to see Sabrina and Paolo as they came out. But what met her eyes when she reached the corner was a shock.

The *campo* in front of the church looked like a flea market, a *mercantino.* There was furniture everywhere, with children and old folks posted like sentries beside the different stockpiles which husbands and wives and teenagers were adding to as fast as they could. They were hurling magazines and mirrors onto chairs or the ground, while the sentries tried to keep things in order within their proper zones. From the passageway, two boys came staggering out with a sofa, giggling and tripping as they struggled with the weight. All at once the boy at the front lost his grip and the sofa's rear leg hit the pavement with a crunch, causing the boy at the other end to lurch forward and fall over the arm. The leg broke with a loud crack and the two boys flung themselves, laughing, onto the sofa, which rocked back onto the broken leg like it was trying to buck them off. They screamed with pleasure. "Let's take it up on the bridge," they cried, jumping up and grabbing the arms. Without ceremony they dragged the ruined sofa up the steps and positioned it on the top of the bridge looking down the *rio.* "*Fantastico!*" they congratulated themselves. "Let's go and get the coffee table to put in front." Rosa stood in a daze watching all the people running back and forth carrying lamps and dishes out into the *campo.* These were the neighbors. Rosa was perplexed and dismayed.

She called to the woman who lived across the hall. "Why is everyone doing this? What's going on?" But she couldn't hear a word over the deafening scream of sirens that rolled over the *campo* from the Rio Nuovo and right down the side *rio* as the fireboat and the police arrived simultaneously.

"Your house is on fire!" screeched the woman, with her nose practically touching Rosa's. "And you're going to lose everything because no one will be allowed to go back in now that the firemen are here."

At that moment the Church of San Pantalon opened its doors, revealing the priest, who stopped, stunned, while his parishioners rushed past him like a river around a snag. Only Sabrina lingered on the step holding Paolo's hand and looking about, bewildered. Rosa went up to her. "Sabrina, our house is on fire; it happened while I was taking Luigi's wallet to him." She put her handkerchief over her face and started to cry. Sabrina patted her shoulder, then rested her hand there to steady herself as she came down the steps. She let go of Paolo's hand as he pulled away to join the other boys. "Come sit down," said Rosa, wiping her eyes and leading Sabrina toward the bridge. Together they climbed the steps and stood before the sofa that Rosa had watched being dragged into place. Rosa looked down at the boys. Seeing the grandmother and the pregnant woman, one by one the boys gave up their front-row seats to the spectacle. She directed Sabrina to the end of the sofa that still had both legs and sat down beside her, exhausted by her exertions. For several minutes the tears wouldn't stop coming, but they finally ebbed to the point where she could see.

From the open space between their kitchen shutters, thin gusts of smoke like innocuous wisps from a toaster drifted away into nothing. The gondolier's wife and the gondolier himself were squeezed together in the window opposite, straining to see through the crack in the shutters. Rosa was glad she'd pulled the shutters to and would have liked to shout something at the gondolier and his nosy wife, but they were too far away. Above the kitchen window something was happening: through cracks under the roof, gray smoke was forcing its way out in thin, swift jets, like a spray under high pressure; it looked as if it were building up to a piercing whistle or a high scream. Down below, the firemen had got the watergate open and were playing out hose from the boat into the building. Rosa held her handkerchief over her eyes and let the long months of unhappiness come rolling out in tears.

Sabrina sat beside her crying silently. "Do you think they'll be able to put it out in time?" she asked in a trembling voice.

They were crowded so close that Rosa could feel the new baby inside Sabrina's belly jumping with excitement, for all the world as though it were celebrating. Rosa sniffed and struggled to give an answer. She had marveled many times at how her daughter-in-law, like those people at home who never opened the door for fear of a subpoena, couldn't bring herself to face anything.

"I'm afraid," said Rosa in little jerks, "if they put that . . . spinach water on it . . . to put it out . . . it will be a lot of work to clean it up."

"Well what will we do?" she wailed.

That was more like it. "Wait for Luigi," Rosa said,

reaching into her pocket. She opened Sabrina's hand and dropped the wedding rings into it.

Sabrina gasped with joy and squeezed her mother-in-law's hand. "Oh thank you, I thought they were lost with everything else. That gives me hope."

"Don't worry," said Rosa. "Luigi will fix everything."

She looked at her watch. It was still only quarter to one, but when she looked over the *campo,* there was Luigi, with his hands in his pockets, lumbering toward them, trying to look relaxed. But she could see that he was nervous. Somebody must have told him, poor thing, and he'd come home early because he loved her fried potatoes. As he climbed the bridge he looked first at Sabrina and then at Rosa.

"What's happening?" he frowned. But before they could answer, Paolo ran up, shouting, "Papa, Papa, our house is burning down!"

"Is it really *our* house? What happened? Whose fault is it?"

Rosa wiped her eyes. "Not mine, I hope. It happened while Sabrina and Paolo were at Mass and I was bringing your wallet to you."

"My wallet! That wasn't my fault!"

A *vigile* stood behind Luigi, listening. "Are you the owner of the apartment that's on fire?"

"Yes. Well, no. Not the owner; just the tenant."

"Do you know what caused it?"

"No, everyone was out. My mother had started to make lunch, but she doesn't remember turning on the stove."

Now that was clever, thought Rosa; she hadn't even told him that.

"One of those reflex actions," the *vigile* nodded. "Aside from gas leaks or short circuits, most fires come from old folks being absentminded. Tell your mother not to worry too much; generally the authorities don't really hold them responsible because they suffer more than anybody. Looks to me like you'll be lucky to salvage anything. One thing's for sure: you won't be going home tonight. Do you have any relations or friends who can help you out, who can give you a place to live until you can find another apartment?"

"My wife's got an uncle, but he wouldn't have us. And her parents would rather burn their own house down than give us a roof. They didn't want us to get married."

Rosa and Sabrina watched the firemen appearing here and there, opening windows and letting the smoke pour out while they caught their breath before moving on.

One of the firemen on the boat had hooked up another hose and was spraying into the windows as they opened them.

"Oh look, that's the Vianellos' apartment," said Sabrina, holding her handkerchief to her mouth as she watched the fireman spray canal water into the window of the couple who were so nasty about Paolo's toys in the entrance. Somehow at that moment she felt her misery change perspective and the deadweight of despair lift a little from her heart.

Paolo leaned over the parapet with his friends.

"That's my house burning. My LEGO is in there. And all my comic books. I had a collection of about fifty, or a hundred."

"I can count to sixty," offered a small boy, pulling on Paolo's shirt.

"Last time I counted I had almost two hundred, or more," answered Paolo. "I can count as far as I want."

One of the boys from the building next door shook Paolo's arm. "My father says our stuff is insured, is yours?"

"Oh sure," said Paolo, throwing his mother a clownish, questioning look.

"This is subsidized housing, isn't it?" continued the *vigile* to Luigi. "The irony is that these buildings certainly don't meet any current standards. The city will probably decide to restore that row of buildings all at once. How many are there in your family?" The *vigile* looked from Luigi to Paolo to Sabrina to Rosa. "Four? Almost five? You won't get a subsidized house with three bedrooms in Venice, or Mestre either. You're going to have to go out to one of the villages on the mainland. I can guarantee it."

"Oh!" gasped Rosa, covering her face.

"The thing is," reassured the *vigile*, "you can probably come back here if you want to, but these restorations take years. By that time you could have two more children. On the other hand, by that time you could probably have your choice of any apartment in the building. People never come back from the mainland. Once they get settled there, they can't give up the convenience."

"My wife will be sad," said Luigi, "she's Venetian. But I'm not."

"No, of course not," said the *vigile.* "Anyway, for tonight they'll get you into a hotel somewhere not too far away, then you'll have to go in and make reports tomorrow and ask for housing. The Red Cross is coming to organize some clothes and things for tonight."

In fact, Rosa wished she had a place to go lie down right now. She was tired and hungry and the ache in her throat from all the crying was taking her back to those last days in Naples when she was packing up and selling everything she couldn't take to Venice. She remembered standing under the trees with the banknotes in her hand as she watched the new owner climb on her old Vespa and take it rumbling down the hill with all her memories. Listening to the sound, she thought her heart would burst. Nando had called it the Laughing Coffeepot. She strained to hear it long after it was out of sight and lost in the sounds of the afternoon. A convict heading for prison couldn't have felt less joy in his prospects than she in hers that day. And had she not run straight to church and promised with a candle in front of the Madonna that with God's help she would get another Vespa exactly like it within the year, she never would have mustered the courage to go on uprooting all the tangled memories of a lifetime and move to Venice.

Luigi sat down on the railing of the bridge. He'd never seen a fire in Venice before. They were pumping water from the *rio* and playing it on the kitchen shutters. The gondolier at the window opposite shouted at the fireman with the hose and pointed: "Get the water inside! It's burning inside!"

The fireman took one hand off the hose and cupped it behind his ear with a daft smile as the hose swung in an arch over the gondolier and his wife, soaking them both.

"*Scusami, scusami,* so sorry," laughed the fireman. "I shouldn't have taken my hand away."

A photographer for the *Gazzettino* came up to Luigi and asked to take his picture. Luigi got down from the railing and went over to stand beside the *vigile,* inviting him to be in the photograph with him.

Now just look at that, thought Rosa: see how a little success improves a man's character.

Don Giuseppe came up the steps of the bridge and leaned over Sabrina.

"I'm offering some lunch, if you'd all like to come over. It's a little impromptu. Loaves and fishes." He patted her shoulder and moved on to another family.

His kindness prompted Sabrina to turn to her mother-in-law. She put her hand on her arm. "Don't worry, Rosa.

We could all be better off in the end. Lots of times misfortunes have a funny twist in them. You'll see."

"It's true," sighed Rosa. "You know something made me stop and buy a whole tray of pastries for lunch. We should go and share them with Don Giuseppe and the others."

As she spoke, three firemen appeared at the window directly under their kitchen window. The smoke issuing from between the shutters was becoming dense. One got on the window ledge with a long pole while the other two held his legs. He poked at the latch holding the shutters until he released it and pushed the shutters wide open so the fireman below could shoot the water inside.

Above the window, gray smoke gave way to billows of black smoke rolling from under the eaves into the sky. Oh dear, thought Rosa, could that be the motor oil? A second later the roof sank with a great *whisssssssh,* letting loose a geyser of sparks and flames shooting high into the sky. From both sides of the Rio Nuovo, all the way back into Campo Santa Margherita, an admiring gasp went up from the crowd, followed by whistles and cheers. Rosa blushed and put her hands over her eyes.

It was her brother who deserved the credit. When he couldn't get his plans authorized to modernize his restaurant, he was seething with frustration. After a while, he seemed to accept it and took on some new staff, among them a retired cook to help him on weekends. One Saturday night at going-home time, following the old man out he turned the knob under the deep fryer. After putting out so many accidental fires over the years, he'd finally recognized that burning oil left to its own devices would burn straight up through the roof and do a nice, clean job. The insurance built him a new restaurant. She wished she could ask him why his fire never burned the neighboring buildings. Well, anyway, these people would all be better off getting out of Venice. Even the *vigile* had said so.

Sabrina too was tired and hungry.

"There's nothing more to do here, Rosa," she said, struggling to get up. "We'd better get some lunch and try to find a place to stay." She went to collect Luigi and Paolo to go to the *parrocchia,* while Rosa took her cakes and handbag and picked her way through the crowd down the steps of the bridge. It would soon be a year that she had been keeping to her promise, every day of which she'd had to fight back the temptation to break into the bank account which held her *buona uscita,* the money the owners of her apartment had paid her for leaving when by law she could have stayed for the rest of her life. No one, not even Luigi, knew why all at once she had stopped fighting against eviction and agreed to leave Naples.

Tomorrow they would all wake up in a strange place and begin a strange new life. The omens were good. As she walked along, she could almost feel herself riding down the hill to town, and like the best years, when Coffeepot was

new, roaring up the hill from school, with little Luigi holding on behind and calling, "Faster, Mamma, go faster, go
faster, as fast as you can go!" She prayed that it wouldn't be
more than a few days before she could walk into that shop
in Mestre and put down the money for the Vespa. It wasn't
exactly like Coffeepot as she'd promised; it didn't sound
the same, but it had had a nice feel when she'd ridden
it around the block to try it out. It was, she had already
explained to God, the closest she could come. He understood. After all, she wasn't the same either. Those happy
days were gone. But she could still have fun going to the
shops. The best part, the exciting part, would be watching
Luigi's family find out what it felt like to be free. For a
change she found herself wishing she could turn the clock
ahead instead of back. In her mind, she knew how it was
going to work: she would stay home and mind the baby.
Everyone would take turns with the Vespa. Sabrina and
Paolo were the ones she couldn't wait to see converted:
they had no idea what joy this day was going to bring
them. And it would all be thanks to Rosa Maria Rosario,
widow Esposito, displaced person. She put her handkerchief to her mouth. She knew she shouldn't smile at a time
like this, but she couldn't help it.

Jane Turner Rylands grew up in Ohio and graduated from the College of William and Mary with a degree in English literature and did graduate work at Boston University and Temple University. She taught English in the University of Maryland's European division for seventeen years, the last twelve in Italy. She now lives in Venice with her husband, Philip, and their son, Augustus.